TWILIGHT IMPERIUM

From the glittering halls of Mecatol Rex, the powerful Lazax Empire rules supreme across the galaxy, enforcing an ancient doctrine of strength and peace.

But their once-mighty rule is failing.

In the shadows, the Great Civilizations plot against the crumbling regime they are bound to, determined to break the chains of their authoritarian masters, claim their independence, and destroy anyone who opposes them.

But their freedom comes at a heavy price. Once the spark of war is ignited, it will consume everything in its path until nothing remains.

The galaxy will burn.

And the empire must fall.

MORE TWILIGHT IMPERIUM FROM ACONYTE

The Fractured Void by Tim Pratt
The Necropolis Empire by Tim Pratt
The Veiled Masters by Tim Pratt

The Stars Beyond edited by Charlotte Llewelyn-Wells

TWILIGHT IMPERIUM™

THE TWILIGHT WARS

EMPIRE FALLING

ROBBIE MACNIVEN

ACONYTE

First published by Aconyte Books in 2023

ISBN 978 1 83908 237 5

Ebook ISBN 978 1 83908 238 2

Cover art by Tobias Roetsch

Galactic map by Ryan Hong

Distributed in North America by Simon & Schuster Inc, New York, USA

Printed in the United States of America

9 8 7 6 5 4 3 2 1

ACONYTE BOOKS

An imprint of Asmodee Entertainment Ltd

Mercury House, Shipstones Business Centre

North Gate, Nottingham NG7 7FN, UK

aconytebooks.com // twitter.com/aconytebooks

*Dedicated to the fans of Twilight Imperium,
pursuing "magnificent peace, glorious war"
for the last two and a half decades.*

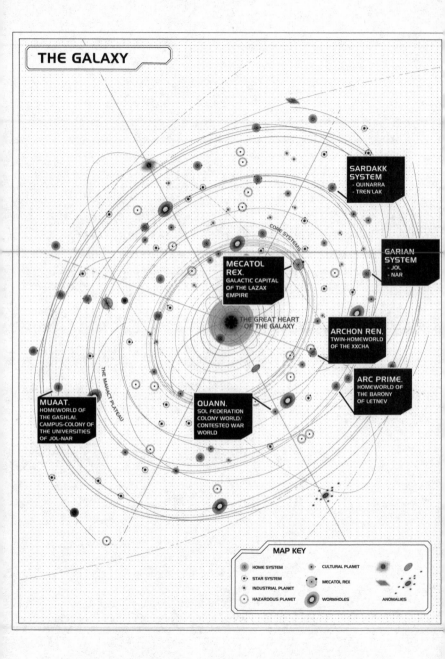

PART ONE

PART
ONE

CHAPTER ONE

The end began while Zara Hail was waiting for her family at Aruzoe Prime Gateway.

She didn't notice it at first. She had uncoupled her savant from her forearm and slipped the personal communications device into her jacket pocket. She was unwilling to let it disturb this moment, but was simultaneously still too wired in to the colonial administration to risk actually deactivating it entirely. A half-day's leave had been prearranged, but for someone of her standing – chief of staff to Willim Forebeck, Governor of Quann – there was never really such a thing as time off.

Her hand strayed instinctively toward the savant, but paused when the Gateway's speaker system went off, a loud chime followed by an automated voice announcing an arrivals update. The landing shuttle from *Star Pilgrim* was inbound, estimated docking in five minutes, Jord time. It was ahead of schedule.

She wasn't ready. It had been over three years since she had last seen Hiram, her husband, and their son and daughter,

Macks and Elle. There had been viz-calls, of course, but they could never compare to being there, to feeling the warmth of a hug or catching the gleam in smiling eyes.

It had been a nightmare, being absent, but she hadn't admitted it to anyone, not even to them, or to her father, who had promised to look out for her family while they were back home on Jord and she was out here, at the end of the full, grasping extent of the Federation's reach. Quann, the jewel in the crown of Sol expansionism, an outpost that, thanks to the ease of travel through the neighboring wormhole, had become a bustling hub of human colonization. All the successes of the last few years meant the administration staff sent from Jord had been worked off their feet. It had been impossible for Zara to get leave to go back to the motherworld, or even to find time to bring her family here. Until now.

She felt her savant go off again, but resisted the impulse to check it. This was her time. For months she felt as though she had been chiseling off fragments of her soul and using them to fuel Quann's government. Forebeck was a formidable figurehead, but like all politicos, he relied on his staff to actually run the show, day to day. That made Zara the head of the whole operation, or at least that was how she felt. As chief of staff she oversaw everything from habitation allocations to zonal disputes, the issuing of new trade and settlement dockets, the collection of tithes to be passed on to Lazax imperial officials, and the distribution of sustenance allotments. The founding of a colony was a life's endeavor, and for a while it felt like she had forgotten she also had a life outside of it.

People were starting toward the main arrival archway, the hubbub of voices and further speaker updates competing with the sounds of construction work emanating from a sealed-off section of the dome. Prime Gateway was the main planetside spaceport in Aruzoe, Quann's burgeoning capital. It was rife with activity, mostly inbounds, as ships from the motherworld – Jord – arrived via the Quann Passage wormhole, their holds rammed with hopeful, fearful new settlers and all the products and produce necessary for their survival.

Zara normally stayed away from the place unless she had official business. The port had grown exponentially in the past few years, from a few warehalls and shacks beside a docking strip to multiple dome terminals, raised landing struts and shuttle bays the size of stadiums. She had ratified a redevelopment package for the Gateway just a month before, authorizing further expansion.

Everything on Quann was expanding, fed by the burgeoning trade from the Passage. Zara felt like it would do so with or without her consent. All she could hope to do was channel it in the right direction.

She edged forward with the crowd, looking up at the screen above the archway, counting down the minutes until *Star Pilgrim*'s shuttle docked. She had promised to meet them here rather than have them picked up by an administration monoride, but she was regretting it. She was afraid, afraid of how they had changed, of how she had changed, of how time and space might have made strangers of the people she loved. She had caught sight of herself earlier in one of the screens as it had changed display. Even in casual wear, she felt like she looked too stiff, too formal. It was strange seeing herself in anything other than the smart, drab gray suits of the colonial administration. There was silver in her tightly bound-up black hair now, and she had no doubt there were lines in her face that Hiram wouldn't recognize, carved and ingrained by too many long days and sleepless nights.

The dome reverberated and a shadow passed over the crowd. Zara looked up, through the glassplex curve, at the underbelly of the shuttle as it came in to land outside. It was a great, ugly thing, mass conveyance rather than the official, sleek transporters she was more accustomed to. Its bloated underbelly was streaked with grime, and its clusters of thruster units were still glowing red-hot. A rain of dirty meltwater cascaded down onto the dome's surface as it passed, the ice of the planet's exosphere turning to water and slipping from the transport's flanks. This was the reality of arrival for the vast number of settlers who came to Quann, hauled a third of the way across the galaxy on craft that were barely spaceworthy. Just another thing that needed legislating.

She tried to imagine the feelings of those packed into the hold – fear, anticipation, excitement – but couldn't see past her own emotions.

The savant went off again. She was about to glance at it, deciding she had time for just one look, when the dome shook again. The landing shuttle, now about to alight, had to yaw dangerously to one side as a trio of F5 Hurricane Mk5s whipped past it at rising speeds. They were going in the opposite direction, rattling the struts of the dome and eclipsing the sounds of construction work as they punched their engines with a roar, sweeping up in an arrowhead formation toward the low-lying, gray clouds.

Why in the name of the Maker had three escort fighters just scrambled from the military wing of the spaceport? Zara retrieved her savant, no hesitation now as she unlocked the screen. Her nerves transformed into the twitchy gut feeling that came with knowing she was outside the loop.

Her savant had logged half a dozen messages from Traquay in the last fifteen minutes, as well as one from Raja Sing. Traquay was the administration's vice chief of staff, and the closest thing Zara had here to a friend, while Sing was the vice governor. If both were trying to get in touch simultaneously, that was serious.

Before she could read their messages, she got an incoming viz transmission from Traquay. She accepted it, activating the receiver chip in her ear and shifting hastily toward the edge of the arrivals archway so she would be less easily observed by the waiting crowd.

Traquay's three-dimensional likeness beamed up out of the savant's screen, a miniature real-time visualization. Even with the rendering fuzzed by waves of static, Zara could see immediately how strained she looked.

"Where in the Maker's name are you?" the miniature Traquay demanded in her ear. That was rhetorical. Tra' was an excellent administrator, and knew full well that Zara had left her in charge while she went to meet her family.

"Hiram's shuttle is just touching down," Zara said.

"Well, you're lucky it made it through."

"Why? What's happening? I've just seen three F5s take off!"

"There's an incident. A major incident. Are you in public?"

"Yes, but I'm receiving you via my chip. Tell me what's happening!"

"A Letnev fleet just broke out of the Passage. A war fleet. Shields up, weapons active. They're running full-tilt at our high orbit right now. Their vanguard vessels will be within strike range of the exo platforms within the hour."

An icy chill gripped Zara. The other great civilizations of the galaxy had been jostling the human settlement of Quann for years, particularly the Letnev, who claimed to have been the first to set foot upon the planet, but an unannounced, full-fleet incursion was unheard of. It could surely mean only one thing.

Humankind was about to go to war.

"Forebeck has ordered all military assets to beat to quarters," Traquay was saying, her words piercing the surge of panic threatening to overwhelm Zara.

"Have you tried hailing the Letnev?" she asked, noticing as she spoke that the nearest people waiting at the arrivals arch were beginning to look her way.

"Yes. No answer."

"I'm inbound."

"Good. Things are wild here. Smyth is recommending we deploy a missile launch immediately. Forebeck is freezing up. We need you."

"I'll be there in twenty," Zara said, and cut the transmission after Traquay had acknowledged. She strapped her savant back to her wrist and turned, pacing through the crowd toward the dome's exit, fighting the urge to run.

One person, recognizing her as a senior official, called out, asking what was happening. She ignored him. Voices began to rise behind her, but she had no time for it. She tapped her savant again, trying to call Hiram as she reached the edge of the terminal, praying the landing shuttle's in-flight protocols had ended and that he was able to receive her call.

Nothing. The transmission failed to find Hiram's signal, meaning he was still onboard. She cursed under her breath.

She didn't want to do this, but she didn't have a choice. She couldn't wait, not now.

"It's me," she said, leaving her husband a message instead. "Something's come up. Something major. I'm dispatching a monoride to collect you and the kids from the terminal. It'll take you straight to my hab. Use the gene key to get inside and then go straight down to the basement and seal it. Send me a ping when you're in. I'll call you when I can. I love you."

She cut the transmission as she strode out of the terminal. People were milling around the transporter line, oblivious to what was happening. The news would start to break any moment.

She pushed her way through the crowds waiting for a line of carrums, toward the fleet of sleek, automated administration monorides parked up at the far end of the row. Using her savant, she unlocked two of the transporters, leashing one to Hiram's own savant signal for when he arrived and inputting the coordinates of her home, before setting the second on a course for Aruzoe's government quarter.

As she clambered in, a second flight of F5s lashed overhead, startling the crowds, the thunder of their supersonic engines clapping back off the surrounding concrete. As though in sympathy, an emergency system somewhere began to sound off, the alarm pealing out over the starport and then the wider city.

The door to the monoride hissed shut, but couldn't quite cut off the mournful wail. Zara clipped on her safety restraint and sat back, listening to it.

It was, she realized, the sound that changed everything.

The administrative quarter of Aruzoe and the adjoining official habitation blocks had been Zara's home since her arrival from Jord. In the early days the buildings themselves had been crude affairs, with the regular loss of everything from communications to clean, running water. Now though, something more permanent was starting to take shape, even as the ever-expanding sprawl of the surrounding city remained comprised mostly of standard prefabs and imported Jord habitation units.

The heart of government itself, the Federation Hub of Quann, was currently being transformed from a drab series of steel and concrete blocks into a nu-classical structure befitting the center of colonial rule. Much of its façade was still covered by scaffolding as Zara got out of the monoride and began to mount the steps to the main doors, a flight of fresh, white Jord marble imported from the motherworld.

She could see immediately that Traquay hadn't been exaggerating. The Jordian Guard protecting the steps had tripled in number, their visors down and weapons unshrouded. The main doors, normally bustling with administrative staff, were shut.

Ruko, captain of the guard, was standing before them. He raised his visor as a mark of respect.

"Chief of staff," he said. "I'm afraid I'm required to scan everybody leaving and entering the FedHub."

"I understand," Zara said, knowing he was only doing what the security protocols mandated.

Ruko produced a scanning bar and ran it briefly over her,

checked her formal identification via her savant, and ordered the doors to be opened. Zara strode in, heart racing. She had little idea what waited for her inside.

When it was fully realized, the entrance hall of the Federation Hub would be a grand place, befitting the heart of Sol governance on Quann. A ceiling dome with a spherical stained glassplex center stained to look like a representation of Jord looked down on an expansive floor ringed with control nodes and computation systems. At the moment however, much of the echoing chamber was still covered by tarpaulins or scaffolding, the digital systems were as-yet uninstalled. The actual work of government was conducted in the somewhat less-grand adjoining annex. For the past few months it had only been workmen and construction mechanimiliars in the hall, but the guards had obviously cleared them out – the space was empty, apart from a single notification familiar hovering just beyond the doors.

"Zara Hail, please proceed to the control center immediately," the small, airborne automaton said after it had scanned her. Zara acknowledged it with a gesture, already heading toward the stairs at the opposite end of the hall. They led down toward another guarded door, this one blast-plated.

Beyond was the control center, the inner core of government on Quann. It lacked the grand ambitions of the rest of the building, a cramped, low-ceilinged room dominated by a circular viz display projector. As Zara stepped inside she was hit by noise and heat – the space was full to capacity with staffers and administration members, the recycled atmosphere stale and busy with chatter, the thrum of the projector, and the laboring efforts of the air scrubbers. She had never seen such a frantic level of activity before.

The guards closed and sealed the doors behind her as she made her way through the crowd. The projector itself was active, beaming up a visual of Quann and its space stations and exo ports, along with the edge of the neighboring wormhole. The familiar faces of her staffers surrounded her, but none spoke to her until Traquay materialized from the press and snatched her by the arm.

"Thank the Maker you're here," she said over the hubbub. She was perspiring into her gray formals, and a strand of her twisted locs had fallen free. She helped steer Zara to the edge of the projector.

"What's happened?" Zara asked as they went. "Have the Letnev opened fire?"

"Not yet, but they're still heading straight for us at attack speed. Estimated contact in fifteen minutes."

They neared the projector and the inner circle of officials surrounding it just as a stentorian voice boomed out.

"Unconscionable! Firing first would be suicide. Not only would that Letnev fleet destroy us, but the Lazax would then view us as the aggressors."

Forebeck was the one speaking, bathed in the green light of the slowly rotating system projection. The governor of Quann was in an unusual state of disarray, jacket cast off, shirt partially unbuttoned, and sleeves rolled up. He was a big, strong man, passing into his later years with more grace than most, his broad shoulders and silver hair lending him a patrician quality he had used well throughout his political career. He was considered by some to be a poor administrator, but he was talented when it came to delegation, picking an effective team to work under him and keep Quann running and on track. He was bluff and, for a politico, honest, and Zara liked him.

She could not say the same for the man Forebeck was addressing on the other side of the projector. Hektor Smyth was a Sol delegate, and he had arrived direct from Jord a month earlier. His family's reputation had come with him. Almost two decades prior, Welmar Smyth, the family patriarch and Smyth's uncle, had been convicted of plotting dissent against the Lazax empire. It had been huge news at the time. Zara remembered watching the caster reports on it while she had been taking her junior Federation administrator exams. Welmar had been tried in a Sol court, but there was pressure from certain Lazax officials to have him found guilty. Only a single Lazax, an ambassador by the name of Syd, had gone public in trying to have the severity of Welmar's sentence reduced. In the end though, he had been executed. The remaining Smyths had suffered a period of disgrace, but now the family was resurgent, Welmar's legacy of rebellion foresworn. Hektor Smyth in particular was known among Federation officials as an ambitious climber.

The purpose of his presence on Quann was to assess the ongoing development of the colony, audit it, and report back to the Federation government on Jord. So far he had lived up to Zara's expectations. He had become a perpetual background presence, sitting in on meetings, requesting reviews of legislation and questioning Zara's staff about seemingly every detail of the colony's running. She had complained off the record to Forebeck, but the governor had claimed his hands were tied. Smyth was still young, handsome, and had far too many connections in the political scene back home. Quann was required to submit to delegate oversight every two-year cycle, and Smyth was the man they had sent.

"Launching a preemptive strike is the only way to make the Letnev check their course," he was currently saying in response to Forebeck. They had clearly been at it for some time, both of them flushed with anger. Despite it, Forebeck cast a look at Zara as the inner circle made room for her and Traquay.

"Hail," he said, acknowledging her rather than replying to Smyth. "Good to see you. Did your family make it through?"

"Yes, governor," Zara said. "At least, I hope so. The shuttle they should be on was docking when I got the news. Apologies for my absence."

"Couldn't be helped," Forebeck said gruffly, casting a glance back at Smyth. "Nobody saw this coming, not even our esteemed colleague from Jord."

"How is that possible?" Zara asked, not giving Smyth a window to speak. It was something she had been wondering during the monoride from the spaceport. "How can a Letnev war fleet assemble and make the jump through the Passage without prior warning reaching us? Are there not delegates on Arc Prime? Does the Federation not have its intelligence assets?"

"Something somewhere has gone wrong," Smyth said, speaking up. "And I will be conducting a full inquiry at the first opportunity. But what matters is the here and now. We have to act, not sit paralyzed while they bear down on us. These few minutes we have are crucial. All of our lives may depend on them."

"On that we are agreed," Forebeck said, gripping the rail around the circumference of the viz projector. "But let me ask you, Delegate Smyth, have you had many dealings with the Letnev?"

"I know them well enough," Smyth said. "They're one of the great civilizations–"

"My great grandfather was on Arc Prime when the Letnev last rebelled against the Lazax," Forebeck said, cutting off his bluster. "My family knows them more than 'well enough.' The other species in the empire may decry us humans as militaristic and expansionist, but we are nothing compared to the arrogance and the warlike nature of Letnev. There is no other part of this empire quicker to anger or more relentless in the destruction of its enemies. The appearance of a Letnev war fleet is a harbinger of devastation, and I can assure you, the last thing we would want to do in this situation is fire the first shot. They will annihilate us without a moment's pause if we prove hostile."

"They look set to annihilate us regardless," Smyth pointed out.

Anything more was cut off by a gesture from the communications officer manning the viz projector's control panel.

"Signal from Commodore Yarrow, governor," she said.

"Put him on," Forebeck said immediately. All eyes turned to the center of the projector as the visualization of Quann and its surroundings blinked out of existence, replaced a moment later by the transmitted figure of Yarrow, commander of Quann's garrison fleet.

"Commodore," Forebeck said. "What news from orbit?"

"Nothing positive, governor," Yarrow said, voice clicking over the speakers built into the projector's flank. He was grim-faced, and it looked as though he had thrown on his Sol war fleet uniform in a hurry. "My flagship *Imperious* is cleared for action, and I have the two Thunderhead dreadnoughts *Fist of Jord* and *Divine Intercession* currently running out their guns and activating shields. Nothing else besides the escort squadron will be ready in time. All other capital and the strike carriers are either currently fitting for repairs or caught on the far side of the planet. Even the ships I have are only manned by skeleton crews. All planetside leave was canceled as soon as the system sensors detected a major incursion via the wormhole, but the garrison fleet won't be fully cleared and prepped for at least six more hours. It's likely to be closer to twelve."

"And what of the Letnev?" Forebeck asked.

"Still bearing down on us at full speed. I've deployed a cordon of escorts and interceptors beyond Exo Platform Nine-Six. They will be in range of the Letnev's vanguard weapons systems in approximately seven minutes. If the Letnev decide to open fire, that cordon will cease to exist in about the same length of time."

"Do you have a data update on the size of their fleet?"

"Yes, governor. I'm transmitting our latest scans. We estimate thirty-four capital ships and carriers, including six *Murmanifique* super-heavy battleships, and that's only if they have nothing else cloaked. We're still computing cruiser and frigate numbers, not to mention escorts."

Yarrow didn't need to spell out the odds any more clearly. At full strength, Zara knew Quann's standing garrison fleet consisted of three capital ships, two strike carriers and two cruisers, plus their attendant escorts. They were hideously outnumbered and outgunned.

As if to drive the point home, the slowly rotating image of Quann replaced Yarrow once more, this time overlaid with void vessel positions. *Imperious* and the Sol dreadnoughts, represented by small blue triangles, were clustered just above Quann's northern hemisphere, a string of escorts spread out ahead of them, shielding the space stations and exo platforms that hung in the planet's high orbit. Approaching them, from the direction of the wormhole, was a vast spread of red markings – the individual Letnev ships, as mapped out by the scan sweeps. Even more were continuing to appear as the data was fed through, along with arrows and trajectory arc overlays.

"Maker preserve us," Traquay murmured beside Zara.

She felt a moment's utter despair, and found herself gripping tightly onto the projector's circumference rail. How could this have happened? How had the Letnev been able to deploy such a significant fleet without even a hint of warning? And why?

She looked at the display again as Forebeck urged Yarrow to continue to marshal his forces and hold his fire unless fired upon. Zara did not come from a military background, but she had paid attention during the emergency briefings, when the administration had run mock invasion exercises and tried to plan out how Quann would be defended from any one of the galaxy's great powers. And in all of them, there had been something that was now absent from the real thing.

"There are no troop transports," she said, interrupting Forebeck and Smyth as they descended into another argument.

Those around the projector looked at her. She took a second to check that what she had said was true, taking in the horrifying bulk of the Letnev fleet again and noting the ship designation tags applied to each one. She was right.

"It's a void fleet only. No dedicated transports. No ground-pounders."

Most of the colonial administrators on Quann had little to no military experience, but even the most oblivious wouldn't miss the importance of Zara's realization.

"They mean to obliterate us from orbit," Smyth said. He leaned forward and smacked a palm off the glassy surface of the viz projector, causing the image rotating above to fuzz and distort for a second. "In the name of the Maker and the Federation, you must strike now, governor! At least give them pause!"

"If they mean to destroy us so thoroughly, a missile launch will not stop them," Forebeck pointed out.

"So you would just meekly acquiesce to our own deaths? As Federation-appointed governor, you have a duty to defend this world and every human on it!"

"Do not presume to tell me my duty, Delegate Smyth," Forebeck barked, causing a hush to fall through the packed, sweltering room.

"Governor, I'm receiving a transmission," Yarrow's voice clicked. "From the Letnev flagship."

All eyes turned to Forebeck. His face, flushed with heat and anger, became stony and guarded.

"Patch it through," he told Yarrow.

The Quann display vanished, replaced by another figure that flickered and distorted before the link finally locked on. He was Letnev, with the pallid blue skin and naturally haughty features of his species. He stood straight-backed and unyielding, legs planted, hands behind his back, clad in the blue uniform and gold-plated demi-armor that characterized his people's military dress. He seemed to take a second to assess what he saw, before speaking, his voice coming in via the projector as cold and precise as a scalpel.

"My name is Grand Admiral Daz Arrokan of the Great Warfleet of the Barony of Letnev, onboard the baronial flagship *Magnificatum*. Whom do I address?"

"Willim Forebeck, governor of the Sol Federation colony of Quann," Forebeck replied. Despite the strain on him, despite his partially buttoned shirt and sweat-drenched brow, right then, when it mattered, he somehow still managed to cut just as strong and proud a figure as the Letnev.

"Governor Forebeck, this will be my first and final warning," Arrokan said, his projection distorting again briefly before resolving. "Do not attempt to resist. Do not attempt to evacuate. We have come here to neither kill nor conquer, but we shall, if you do not follow these simple instructions."

"And who are you to make such demands?" Forebeck asked fiercely.

"I have already introduced myself, human," Arrokan replied. "I am not here to bandy words. You are safe if you remain upon this planet and your garrison ships return to their orbital docks. If any vessel attempts to leave, civil or military, it will be terminated. If any vessel attempts to make use of the Quann Passage, it will be terminated. That includes any ships approaching from the opposite side. There will be no compromises."

"Why?" Forebeck demanded. "Why are you doing this?"

Arrokan did not answer, and his projection blinked out of existence. Zara looked to the communications officer, half thinking there had been an accidental interruption, but the woman shook her head.

"He's cut the link," Yarrow's voice confirmed a moment later, the naval officer reappearing on the display.

The room was utterly silent. Despite the heat, Zara felt a bitter coldness in the expressions all around her, a chill left in the wake of the Letnev's terse ultimatum.

"May the Maker preserve us," said Forebeck eventually, to no one and everyone. "It's a blockade."

CHAPTER TWO

MECATOL REX,
GALACTIC CAPITAL OF THE LAZAX EMPIRE

The Chamber of the Galactic Council was considered by many to be the very heart of the universe. Ibna Vel Syd remembered reading those words as a child in his digi-copy of *The History and Origins of the Great Factions of the Chamber*, a secondary work of the influential Winnu political historian Meyer Malen. It had only been part of his school's optional reading, but he had devoured it from start to finish. When his father had seen what he was reading, he had laughed and said, "Seems this family has another ambassador in the making."

He had been correct. Syd had served Emperor Salai Sai Corian and the Lazax empire since he had graduated nearly two decades ago, first as an ambassador, and more recently as a new member of the imperial council. In that time he had traveled the length and breadth of the Lazax's galaxy-spanning fiefdoms, protectorates, and colonies, met with a hundred different species of sentients, stood upon a thousand foreign worlds, and gazed up at the constellations from a thousand unique angles, but always he loved to return here, to Mecatol Rex, to the chamber, seat of the imperium his ancestors had founded and now strove so hard to maintain.

He sat at that moment, fighting not to let his attention be drawn once more to the architecture of the great building. The design of the oratorium that housed the Galactic Council, much like the noble values of the Lazax themselves, had been copied in systems from the Mahact Plateau to the Unicorn Nebula, but never bested, never improved upon. The structure was a vast, circular space, bound by soaring walls leading to an arching roof, all built from millennia-old white Mecatol permacore, cracked and worn but still as strong as the day it had been hewn. Loges were set into the walls at heights from the ground level to where the curvature of the ceiling began, enough to house each of the fifty-thousand council delegations. Syd had only been present when it was full three times – when his father had taken him, as a child, to witness the coronation of the new emperor, during the Shaleri Taxation Crisis, and for the celebrations that had marked the one-thousandth year since the Galactic Council's founding. Today, fewer than half the viewing boxes were full, though remote attendance via viz projection accounted for another quarter.

Syd sat alone in his own loge, listening to the ongoing debate even as he gazed up at the ceiling, using the optic enhancements provided to those attending in person to inspect the frescos on the great dome. They showed each of the empire's chartered planets, arrayed in a mirror constellation. Architects and historians, most of them Winnu, debated endlessly just how many planets were displayed within the chamber, with several fiercely opposed numbers given. Syd himself had tried counting them on many occasions, but had never gotten close to halfway before duty called him elsewhere.

The voice of one of the debaters, carried over speakers set into each loge balustrade, rose as she met a point of contention. Syd glanced down, sensing matters were slowly coming to a head.

The speaker was Hacan. The golden-furred leonid was dressed in the red and gold robes of her people, her bearing strong and proud, her voice brooking no argument. Still, the one who had risen to challenge her was trying. He was a Ral-Nel, a reptilian-like being, one of the lesser civilizations who, today, was acting out the role of pawn in a greater game.

Syd had familiarized himself with the logistics of the debate before taking his seat, as was only proper. The dispute was essentially legalistic and patent-related, likely more suited to the galactic courts than the council, but as with anything on Mecatol, there was more at play than it first seemed. The Hacan, considered by many within the empire to be the cleverest and most ruthless traders of any civilization, were attempting to corner the market that had risen up around the exportation of basic microprocessor units used in savants and other computational and communication devices. Their own product was cheaper than those already available, and was growing in popularity across the empire, but recently the Ral-Nel had begun producing their own microprocessors and starting to undercut the Hacan. "Recently" was part of the contention, as the Ral-Nel claimed they had been making the chips for decades.

All that was convenient, given that the Hylar universities of

Jol-Nar were currently exerting control over the Ral-Nel who, as one of the smaller sentient groupings in the council, had little option other than to seek the favor of one of the major galactic players. It seemed more than likely the Hylar, responsible for most of the advanced technology that proliferated across the empire, were angry at the Hacan for marketing alternative products, and had provided engineering assistance to the Ral-Nel in order to combat Hacan trade expansionism without dirtying themselves with a public head-to-head.

It would have all seemed very petty, were it not for the fact that tens of thousands of livelihoods – Hacan, Ral-Nel and Hylar – as well as the prestige of the major factions depended on the outcome of the dispute, and whether it could be solved within the Galactic Council or would have to go before the courts.

In truth Syd had not chosen to attend the council that day because he was invested in the future of microprocessor technology and production. He had spent the past month on leave, most of it visiting friends in the Kingdom of Xxcha. He always enjoyed his rare time there, especially in the company of Tutur, an old, experienced diplomat who had provided him with critical advice when he had first started his service to the empire. He found the likes of Tutur and another colleague, Atz – the reptilian Xxcha in general – to have many characteristics he admired. As one of the oldest sentient species in the galaxy, they were slow to anger, thoughtful, and took a measured approach to life that Syd wished he had the opportunity to emulate.

The break had been welcome, but duty had called, and Syd was nothing if not dutiful. The empire ran on duty, or at least he believed it should. The duty of the Lazax toward the disparate peoples of the galaxy, guiding them in the quest for peace and prosperity, and the duty of those same hundredfold species to uphold the peace the Lazax had created and adhere to the beneficent rule of their imperium.

That, of course, was not how things really worked. Syd knew this, and so he had forced himself to attend the first meeting of the Galactic Council the moment he was back on Mecatol. He had spent too long with his guard down, in Tutur's good and honest company. He had to find his edge once more, and there was no place sharper than the chamber.

Throughout the exchanges between the rival factions in this current dispute, he had been attempting to work down to what lay beneath the surface, reviewing everything from those councilors who had chosen to attend the debate, to the body language of the speakers and the reception their words received from the so-called neutrals. While the Hylar's play using the Ral-Nel seemed transparent, Syd was certain there was more to the Hacan's own protests than met the eye. They had allies too, somewhere. Syd just hadn't yet worked out who. To do his duty as an advisor to the emperor, he had to be capable of understanding those sorts of elements.

"Eminent councilor," said a soft voice. It was Onni, his Winnu assistant, communicating via Syd's savant.

"Go ahead," Syd prompted, turning his head to one side as a declaration from the Ral-Nel section of the chamber drew a spattering of boos and jeers that echoed back from the high ceiling.

"We have just received an in-person meeting request from Eminent Councilor Atz," Onni said. "Its purpose has been left blank. The time is unscheduled besides 'immediate,' and it is marked with a vermillion priority warning."

Syd took a second to digest the news. Atz was a trusted peer and, Syd hoped, a friend. A former Mirritan, one of the emperor's personal ambassadors, he was currently the only non-Lazax member of the imperial council. Like Tutur, he was a Xxcha of steadily advancing years, and had been honored with a place among the emperor's court after numerous acts of diplomatic service for the empire. When Syd had first become an ambassador he had mentored him in the ways of the imperial council, a very different beast from its galactic equivalent – besides Atz it was comprised exclusively of senior Lazax, and provided private advice to the emperor himself. Syd was thankful Atz had taken him on, but he suspected a summons such as this would not be some idle reunion. Vermillion was used by imperial administrators to indicate a matter of the utmost urgency. It was generally reserved only for a crisis. Why would Atz need to see him so urgently?

"Where is the meeting location tagged to?" he asked Onni.

"The imperial gardens, sir. I have the specific quadrant."

Another ominous sign. Atz would only meet with him there if he had something he didn't wish to discuss in the halls of the council building or the chambers of the imperial palace. It had the ring of the clandestine about it, something Syd disliked.

"Send a response to the eminent councilor confirming the meeting, post haste," he instructed Onni. "And meet me outside the council dome. Let me know if Atz provides any further updates."

"Affirmative, sir."

Syd rose and bowed toward the imperial throne. It sat in the center of the chamber's pit, a copy of the one in the neighboring palace, a great, arching block of dark metal accentuated with gold, silver, and admanite, gleaming brilliantly in the shaft of light beaming down through the hole in the dome's middle. Emperor Salai Sai Corian was formally invited to every meeting of the Galactic Council, but no Lazax emperor had attended one or occupied the empty throne for almost two centuries, except during a coronation. It was, according to some, a sign of respect for the quasi-democratic workings of the council and, according to others, an indication of how little the rulers of the empire now cared for the trials and tribulations of their subjects. As ever, there was some truth in both.

Obeisance made, Syd departed, exiting out the rear of his loge. As he left, he could hear the main Hacan speaker skewering the Ral-Nel's claims, to rising applause. Ordinarily he would have been displeased at having to leave just as one side was making their play, but all thoughts of microprocessors and trade wars had been banished by Atz's summons. There was something ominous afoot.

Onni met him in the great, curving hall that encompassed the circumference of the council chamber's exterior. Like many of the administrators and assistants on the capital world, he was a Winnu, part of the officious species who had the distinction of being the first sentients to request formal annexation into the Lazax empire. Their diligence and loyalty made them effective civil servants for the empire, and Onni had been serving as Syd's assistant for almost two decades. He stood now waiting for the councilor, the restrained colors of his formal gray waistcoat and deep purple sub-garments offset by the gold and ruberite-jeweled chain and earrings worn as a mark of his rank and status. He offered a short bow as Syd approached.

"No update from Eminent Councilor Atz, sir," he said. "I have ordered a monoride to collect us."

"That won't be necessary," Syd said. "The gardens aren't far, and I wish to run possible scenarios past you before we arrive."

"Understood, sir," Onni said, tapping the savant worn on his forearm and canceling the ride. Syd motioned to him, and they stepped out through the nearest of the council building's towering door arches, passing by the N'orr auxiliaries guarding the chamber's exterior. Onni walked to the left and a half-step behind Syd, the natural position of a diligent Winnu assistant.

"Atz would not normally summon me like this," Syd said as they took a route along the statue-lined bridge that crossed the black waters of the Dorus River, connecting the council building to the imperial palace complex and its formal gardens on Dominus Island. The digitally projected renderings of a hundred Lazax emperors were beamed from their viz-plinths on either side of them, gazing down with haughty indifference. "I had not even informed him about my return to the capital."

"It would seem to be a matter of grave import," Onni observed. "Previous meeting logs with this particular eminent councilor show that he has never requested an immediate, unscheduled audience."

"And the vermillion status confirms it," Syd said. "Something drastic has occurred, and news has only just reached Mecatol."

"The question is, what?" Onni wondered, knowing Syd wished to have his own thoughts teased out.

"It could be anything," Syd admitted. That was the unpleasant truth. Every year it seemed the Lazax ambassadors who maintained the empire's peace and the councilors who advised the emperor were having to contend with greater difficulties. It was easy to become focused on the present, to disregard wider trends, but since he had first become one of the empire's representatives, Syd could detect an upturn in what other senior Lazax often dismissively referred to as a "crisis."

The Arcturus Dispute, the Mordai Annexation, the rise and fall of the Vornel Confederates, the assassination of the Carro Primus, the passing of the Charter of Expansion bill and the schisms it had caused, the rebellions on Zonda and Hiyrel – all of these had occurred within the past ten years alone, and each one had looked as though it might fracture the empire. Where once peace and stability had been the watchwords of Lazax rule, now it felt as though the galaxy was caught in the tremors of a slow but continuous quake, one that was gradually crackling the foundations of the imperial edifice.

To make it worse, rather than face each crisis head on, the upper echelons of the empire's government had become increasingly withdrawn, unwilling to become involved in the petty politicking and disputes that were multiplying among the greater and lesser civilizations. Syd understood that such an attitude could be alluring. Whenever the Lazax intervened or mediated, relations with the faction that felt as though it had lost out deteriorated further. If we do not involve ourselves, Emperor Salai Sai Corian had once said, then they cannot blame us. In Syd's experience the opposite was true. If the Lazax did not fulfill their duty as custodians of the empire, everyone would blame them.

"Perhaps the pirate systems have launched another raid

toward the core?" Onni said, addressing the latest rumors that had been swirling around the imperial capital in recent weeks. "Or the Hylar have finally made a play against Sardakk encroachment?"

"Perhaps," Syd allowed, mulling through the possibilities as they reached the triumphal arch that marked the eastern entrance into the gardens. Many senior Lazax wouldn't brook idle speculation among their Winnu staff and servants, but Onni had been in Syd's service for long enough for him to appreciate his incisive mind. He was, in his own way, a fine diplomat, and his thoughts were an asset.

Still, none of his suggestions sat right this time. It felt like something unanticipated, another ill rising up unexpectedly from the depths to gnaw at all Syd held dear.

"We will find out soon enough," he told Onni noncommittally as they entered the gardens proper. The expanse of greenery sat upon the flat, elevated plateau overlooking the Dorus and the rear of the imperial palace complex, at the center of Mecatol's ecumenopolis. Like many Lazax officials, Syd enjoyed walking among the precisely cultivated clid and xylex trees, the hedgerows and the elaborate ornamental displays, but the most impressive aspect was the view of the surrounding city.

The entirety of Mecatol Rex's surface was dedicated to the function of empire, and housing those who made it run. This particular area was often known informally as the Core, and it consisted of a bristling array of heavenscrapers and civhabs, arrayed around the palace and the Chamber of the Galactic Council like the vast spears of an army of giants.

Twilight was approaching, and darkness had already started to creep up from the Old Deep and the lower levels of the subcity, shot through with lights from a million windows and the kaleidoscopic, neon luminators reflecting through the smog that was ever-present in Mecatol's guts. Higher up, daylight still held sway, turning those spear tips blood-red and glinting from the glassplex and alloys of the tens of thousands of hovervehicles, monorides, courier darts, and grav-carrums thrumming along the sky lanes between the columns. Above the peak of the highest scraper, the mountainous mega-tower of the Bureaucratic Institute, the sky was turning dark, the twinkling of distant stars creating a halo that sat lightly upon the capital's jagged brow.

Mecatol Rex, the heart of the galaxy, the heart of the empire, in the heart of every trueborn Lazax. Despite his concerns, Syd found himself acknowledging its glory and splendor. It was a sight he had seen countless times before and still, he never ceased to exult in it. This was the center of everything, and while it endured there was hope.

"Atz's locator tag is set to the northeastern quadrant of the gardens, sir," Onni said, preempting Syd's question. They took the required path, through a stand of ri-groves, the air heavy with the scents of the ripe fruits, and past a pair of Winnu garden attendants, sleeves rolled up, scraping around the roots of an old clid tree with trowels. An air-scrubber hummed past in the opposite direction, its Hylar-made systems purring as it fought to keep the wider city's pollution at bay and maintain the gardens' equilibrium.

At the path's end was the centerpiece of the northeastern quadrant, a great moontree, one of the symbols of Lazax imperium. The sunset was still reaching its peak, making its silver leaves look as though they were aflame, casting a shimmering glow that kept the darkness beginning to stretch through the lesser foliage at bay. As Syd and Onni approached a flock of ruvar birds took flight with a clapping of wings.

Esteemed Councilor Tchanat Atz was waiting in the shadows beneath the boughs, standing between two huge roots. Like Syd, he wore the white robes and binding cloths of a Lazax dignitary and a golden datarecorder circlet on his craggy brow, but otherwise their forms could hardly have been more different. He was, like all Xxchaa, reptilian. Even young Xxcha tended to have a wizened look about them, at least as far as most other species were concerned, but in his advanced years Atz's appearance lived up to his "venerable" title.

Atz was not alone. There were two Lazax with him, one male and one female, similarly dressed. The woman Syd knew to be an ally of Atz's, a senior member of one of the eight Kenatar industrial conglomerates and a councilor of the Civita Planetar by the name of Marchu. The male was younger, with a less elaborate circlet, the naturally high-boned, noble features of all Lazax not yet engraved with the lines of care and experience longer-serving officials bore. He clutched an ambassador's staff with one of his four arms.

Syd recognized him, and his mood plummeted to new depths. His name was Sorian Sai Zey, and he was an ambassador to the Mahact Quadrant and second cousin of the emperor himself. He was also one of Syd's bitterest rivals.

"Syd," Atz croaked, slowly inclining his head in a Xxcha greeting. "It does me well to see you. Thank you for coming with such immediacy."

"I believe vermillion requires nothing less," Syd said as he made the Lazax sign of friendship, briefly crossing both sets of arms before doing the same with Marchu. Zey did not do likewise.

Syd stepped in with them beneath the silvery boughs. Atz and the other Lazax had brought their own Winnu attendants, but they stood off at a respectful distance, as did Onni, leaving the four to discuss matters in private. Syd noted that Atz had also triggered a sound dampener and recording scramblers, nullifying any efforts to listen in to their conversation. Between that, and meeting out in the gardens, it seemed he had no wish to be overheard.

"I would not have tagged this meeting as vermillion were it not a serious matter," Atz went on in his slow tone. "We are all acquainted, so I will do without the formalities. Needless to say, nothing we discuss here must leave the gardens."

"Naturally," Syd said, glancing coolly at Zey. The younger Lazax returned his gaze without expression.

"Word has just come through from a sprint courier vessel transmitting to the orbital relay network once it reached the outskirts of the Mecatol system," Atz said. "Three days ago a significant portion of the Barony of Letnev's grand war fleet made a jump through the Quann Passage and appeared in battle array above the system's only habitable planet. It is, as I'm sure you know, currently controlled by the Sol Federation, as ratified by a Charter of Expansion issued by the emperor himself a little over a decade ago. The Letnev fleet has started a blockade of the planet and, more importantly, of all trade passing through the Passage."

Of the many disasters Syd had been attempting to anticipate, that hadn't been one of them. He took a moment to process it, looking again at Zey, though the young ambassador remained guarded and unspeaking. Syd asked Atz the most immediate question.

"Has the barony fleet opened fire?"

"No, at least not as of news reaching us. It was transmitted six hours after the Letnev arrival was first detected. They might well have since."

"How was this not anticipated?" Syd wondered aloud. "A fleet? How many capital ships?"

"At least three dozen."

The information was staggering. In their effort to maintain the empire's peace and unity, the Lazax monitored everything – there was a constant official presence among all of the great civilizations and many of the lesser, from the ambassadorial corps to the tithe and levy department, and that was before even considering the vast, galaxy-spanning network of spies, informants, and monitors the empire employed. Nothing of note occurred across the cosmos without word of it reaching Mecatol Rex in some form or another. So how in the emperor's name had the Letnev assembled so large a war fleet and made the wormhole jump to Quann without even rumor of it spreading?

"We don't know how the Letnev have moved their pieces with such secrecy," Marchu answered when Syd asked as much, speaking up for the first time. "There will be inquiries. The priority now is intervention. We need not spell out the seriousness of hostile Letnev-human interactions."

Indeed she did not. The Letnev were considered by the Lazax to be aggressive, warlike, and had imperialistic tendencies, but if any of the other great civilizations could rival them in those regards, it was the humans of the Sol Federation. If one were to threaten the other, the fallout had the potential to be catastrophic.

"Are we sure this information can be trusted?" Zey said, finally joining the conversation.

"I received it from a trusted source in the Office of Communicators who has it direct from a courier picket. I took it straight to Eminent Councilor Atz," Marchu said. "Not merely a report, but scan data and imagifiers. I will translate them to your datarecorder circlets at the conclusion of this meeting."

"So, this knowledge isn't public yet?" Syd asked.

"No, certainly not on Mecatol," Atz said. "I expect the news to break within the next day-cycle. That is part of the reason for acting so quickly. You both know well enough that the empire always seeks to be ahead of events. Well, right now, we are very much behind. We have to get back in front."

"And we do not know what has prompted this aggression from the barony?" Syd went on.

"No, but that must be identified and the situation defused. To that end, I am authorizing your dispatch to the Quann system. You will leave as soon as you are able. I have already chartered transport, and will assign a Tekklar Elite to guard you."

"We are to go together?" Zey asked pointedly.

"Yes. Syd's experience in matters of negotiation will be crucial, and I want a member of the imperial council present, while Zey, you have spent time assigned to ambassadorial duties on Arc Prime. Your contacts with Baron Werqan could prove vital. The two of you are to work together, for the good of the empire. I'm sure I need offer no further instructions in that regard."

"Of course," Syd said dutifully. "Hopefully, we can yet avert disaster."

"If it hasn't already played out," Zey noted.

"All the more reason to make haste," Atz said. "I have already chartered an imperial sprint-craft. Estimated journey time to Quann is three weeks. The imperial outpost at Dolorum is en route; expect a transmission to be waiting for you there detailing any new developments. I want you to arrive with the most current intelligence."

"And if we get there to find Quann a fire-scoured rock?" Zey asked.

"Then return here with news. If that is the case then we truly will have a crisis at hand."

"Either way, you will be the first to know," Syd said. "Which brings me to one more question."

"Ask it," Atz said. Syd watched him closely as he spoke.

"You said that this intelligence was unknown by others here on Mecatol, and that it was received directly from the Communications Office. Does that mean that other members of the imperial administration are also as-yet unaware of what has transpired?"

"You are correct," Atz said.

"The emperor does not know?"

"No, he does not. I made a decision. A response has to be put in motion. Marchu and I are going to oversee that, but if we seek to do it through official channels, by consulting the emperor, the imperial council, and the ambassadorial corps, it will be weeks at best before anyone with authority is dispatched to Quann. More information would be required, and there would be wrangling over just who should be sent. These events are still in their infancy, and we do not have the luxury of time. Is that something either of you would dispute?"

"It is not," Syd admitted. While bypassing formal channels always made him uncomfortable, he could see that Atz was right. The wheels of Lazax bureaucracy seemed to turn slower by the day, rusting with inefficiency and weighed down by indolence. If the intelligence Marchu had received was accurate, speed was essential.

Zey made a gesture with two hands, a fist clenched in an open palm – a Lazax agreement signifier. Syd swallowed his discomfort at being asked to work with the younger Lazax. He realized he was proud that Atz had come to him. Beneath the layers of concern, he acknowledged a sense of excitement, born out of the knowledge he was about to be at the leading edge of an incident of galactic importance. This would be his greatest test for many years.

"Then it is settled," Atz said. "You will need to retrieve your ambassadorial staff, Syd. There is arduous work ahead."

CHAPTER THREE

"Subject stability, one hundred percent."

As far as Doctor Atak Arr was concerned, that was only good news for the time being. He dismissed the automedicum message that had blinked up across the containment sphere of his enviro-suit, refocusing his attention on the creature before him.

"Creature" was the correct appellation, because Arr refused to grace it with the title of "sentient." It was a hulking monstrosity, almost twice the size of Arr even with his enviro-suit on. Six back-jointed limbs connected to a trunk-like torso, all encased in a spiny, rigid green-and-yellow mottled carapace that, according to his scans, was almost as resilient as tempered steel. Its head matched the rest of it, insectoid, broad, and flat-plated, completed by big, glassy black bug-eyes and twin antennae that, even with the rest of the creature unconscious, continued to twitch.

The subject was a Sardakk N'orr, and Arr hated it with a passion. The N'orr were, according to the official decrees of the Lazax, one of the great civilizations, and a fully integrated part of the empire – indeed, they provided many of the foot soldiers in its military campaigns. To Arr however, they were an infestation, no better than the locust-variants native to so many planets the galaxy over. They swarmed, they multiplied, and they stripped bare all that was good and wholesome. They were so numerous they doubtless had not even noticed the absence of this one particular subject from his home-swarm, snatched as he had been by Hylar tyros during a multi-species trade conference on Kastarene. And Atak Arr knew that he was not alone in believing these creatures to be a blight.

"Begin incision," he instructed one of the automeds hovering over the operating slab. The gleaming chrome medical familiar slid down to a point on the N'orr's lower torso, its focus slaved to the crimson lance of an indicator beam that was picking out an area of chitin just below the subject's primary torso plate.

There was a faint whine, barely audible over the smooth humming of the array of active medical equipment that filled Arr's laboratory. The automed's hydroscalpel initiated, a thin, hyper-concentrated stream of water mixed with microscopic fragments of abrasive garnet, cutting effortlessly though what a regular blade or saw would have struggled to hack open. It left a perfect series of incisions in the mottled carapace, not deep enough to injure the N'orr, but enough for Arr's purposes.

"Begin plate leverage," the Hylar doctor ordered, shifting around the operating slab for a closer look. His enviro-suit whirred as he moved, the hydraulic calipers and structural supports giving him a loping gait. Like all Hylar, he was a cephalopod in what at times seemed like a galaxy of land-born mammalians and reptilians, a soft-boned aquatic who required permanent immersion in H2O – something achieved in his case thanks to his enviro-suit's containment sphere and the dispenser system that kept water flowing across his gray, scaled body.

That body couldn't be more different from the subject – the creature – stretched out and bound before him. That was one of the reasons he hated it. One of many. Dry, hard, rigid, bright, not soft and slick and slippery and dull. It repulsed him, made his gills shudder and his scales crawl. It was anathema to him, as he surely was to it.

A second automed hovered down and attached its surgical foreclaws to the small area of carapace sliced into by the hydroscalpel. It began to apply leverage, the pressure carefully calibrated to lift the plate fractionally without cracking it. Arr intended to do the absolute minimum amount of damage. For now.

"Subject stability, ninety-nine percent," droned the automed overseer running quintisensor diagnostics on the N'orr's vital signs. Arr considered the reading acceptable. He consulted the surgical tray that was floating alongside him on micro antigravetic motors, removing a syringe filled with an oily yellow substance and testing the plunger. Satisfied, he leaned forward over the slab and its prone subject, letting the struts woven into his suit support him as he got the required angle on the opening created by the automeds.

He injected the N'orr, quickly and efficiently, having the overseer automed note that the subject's antennae began spasming as he did so. He then stepped back, placed the syringe into the medical laboratory's incineration chute, and sterilized his suit's arm extensions.

After that, it was merely a case of waiting.

He allowed the lab's advanced equipment to continue monitoring the N'orr while he called up Muaat Campus-Colony's latest collated data review on the screen of his containment sphere, his unblinking eyes focusing through the water encasing him. There were several research pieces on the latest breakthroughs in reappropriated Gashlai hyper-fusion and a transcript of the lecture given by High Scholar Devram following his recent return to the Campus Prime in Wun-Escha. None of it seemed especially revelatory. He spent a little longer digesting a rumor docket that included an account of a Letnev war fleet entering the Quann Passage. It was unsourced and unverified, which made it worthless. Arr moved on, finding the piece that had piqued his interest when he had first glanced through the newly transmitted data.

Muaat had a new arrival. Her name was Harial Tol, and she had been reassigned following graduation on Jol to a previously self-automated Hylar high-orbit station here, on Muaat.

Arr recognized the name. He remembered Tol as a junior student at the Wun-Escha University of Biomedical and Genetic Advancement, when he himself had been a senior lecturer there. Even at a young age she had shown potential, but one of Arr's rivals, that gene-twisting Doctor Mayu, had gotten around her gills early and started sponsoring her research. Arr had forgotten the matter after he had departed the UoBGA to further his own particular strand of medical interest.

Now Harial Tol was a graduated under-doctor in her own right, and seemingly had been doing unspecified research in a solo capacity for the past month on Muaat. That, as much as the name recognition, caught Arr's attention.

Only three types of Hylar came to Muaat. The largest group belonged to the Pan University Fusion Research Initiative, an undertaking sponsored by all the major Jol-Nar institutions. The Initiative had been founded when the universities had first discovered Muaat or, more importantly, the native Gashlai sentients. The High Scholars were fascinated by the Gashlai's natural state – they were creatures composed almost purely of heat, and the cocooning process they underwent at birth, converting raw energy into mass, had profound implications for the state of Jol-Nar medical and technological advancement, and the very nature of the galaxy itself. The Initiative therefore ran a host of research bases on the surface of the volcanic planet, studying and experimenting on the unwilling Gashlai.

The second-largest Hylar group on the planet was the Pan University Military, Jol-Nar's fighting forces. Besides ensuring the protection of the researchers and the subjugation of the Gashlai, the Hylar war fleets had quickly realized the potential of the vast mineral deposits on Muaat. Early deals had been struck with the Initiative and other interest groups, ensuring that the so-called Hacan's share of the natural resources being plundered from Muaat's surface went to the fleets. At that very moment, construction of a vast military dockyard was underway in high orbit, a base that could be used to expand Jol-Nar's deep-space combat capacity threefold.

Lastly, there were the Hylar like Arr, individual researchers who wished to avoid oversight, and so had come here, to the farthest campus-colony from the homeworld system of Garia.

It was not simply that Arr's work was illicit or controversial, at least by Hylar standards. While publicly the universities had subscribed to all manner of inane, limiting Lazax laws, scientific advancement brooked no artificial constraint, especially not one based on the supposed moral code of hypocrites like the Lazax.

The universities understood this, and privately permitted unrestricted research by those Hylar considered talented or senior enough to deserve such leeway. The Black Trench Facility, hidden in the darkest, deepest recesses of the oceans of Jol, was known only to these foremost savants, and provided a safe space for conducting research unfettered by morality.

Arr had pursued his own projects there for a while, but found himself stifled by his fellow academics. He brooked no fools, a prickly disposition that had led to his departure from the University of Biomedical and Genetic Advancement, and funding disputes had made him decide to uproot from Jol altogether and relocate to the edge of the galaxy.

He knew there were others like him on Muaat, experienced, far-thinking researchers who kept themselves to themselves. He respected that. What, however, was someone like Tol doing here? Freshly graduated, with few contacts, working alone on an orbital station that made Arr's own isolated laboratory in the depths of the Praxen volcano seem positively accessible. Was she still Doctor Mayu's protégée? Had she been sent to spy on him?

He forcefully dismissed such a suspicion as a bout of paranoia, but the questions remained unresolved, and a mind like Arr's detested nothing more, except perhaps for the N'orr. He realized he had become annoyed.

"Subject stability, eighty-nine percent."

The dull voice of the presiding automedicum snapped him

out of his reverie. No, he thought. No, no, no. That was far too soon.

"Stabilize," he demanded. The automeds administered further medication.

"Subject stability, eighty-four percent."

It was still dropping, and so fast! This was a disaster. It was the very opposite of what he hoped to achieve.

He didn't want the N'orr to die quickly. He needed it to be slow.

Further precautions were initiated. A breather tube was inserted down the subject's throat. There were more injections, pulse-bursts, plasma and enzyme activators. Deep down though, in what the Hylar called their depths, Arr knew it was useless. He had failed, again.

At fifty percent he cut off medical assistance and allowed the N'orr to expire, watching in bitter silence as its vital signs flatlined. Eventually he deactivated those as well, annoyed by their whining. The automeds dropped into their charging cradles, and a cold silence gripped the laboratory.

Failure. Arr abhorred it. It made his stomach knot up and his scales ache. It haunted him, stalked him, confounded him. Years of research, a vast expenditure of resources, and he was not a step closer to the only thing that mattered – wiping the foul Sardakk N'orr from the galaxy.

He festered in his own anger and misery, until he noticed the words on his containment sphere. The data review was still up, and the brief section on Doctor Harial Tol was still highlighted.

Perhaps Tol could be more than a curiosity, a distraction.

Arr was not impulsive – few of his species were – but in that moment, he made a swift and decisive choice. He moved to his laboratory's communications array, located the high-orbit station taken over by Tol, and pinged a meeting invitation.

Arr worked better alone, but then, maybe that had been the problem all along.

A firestorm was coming, and if Tol didn't hurry she knew she would be incinerated.

The problem was that she hadn't finished harvesting yet, and she refused to turn back until she had what she needed. She had identified a growth of hardy zantu moss blooming along one of the upper ridges running down from Doolak 7. It was just what she had been looking for, but getting there was proving easier said than done.

On a planet covered by rugged mountains, plunging fissures and vast volcanos, the Doolak range was the biggest of them all. Spanning over half of Muaat from one polar cap to the other, the great highlands were the oldest geological strata and, consequently, the least active. While so much of Muaat's surface consisted of broiling magma lakes, erupting fire-geysers, sulfur smogs, and continent-covering clouds of black ash, the Doolaks stood proud of it all, a jagged spine rising up like the back of some monolithic god-beast, breaking out from the sulfuric depths. At the right altitudes, rain even fell here, and where there was rain, there was life.

That was what Tol was investigating. While the Universities of Jol-Nar had been drawn to colonizing Muaat due to its abundance of minerals and the strange nature of its native species, Tol was one of the precious few Hylar who saw value in what was otherwise overlooked – in this case, the many strange and varied forms of mosses and fungi that bloomed in the rare environment created by the Doolaks.

She began to climb toward the ridgeline, her enviro-suit whirring as its hydraulic joints and struts gave the support her otherwise-frail body needed to make the trek. As she went, the suit's gorget rim released a puff of misted water into her face, moistening her eyes and gills.

She was a Hylar, but unlike most of those occupying Muaat, she did not hail from Jol, but from the sister world of Nar. The Hylar possessed great racial diversity – not for her the clammy gray scales and skin of the Jol peoples, but rather the brilliant orange and blue stripes and crested head-fin of Nuun-Dascha, the capital of Nar. While the waters of Jol were deep, dark, and frigid, the seas of Nar were comparatively shallow and temperate, leading to further dimorphism. Tol was capable of breathing air for prolonged periods, and needed only semi-regular bursts of moisture to remain comfortable, rather than the full liquid immersion required by many Hylar. She did not find it particularly pleasant, especially on Muaat, where even at high altitudes the air was abrasive and warm, but it still made things easier.

She paused briefly to check on the progress of the firestorm. In the past month she had made advances with the plant life higher up the range, but zantu moss liked the heat, and it grew lower down the slopes. This was the furthest down she had yet traveled, and it was bringing her dangerously close to the fire layer, the point at which Muaat's true heat began to take over.

From a spur of rock, she took in the sight of the storm. It was rising up out of the low-lying ash banks that hung perpetually around the feet of the mountains, multiple points of angry red and yellow, flickering with wrathful intent. They began to glow and spread, accompanied by a distant, throaty roar that carried on the baking breeze.

Nar was popularly considered one of the most beautiful worlds in the empire, if not the entire known galaxy. Its warm, clear oceans glittered in the light of the Garian star, its depths teeming with multi-hued life and entire mountain ranges of brightly colored coral. Its islands were small, consisting of perfect white sand ringing blooms of verdant greenery. To visiting offworlders and foreign sentients it was considered a paradise.

Nar could not have been further from Muaat's appearance, and yet Tol found herself relishing the alien view as she watched the rising storm and took in what lay beyond. Other mountain ranges studded the horizon, many of them illuminated by the crimson glow of erupting volcanoes, adding their ash plumes to the dense miasma that shrouded everything beneath the Doolaks. It was a primordial realm, rugged and wrathful. In its natural smelters of molten stone and seething lava, Muaat forged the minerals that had so drawn the Hylar to it, but it also created the conditions for the resilient plant life that Tol hoped could lead to a medical breakthrough. If Nor was a paradise, pleasant and languid, then Muaat was a vast manufactory, hammering and burning out the raw materials necessary for further advancements.

"You probably shouldn't just stand there staring at it," said the voice of her mechafamiliar, ZALLY, in her ear. The little automaton was back manning the shuttle, but could track her via her savant's wireless uplink.

"Noted," she responded. The familiar was right, she was

taking too long. She tore herself away from the view and began to climb with renewed urgency. This was only her ninth visit to the planet's surface, but already she was well aware that, for all its hellish beauty, a firestorm was not to be trifled with. They rose hot and fast along the lower slopes, and even with her enviro-suit, she would be completely incinerated if it caught up with her.

The ascent was difficult. The black, rough stone beneath her kept crumbling and giving way, threatening to send her tumbling. She wished she had an anti-grav thruster or even an ascender kit, but she couldn't afford anything like that – she was just thankful she had a shuttle capable of getting her to and from Muaat's surface at all. She looked up as she went higher, hunting for a sign of the zantu moss she had identified earlier.

There it was, just a little farther up. Like most species of plant life clinging to Muaat's rocky back, the moss was long, pale, and brittle. So much as a breath of hot air could ignite it, but it also regrew in the aftermath of each conflagration, feeding off the rich ash blown up by the storms.

Tol scrambled the last few meters up to a small plateau that was thick with moss. Her scales were beginning to feel dry and uncomfortable in the mounting heat, but she didn't dare increase the frequency of her water bursts, for fear that she might run out before getting back to the shuttle.

She opened one of the specimen pods strung around her waist and began uprooting fistfuls of zantu, scientific finesse momentarily abandoned in favor of pressing urgency. With the pod rammed full, she resealed it and turned toward where she had downed her shuttle across the slope, on the only patch of ground flat and firm enough to effect a landing.

Too late.

A tongue of flame had surged up the mountainside, questing out like a blazing outrider from the main body of the advancing storm. A river of fire now lay between her and the most direct route to the shuttle.

She would have to cut around. She began following the ridge line, hoping to outrun the flames, her suit whirring loudly as she pushed it to the maximum. She felt the heat increasing, and realized that the moss left behind her had started to combust.

"Oh my sweet gills," she exclaimed, as the seriousness of the situation became truly apparent.

What a fool. She had gone too far, as usual. Clenching her gills, she put her head down and went as hard and fast as she was able, her soft bones beginning to ache. Fire was now catching and flaring up, the brittle zantu igniting like tinder.

Strange irony, Tol thought as she ran. An aquatic, meeting her end on a fire world. She found herself wondering if a Gashlai had ever drowned.

"ZALLY, get the engines fired up," she shouted into her savant.

"Possibly a poor choice of words," the familiar responded. "But noted."

She stumbled, almost plummeting back down the side of the ridge. She had to cut through the spur of fire between her and the shuttle, or she wasn't going to get above it and back down again before the main body of the storm caught her.

Without giving herself time to think, let alone panic any more, she charged the barrier of flames, hitting her aquifer and raising her forearms in front of her face. Her suit blasted the last of its water supply over her, the welcome relief replaced immediately by the choking, searing intensity of smoke and heat. She half fell, half threw herself through the curtain of flame, hissing with pain as it singed her feet and arms even through the protective layering of her suit.

Then she was through, and still running. The flames had snatched her, but had relinquished their grasp as soon as she reached the other side. The shuttle lay just ahead, a miserable old second-hand mono transporter that she had bought with the last of her saved university credits. The crawling edge of the firestorm was just meters from its lowered landing prongs.

Tol forced herself the last few paces, her whole body aching, a deadly, gagging dryness beginning to set in. She banged desperately on the cockpit access hatch, and ZALLY unlocked it from the inside, allowing her to scramble up and into the blister. Already, the firestorm had started to sweep around the shuttle, flames rising to engulf it. She was just thankful it was built for atmospheric exit and re-entry; otherwise she suspected it would already have started to melt under the furious heat.

"Engines up and running," ZALLY said, the fist-sized little chromatic familiar hovering on tiny anti-grav units alongside her in the cockpit. "Some systems still waking up though. Recommend you punch it."

Tol hit the cabin mister she had installed, giving herself another welcome dose of water. Everything beyond the cockpit's glassplex was now completely obscured by a wall of gray ash, shot through by fire. Warnings blinked across her display systems, but she overrode them with a series of vicious stabs before manually linking ZALLY as copilot and hauling back on the throttle.

The noise of the engines rose up to compete with the roar of the storm, ash, and burning embers billowing around them. Tol felt a moment's weightlessness as the shuttle began to lift off, clenching her gills again as she prayed to every aquatic deity she knew of. She retracted the landing prongs and kept the flier going up, hoping she could clear the cloud without hitting anything.

The engines began to cough and choke, filling with burning debris. More warnings appeared on her screens. But then, suddenly, the ash was gone. She could see pallid gray sky ahead, and Muaat's star, Mashaak, blinding her. Relief flooded her as she purged the engines and got her bearings.

"Silly Tol," she murmured to herself, repeating the phrase her mother always said when she made a mistake. Growing up, those mistakes had admittedly never been quite as severe as getting caught in a raging firestorm.

"Agreed wholeheartedly," ZALLY said snidely.

"Any damage?"

"Besides my nerve-circuits and the paintwork, which was never up to much anyway, no. We probably shouldn't make a habit of this though."

"Agreed."

Tol set the pre-logged flight coordinates to Exosphere Pod T19 and allowed herself to sit back in her seat. Behind her, the storm continued to rage, but it rose no higher, impotent and constrained.

Discounting the near-death experience, she decided that had gone quite well. She checked her specimen pod, thankful to find the zantu hadn't ignited inside it.

As she looked down at the pod, she spotted her savant

again, which was woven into the sleeve of her enviro-suit. Its screen had lit up since she had last used it, indicating a message, though it was too befouled by grime and ash to read. She wiped it clear with another cockpit moisture burst, peering at it.

While she had been scrambling up into the shuttle, someone had sent her a meeting request. She recognized the name. Doctor Atak Arr. He had been a senior lecturer while she had been at the University of Biomedical and Genetic Advancement, on Jol. He had taught disease and genetics, the same courses Tol had taken, but their paths had never crossed outside of the lecture domes and tuition pods. She remembered him as a cold, prickly Hylar, even for one from Jol's joyless gray depths. Rumor had it he had been a senior weapons developer with the Pan University Military before he became a lecturer.

She felt a moment's panic. Why was he out here, on Muaat, and why did he want to meet her? He must have heard about the incident at the university through old contacts. He surely knew she had been banished here? Was he going to chastise her, issue a Restriction of Research Edict? What if he had been sent by the university to track her down and rescind her doctorate? She had been told that wasn't going to happen, provided she caused no further trouble. Surely no one minded the research she was doing now, all the way out here? She had promised not to interfere in any way with the running of Muaat's campus-colony. By the Great Deeps, she had barely spoken to another Hylar since arriving, and had only seen the native Gashlai from a distance.

The shuttle began to rattle as it approached orbit, the sky

darkening. Twilight lay ahead, a twinkling sea of stars in positions she was still getting used to.

She did her best to quell her fears and settled back in the pilot's seat, buckling up. Then, she glanced back down at her savant.

"You're being irrational," she said out loud. There was only one way to actually find out what Doctor Arr wanted with her.

She opened the response section of the meeting request, and hit "attending."

CHAPTER FOUR

QUANN,
SOL FEDERATION COLONY WORLD

Zara embraced Hiram, closed her eyes, and for about five seconds, allowed herself to forget everything else.

"Any news from the control center?" her husband asked, breaking the moment.

"No change," she replied, in turn breaking the hug. "No further contact from the Letnev. I'm sorry, about all of this."

She had lost count of how many times she had said those words over the past few weeks. By day she occupied the sweltering depths of the government's control center, straining to keep Forebeck and Smyth from each other's throats while constantly expecting the viz projector to show the telltale signs of the Letnev vanguard ships opening fire. By night she returned to her hab and her family, and said sorry for bringing them to a world that seemed now to be on the cusp of obliteration.

"Stop saying that," Hiram said, pressing his forehead briefly to hers. He was tall and dusky, and still as handsome as the day Zara had met him back on Jord, though middle age had put a streak of gray through his swept-back, dark hair. "You told us, not even the Federation's intelligence agencies predicted this. How could you have known?"

"This is a frontier world," Zara replied, her husband's words doing nothing to lessen her guilt. "Places like these are never truly safe. I should have held out until I could get back to Jord."

"I'd much rather be here with you," Hiram said, "than back there hearing about it on the newscasters. I'd be sick with worry."

"But what about the kids?" Zara murmured, glancing through to the spare room. They had been doing their best to downplay the seriousness of the situation and keep them distracted. Macks, the younger of the pair, was happy to spend all his time on the SimTrix game console Zara had bought them before they arrived, but Elle had taken to sitting and staring out of the window, not at the neighboring buildings of Aruzoe's government quarter and the half-built dome of the Federation Hub, but at the sky. There were new stars there, visible during the day as well as the night – the Letnev Grand War Fleet.

"We're all in it together," Hiram responded quietly as they looked together down the corridor and into the kids' room. It was one of his favorite phrases. "And it's for the best."

"It's past their bedtime," Zara said. "That console screen is going to give Macks brain-rot."

"You let me worry about that," Hiram said. "So you can worry about everything else."

She nodded, told him to say she would be through in a moment to wish them goodnight, then kissed him and headed through to the kitchen unit. The family's household familiar

was just finishing the washing up. Its battery pack was low –
it never lasted more than an hour before it had to go back in
its charge cradle. Back on Jord, a government official like her
would have had half a dozen top spec familiars performing
housekeeping duties, but out here she had only been able
to afford this old, beat-up unit. She knew she shouldn't be
ungrateful. Life on a new colony was hard for everyone, and
she was more privileged than most.

She sat down at the dinner table and put her head in her
hands. She had cried a few times since it had all begun, just not
in front of anyone else. She felt too tired for tears tonight.

It wasn't just the obvious strain of the Letnev fleet hanging
like an executioner's axe, poised above them all. It was the
borderline collapse of the administration that was wearing
her down. Nobody seemed to know what to do. Forebeck was
doing what he did best, putting up a strong front for people
to rally around, and his public appearances had done much
to keep the populace calm. Zara had a seat backstage though,
and she could see the reality of the situation. Despite repeated
pleas for instructions and assistance to Jord, courier ships sent
from the Federation had given almost no advice besides the
fact that help was on its way.

Zara didn't know why the Federation was gripped by such
lethargy. She could only assume, from experience, that rival
political parties were arguing over a coordinated response,
probably not helped by meddling from High Minister
Hammid. It was probable too that they were having to explain
the situation to the Lazax oversight committees, who were
somehow even more bureaucratic in nature. That, combined
with slow fleet mobilization times, meant the Federation was

likely currently paralyzed, but didn't want to admit as much to its colonial administration. For all the difficulties of frontier life, Zara was sometimes glad she had left Jord behind.

Her savant buzzed. It was Traquay. She opened it in a flash, afraid of what the message might contain.

Put your caster on.

"Caster activate, news one," she said hastily, the viz monitor on the kitchen wall blinking to life. A report was just coming in. The newsreader looked as tired as Zara felt. He was busy saying something about footage newly transmitted from a courier vessel arrived from Arc Prime.

Zara verbally ordered the sound up. Arc Prime was the Letnev homeworld, the seat of their baronial government.

The view changed to a gaunt figure, long, white hair swept back from her high scalp, her flesh a blue-gray hue. She was dressed in a panoply of military finery, a blue dress jacket thick with golden brocade, a purple sash, and chest full of medals. She glared with fearsome imperiousness at the recording device for a moment, before speaking in univoca, the universal language used throughout the Lazax empire.

"My name is Baron Dazie Allic Werqan, Sire of Arc Prime, Supreme Admiral of the Grand Fleet, Supreme General of the Grand Army, Baron of Letnev. I am at this moment addressing Emperor Salai Sai Corian, the Lazax empire as a whole, and those disparate sentients that comprise it, including the humans of the Sol Federation and their colony on Quann.

"Two weeks ago, elements of the Grand Fleet were deployed to the terminus of the Quann Passage with instructions to effect a blockade of the Sol Federation's colonial holdings there. No harm is intended upon the people of Quann or the

Twilight Imperium

Federation at large. This action has been ordered by me with regret, but it is a desperate necessity.

"The blockade will remain in place until the following terms are met; the Lazax will withdraw their oversight forces from both Arc Prime, and all Letnev colonial possessions. The Lazax will cease their excessive tithing of the Letnev domains and lower the taxation grade to Level 2, in line with other major powers. Finally, the emperor will issue a public apology toward the Letnev as a whole for the lives taken and the damage done during both the First and Second Conflict of Lazax Aggression. All of these terms I submit now, verbally, to Emperor Salai Sai Corian. They will be supplied in written form at a later date.

"As long as any one of these terms remains unfulfilled, the blockade of Quann will continue. I reiterate, no harm is intended upon the humans of Quann, or the Federation generally. Any suffering that they experience must be laid wholly at the feet of the emperor, his imperial council, and the Lazax. For too long they have fettered and abused not only my people, but all the great sentients of this galaxy. We seek not their blood, as in ages past, but only honest redress of their injustices. If that is realized, the Quann Passage will be reopened, and these parts of the galaxy will enjoy the trade and prosperity Lazax dominion has thus far denied them."

The transmission cut out as abruptly as it had started, returning to the harried-looking news anchor. Zara simply stared for a while, trying to digest what she had just heard.

It was common knowledge that the proud Letnev railed against the oversight of the Lazax. They had twice rebelled, and twice been defeated, and now suffered the ignominy of an occupation force and higher taxes as a result. That they were demanding an end to both seemed outrageous, but the fact that they had made a play against the emperor by blockading Quann was even worse. What in the name of the Maker did any of them have to do with Lazax imperialism?

She called Traquay on her savant.

"You saw it all?" Traquay asked.

"Yeah. They're holding Quann hostage, and expecting the Lazax to pay up."

"It's wild," Traquay said. "Forebeck is going ballistic, and I don't blame him."

"Surely the Lazax will enter into talks?" Zara wondered out loud. "Now that the baron has called them out, this could threaten the stability of the whole empire."

"Since when did the emperor grant concessions to anyone, let alone the Letnev?" Traquay pointed out. "We'll be lucky if another war fleet isn't already on its way to Arc Prime."

That was true – another rebellion would surely see Quann caught up in it, and who knew how the Federation government back on Jord was going to respond to all this? Support the emperor? Let the Letnev use them as a bargaining chip? Lazax suzerainty was hardly popular in the Federation, and while the Letnev were considered unattractive allies, Zara had no doubt some would welcome any challenge to the emperor's authority. And if that challenge required a far-flung colony to suffer, they wouldn't lose much sleep.

Zara abruptly felt more isolated than ever.

"I'm coming back to the FedHub," she said, beginning to head for the door.

"Why?" Traquay asked, checking her. "That message was recorded and dispatched via courier from Arc Prime. There's nothing more you can do right now. Nothing more any of us can do. At least now we know why they're here. We're their hostages. There's a positive to that."

"A positive?" Zara asked incredulously.

"Yeah. If they kill us, they don't have anything left to bargain with."

CHAPTER FIVE

Dolorum,
Lazax Imperial Waystation

There was a message waiting for Syd and Zey at Dolorum.

The voyage there had been relatively brief but unpleasant. Sprinter spacecraft were among Syd's least favorite. They might be fast, but there was barely even room onboard for his spacer trunk – they were invariably small and cramped, and that meant a great deal of close proximity to Zey and his Winnu aide, Nauru. There was also the rather disconcerting presence of Chal, a Sardakk N'orr warrior of the prestigious Tekklar Elite, reassigned from praetorian duties on Mecatol Rex to guard the two Lazax during the expected negotiations. He was, like all his kind, a hulking, chitin-plated brute, so large he barely fitted into his assigned berth on the sprinter. The ticking and chirring noises made by the Sardakk N'orr were translatable into univoca by the "ambassador" device Chal wore around his thorax, but thus far he had hardly said a word, and seemed content to remain in his assigned space until they reached their destination.

For their own part, Syd and Zey had, up until Dolorum, settled into an acceptable compromise to the problems of sharing the small ship – they simply didn't talk to each other. Syd realized it was churlish, but he also considered it a necessity. When they reached Quann they would be required to work together. For the good of the empire, they had to set aside their differences, and the best way to do that was to not air those differences in the first place.

Syd had not known Zey long. He had first joined the ambassadorial corps a mere decade earlier. Zey came from wealth and privilege. He was a cousin to the emperor himself, and possessed all the contacts that entailed. Foisting relatives of the imperial household on the corps was common practice. At best, diplomatic duties could be used to teach the skills vital to those in positions of power throughout the Lazax hierarchy. At worst, it was an excuse to send youthful troublemakers off to some distant star, where they could cause less public drama.

Sadly, Zey's fate had not been some frontier dirt-hole. He had secured major ambassadorial rights, first among the Letnev on Arc Prime and then to the tri-system of Hacan, one of the most prestigious appointments in the empire. Syd knew several other worthy senior ambassadors who had been passed over for both roles. The imperial council – at least, elements Syd counted himself a part of – had worked hard to ensure the emperor did not slip into nepotism, but with Zey they seemed to have failed.

That would have been a point of contention, but if Zey proved to have a talent for his duties, it could have been overlooked. And Zey was talented, but he held views that Syd detested. He was a leading Accelerationist, a faction within the Lazax political sphere that Syd considered dangerous and radical. They believed that the empire's current trajectory was fatal and beyond correction, and that the best way forward was to tear down the structures of imperium and remake them. Zey was emblematic of what he had heard Atz's colleague, Marchu, disparage as the "new Lazax," a generation that saw and acknowledged the slow decay of their species' authority, but believed that the only cures were greater control and less autonomy for the greater civilizations.

That was the sort of attitude that Syd believed was contributing to the collapse. In centuries past, the Lazax had been respected as the liberators of the galaxy. They were the ones who had stood against the tyrannical kingship of the Mahact Gene Sorcerers. They were the ones who had rallied the other civilizations and destroyed the oppressors. And, after winning the war, it was the Lazax who had forged the peace, creating an empire based not on oppression or coercion, but upon the mutual benefits of shared, harmonious advancement for all species.

That was what the histories claimed, and it was an ideology that Syd believed in to the very core of his being. Pax Magnifica, magnificent peace, the motto of the Lazax empire and the foundation of Syd's commitment to unity and shared prosperity. As the galaxy grew more fraught, measured responses were needed – the Lazax couldn't deal with every crisis; they needed to work with the other civilizations and foster wider cooperation and understanding.

Not so for imperial officials like Zey. Tax increases, military expansion, greater oversight, those were his solutions. They found favor with those factions of the imperial court who believed the Lazax superior to their kindred sentients, and who viewed the imperium as their birthright, an inevitability, a strong, immovable citadel, rather than the fragile construct that Syd knew it to be. The attitudes of Lazax like Zey were dangerous.

Syd, and other moderates like Atz, had claimed as much, and he and Zey had sparred with increasing ferocity in recent years, both within the imperial council and when called up to the wider Galactic Council. Their rivalry was developing a reputation. Syd half wondered if Atz, ever the clever diplomat, hoped that by assigning them to their duties together, they might find common ground or a level of mutual respect. Perhaps he intended Syd to ameliorate the worst beliefs of the younger Lazax. So far, they had succeeded in avoiding any of that.

It was at Dolorum that things began to escalate. A Lazax-controlled waystation and communications picket relay point on the edge of an otherwise-uninhabited system of gas giants and void debris, the commander there reported to Syd and Zey – together – that he had received a communique from Mecatol Rex a few days prior to the sprinter's arrival.

Syd unsealed it, discovering a verse viz transmission of Atz reporting the developments they had missed while en route. Syd had worried that a war between the Letnev and the humans would have already broken out by the time they reached Quann, but thankfully neither side seemed to have been foolish enough to fire first.

Far more concerning was the recording attached to the transmission, a capture of Baron Werqan, ruler of the Letnev, delivering an open address from Arc Prime. The demands she made were simply outrageous, even more so considering she was openly using the human colony on Quann as a ransom. That surprised Syd. On the face of it, the entire thing looked like a serious misstep on behalf of Werqan. It was a risk completely out of step with her more conciliatory efforts in recent years. He felt sure something more was the cause of it.

Along with the attachment, Atz delivered new instructions. With neither side having yet opened fire, Syd and Zey were to redirect toward Arc Prime, where they would seek an official audience with Baron Werqan herself. Atz was unclear as to whether the emperor or his council had actually authorized either of them to negotiate or make concessions, but promised that more information would be waiting once they reached Arc.

"It all seems like a terrible mess, sir," Onni said to Syd in the cramped cabin they were forced to share. The sprinter had just set off on its new course, with a two-week estimated journey time.

"We'll have to make something of it," Syd said, keeping his thoughts even from his Winnu. Onni was right, of course. It was a terrible mess, and Syd didn't like it one bit. It felt as though events were still outpacing them. Worse, they were now being ordered into the Hacan's den, so to speak, to Arc Prime itself. The Letnev had twice risen against Lazax rule, and the first thing they had done on both occasions was slaughter the local imperial delegates.

Since the second uprising had been quashed, the empire had maintained a small but permanent garrison on Arc Prime, making it the only homeworld of one of the greater civilizations to have direct Lazax oversight. According to Atz's report, no aggression had yet been shown to the resident Lazax ambassador, Kwarni, or the garrison force, but that was little comfort.

Zey was obviously having similar thoughts, because on the second day-cycle out of Dolorum, he spoke to Syd properly for the first time.

"Have you ever met Baron Werqan?" he asked as Syd was sitting at the brig cabin's fold-down table, eating a dull breakfast of warka beans and grit bread enlivened a little by the scorch-sauce Onni always brought on voyages.

"I have not," he said, glancing at Zey. While Syd always made sure to dress properly outside of his cabin, Zey appeared to prioritize comfort during the journey. He had removed the datarecorder circlet from his brow and wore a simple off-white shift that Syd had initially mistaken for nightwear. It was, he supposed, just another difference between them.

Zey didn't respond to Syd's answer, and he briefly wondered if he should have offered up the information. He hadn't spent much time on Arc Prime before. He wondered if Zey was intending to use his greater experience with the Letnev as a point of superiority over him.

"I have been considering the… nature of recent events," Zey said eventually, the grandiosity of his turn of phrase almost making Syd scoff. "I have no doubt you have been as well. I think it would be worthwhile sharing our assessment of the situation we are about to enter."

Syd clasped his lower hands together while the upper two continued to work on his breakfast, chewing and swallowing slowly to buy himself time for a measured response.

"I have a number of thoughts, yes," he said. "But given your superior understanding of the Letnev, and as our destination is now Arc Prime, I find myself surprised that you would care for what I have to say."

"To ignore your general experience would be foolish," Zey said, causing Syd to tap his thumbs together – a Lazax equivalent to the pursing of lips seen in many other species.

"Is that an attempt at flattery, Ambassador Zey?" he asked.

"It is a stab at truth," Zey said. "Something we will both need to be conversant in if we are to avoid disaster. You know me well enough already, Syd. I am a pragmatist. I will do whatever it takes to uphold the empire. And right now, it seems best for our beloved imperium if we set aside our differences and pool our abilities."

"Fine words," Syd said, still guarded. "But I always intended to work with you, Zey. It is my duty, and the empire runs on Lazax doing their duty."

Zey inclined his head slightly, a rare sign of respect.

"Then how does it sit with you?" he asked, going so far as to take the fold-down bench opposite Syd, uninvited. "All of this?"

"It sits ill," Syd admitted, still trying to decide just how much he truly intended to share. "Matters cannot be as simple as they first appear."

"I agree," Zey said. "The problem is that we must reach the bottom of it by the time we arrive on Arc Prime."

"I doubt that will be possible, but any meeting we have with Baron Werqan will likely be highly informative."

Zey watched Syd closely as he finished his food, Syd refusing to feel uncomfortable. It was clear Zey wanted more – let him be the one to squirm. It occurred to Syd as he slid his plate and cutlery into the wash chute that he hadn't actually seen Zey eating at all since setting out. He either had food in his cabin or was waiting until Syd was asleep. Either way, a curious weakness.

"What are the Letnev hoping to achieve?" Zey said, clearly resolving to press on in his efforts to tease out Syd's thinking. "They must know their demands are utterly impractical."

Syd allowed himself a short sigh as he settled back in his chair and locked eyes with Zey. He was probably right, he privately acknowledged. At some point, they were going to have to start working together, maybe even trusting each other. It was his duty, and he always did his duty.

"I don't believe the Letnev intended to deploy a fleet to Quann and begin a blockade," he told Zey. "At least, not the majority of the Letnev. I think that the commander of their grand war fleet, Admiral Arrokan, took his assets and has invaded Sol-held space unilaterally and is blocking the Passage without instructions to do so. That would explain a great deal of what we are currently seeing."

Zey nodded slowly.

"If Arc Prime was unaware of the deployment of the Grand Fleet, then Ambassador Kwarni, the empire's spies and officials, and the usual rumormongers would also be unaware," he said. "That is why everyone was caught off-guard."

"It also explains why Baron Werqan was silent for two weeks after the fleet's arrival at Quann," Syd carried on. "She will not wish it to become public knowledge that the greater part of her space assets have just gone rogue. She has to maintain the appearance of strength and unity. She has no choice other than to claim the fleet has moved on her orders, and now she has further cemented her authority among her own people by issuing bold, public demands."

"Admiral Arrokan is a known agitator," Zey said, finally offering up knowledge of his own. "He is a senior member of the Letnev faction trying to roll back Lazax authority, known as the Resurgentists. If they get their way, there will be a third rebellion. Most know this, and are part of the more gradualist majority that wants to see redress without resorting to another conflict. The baron herself was part of the gradualist group, though seemingly no longer."

"Arrokan has forced her hand," Syd observed, thinking it through. "By making this play, he has left the Letnev government with no choice other than to back him or admit to a schism. Baron Werqan has chosen the former. A dangerous choice."

"It is beyond dangerous," Zey said. "The majority of the Letnev armed forces are Resurgentists. They would back war against the empire in spite of the Arc Prime public's desire to avoid it. It will be the military's support that Arrokan will be counting on, and they will be the ones Baron Werqan is attempting to win back with her harsh rhetoric. And strangling trade to this sector of the galaxy via a blockade of the Passage ensures time is on his side."

"Our course is clear enough then," Syd said. "We must convince the baron to reverse her stance. Out Arrokan as a rogue element, convince her that now is the opportunity to rid herself of the Resurgentists and secure peace for a generation. Once Arrokan is isolated, he can be dealt with."

"Can he?" Zey asked, the question catching Syd by surprise. He realized the angle of Zey's thinking quickly enough.

"There are precious few imperial fleet assets within easy striking distance of either the Quann system, or the far side of the wormhole," Zey said. "The recent budget cuts and the redeployment of Commodore Varnak to the Mahact Plateau have made sure of that."

Of course that was something Zey would complain about. He and his other Accelerationist allies were constantly agitating for greater military spending and a more aggressive, interventionist policy. Syd wondered if he realized how closely related his ideology was to the likes of Arrokan and his Letnev Resurgentists.

"We will make use of the Federation fleet," Syd pointed out, refusing to give Zey's grievances any consideration. "Given it is their colonial holding currently blockaded, and their trade that languishes, I imagine the humans will be happy enough to join with what fleet elements we have in the sector to form an imperial reaction force. That will be a match for the Letnev's so-called grand fleet, especially if Baron Werqan renounces them. Their disunity will be their downfall."

"Do you think the other great powers will stand by and watch this play out?" Zey asked. The question sounded sincere, and it was something Syd himself had been mulling over. Laying plans was one thing, but anticipating the domino effect they could have on the other great civilizations and the factional blocks throughout the empire was quite another.

"I'm sure the imperial council will make certain that no other civilization is foolish enough to speak out in support of the Letnev's current demands," he said. "Beyond that, it will depend how quickly and efficiently we deal with this. If matters go as we hope, I doubt there will be major repercussions. If we misstep, or things escalate further, other groups may see an opportunity. I find the recent discord between Jol-Nar and the Sardakk N'orr particularly concerning. There is only so much we can account for, however. The important thing is to continue to move quickly."

"Get ahead of events," Zey said thoughtfully, echoing what Atz had said.

"Exactly." Syd nodded. "Now, if you will excuse me, I have further data to review before our arrival on Arc Prime."

"Further data?" Zey wondered aloud.

"Reading, on Letnev current politics," Syd said. "We may have reached a temporary accord, Ambassador Zey, but I don't wish to be conducting affairs on Arc Prime relying solely on your knowledge."

CHAPTER SIX

Since getting back to Exosphere Pod T19, Harial Tol had barely slept. The message from Doctor Arr played on her mind constantly. It seemed more like a summons than an invitation. She felt like she was a young spawnling again, being ordered to her junior head-scholar's dome because she had been caught letting other pupils copy her homework.

She had exhausted the possible reasons Arr wanted to see her, so when the time came to return from the exosphere to Muaat's surface it was almost a relief. She embarked on her shuttle, triggering the autopilot and strapping herself in. ZALLY was, as ever, upbeat.

"Maybe he wants to give you a job?" she wondered via the comms link connecting the shuttle to T19. Tol had left the familiar behind this time to oversee the station. She didn't really think the doctor would appreciate her company.

"As long as he lets me continue my own research," Tol said, privately thinking an offer of employment from Arr was unlikely. She had done her reading on him. There had been several public spats between him and other academics while she had still been a student on Jol, though she hadn't really crossed paths with him in person. How he had ended up on Muaat, on the edge of Hylar-controlled space, hadn't made it into the public sphere. It seemed likely though, given his background, that it had something to do with Jol-Nar weapons research and production.

The shuttle's descent path took it past New Escha. That was the name the Jol-Nar war fleet had given to the vast manufacturing dock still being constructed in Muaat's high orbit. When it was complete it would be the single largest Hylar military installation anywhere in the galaxy, larger even than the Pan University Fleet Headquarters above Jol itself. It was a vast crescent of terridium and galvanized voidsteel, much of it still a skeletal framework, surrounding by the running lights of the tens of thousands of automated construction familiars and tech-labor vehicles, clustered around it like the minnows that latched onto the great fin-behemoths or depth-surfers of Tol's homeworld. It was bigger than any of Muaat's moons, and already it was beginning to produce new warships, half-completed void hangars housing the chassis of future cruisers and frigates, fueled by the raw materials being dredged up directly from Muaat's primeval surface below.

It was a potent symbol of Jol-Nar militarism, and Tol despised it. Her species was one of the most gifted in the galaxy – with their incredible intellect they had given the other civilizations so much, great and small. Everything from the creation of the savant as it was used today, to FTL communication devices no larger than the palm of a generic mammalian sentient's hand.

It wasn't only technology that the Hylar spearheaded either, but advancements across the scientific spectrum, from physics and chemistry to biology and medicine. The lattermost Tol had always taken particular pride in. How many billions the galaxy over were alive today because of vaccines developed in Jol-Nal laboratories, or the dedicated work of the Disease Intervention Units?

So why did some of her kind feel the need to turn their intellect toward the manufacturing of war and oppression?

She knew she was a hypocrite. What were the universities doing here, if not oppressing? Muaat was not some uninhabited ball of fire and rock. When the Hylar had arrived, they had discovered the Gashlai, a fully sentient species. Among the Circle of Regents who governed the Jol-Nar under the auspices of the headmaster, there had been no question about Gashlai autonomy, no consideration for the rights or privileges that inclusion in the Lazax empire supposedly guaranteed them. The planet had been claimed, and a swift and decisive Hylar military occupation had seen the Gashlai suppressed and enslaved. Now they were used as forced labor in the pillaging of their own planet's natural resources.

Tol knew all this, but in the month since she had arrived on Muaat she had never encountered a Gashlai up close, nor witnessed their enslavement first-hand. She had been banished here, consigned to an isolated orbital station for the next year-cycle as penance for what she had done. The Gashlai's subjugation was not her fault.

That was what she tried to believe, though she knew that in truth she was a part of the system of oppression. What could she possibly do about it though?

She again forced her concerns to the back of her mind as the shuttle cleared an ash bank and began its descent over the burning red-and-black expanse of the Molten Eternal. The initial rendezvous she had received for the meeting was close to Muaat's planetary capital, Mavgala, which lay beyond the lava ocean. It was the most populous Gashlai settlement on Muaat, sited at the base of Mount Mav, the greatest volcano in the second-largest range after the Doolaks – the Kormav Mountains. Jol-Nar archaeo-investigators placed the city's construction at three-point-two thousand years prior to first contact. Certainly, the sight of it dispelled any lingering belief that the Gashlai were not an advanced or intelligent group of sentients.

The structures of the city were vast, cyclopean edifices, hewn from the black rock of the mountainside. Their own flanks were in turn honeycombed with Gashlai dwellings and infrastructure and overlooked by tens of thousands of intricately carved bas reliefs and statue columns, many in the shape of the flames-and-eyes, the symbol most readily associated with the Gashlai. The entire city was cast in a lambent red glow by the two rivers of lava that ran past it to the east and west, for Mount Mav itself was still active, its jagged crown perpetually churning forth the wrath of Muaat's core. Huge bulwarks around the uppermost towers of the city redirected the lava flow around its lower portions, though smaller tributaries of the molten rock continued to pass between the towers, the fiery illumination giving the city light despite the pall of ash and black smoke that hung perpetually upon it. The Gashlai traveled between the towers via hundreds of walkways strung between them, some of them so low they barely stood above the bubbling, seething swell of flame.

To a water-dweller like Tol, the lava city was terrifying. The scale of the stone habitation blocks were themselves intimidating, and that was without factoring in the fire and brimstone. She had only visited Mavgala once, when she had first arrived on Muaat and been required to report to the campus authorities. The sight of it had almost convinced her to go rogue and flee the system. While the isolation of Exosphere Pod T19 was difficult at times, she was thankful she was out there, on the icy fringes of space, and not down here amidst the leering statues, choking ash, and furnace-like heat.

The shuttle passed through another skein of ash, and she saw the landing zone marked out by green lights below. Since the Jol-Nar takeover, Hylar installations had been added throughout Mavgala. Now the blackened stone blocks and columns were topped by the bare steel and white plasticon structures – weapons defense systems, landing pads, communications arrays and prefab aqua-dome habitats for the soldiers and scientists that now called Muaat home. Even the walkways and bridges between the towers had been bookended by electro-gates that allowed Hylar overseers to dictate when they were allowed to be used, enacting curfews and restricting travel. It was a city under occupation, and despite its utterly alien nature, Tol couldn't help but feel a pang of sorrow and regret as she again saw the extent of its subjugation.

The landing zone Arr had sent her to was a tertiary strut jutting out of the flank of one of the tower blocks. Besides another, smaller aircraft, it appeared to be abandoned. Tol's old, rattling shuttle settled down with an ungainly thud, and

she spotted something approaching out of the fiery twilight –
a familiar, a chrome-plated greetings unit, its optic clusters
glowing through the ashy pall.

Tol clambered out of her cockpit blister to greet it. She
had chosen to wear her enviro-suit's full head-bowl, partly
to insulate herself from Mavgala's inimical atmosphere of
smoke and ash and flame, and partly because she recalled
Arr was a native of Jol, and therefore had to wear his own
containment sphere constantly. Many Jol Hylar were envious
of their Nar cousins' ability to breathe like land-dwellers for
extended periods, and some even took offense when they did
so in person. At that moment, the last thing Tol wanted was to
annoy a prickly former lecturer, so she had consigned herself
to the full suit.

"Present credentials," the familiar droned as Tol alighted
on the landing deck. She pulled up her data log on her savant
and accepted the familiar's connection request, allowing it to
identify her.

"Credentials verified. Stand by for transmission."

Tol stood dutifully still, and a moment later the small
screen in the familiar's center beamed out a prerecorded viz
projection of a Hylar that she recognized as Arr.

"Welcome to the surface, Harial Tol," the doctor said with a
typically cold, precise Jol accent. "I am sure you are wondering
why a senior academic such as myself has asked to see you. All
will be answered soon enough, in person. Please follow the
familiar to the automated monoride. It is calibrated to take
you to my facility, and will likewise return you to your own
transporter once our initial discussion is completed. Please
deactivate your savant, and do not bring any other log-devices

or familiars of your own. If this is clear and acceptable, please give verbal indication."

"It is clear and acceptable," Tol said, looking at the recording of Arr rather than the familiar beaming it, out of habit.

The recording cut off, Arr's words replaced by the automaton. "Follow."

Tol did so after pausing to make sure the shuttle was locked and secure.

"All okay?" ZALLY asked over the savant, her voice chopped up by the dreadful atmospherics of the Gashlai city.

"Think so," Tol said. "I'm going to go dark for a bit, but don't fret, I'm alright."

She only hoped that was true.

"Deactivate savant before proceeding," the familiar said as they reached the door to the monoride, as sleek and chromatic as the bot.

"Alright, alright," Tol huffed, powering off the wrist device. She climbed in as the familiar settled into the remote pilot cradle at the flier's rear.

The atmospheric sensors on Tol's enviro-suit read a marked change within the monoride, the air cool and heavy with moisture content. She settled into one of the recliner chassis built to hold Hylar enviro-suits and strapped herself in as she felt the ride's engines power up.

It was only as they pulled away that she realized the monoride's windows were black, completely opaque. She looked for an option to change them on the passenger control display, but there wasn't one.

She could guess why. She had already assumed from the nature of the summons and the lack of information on Arr that he was not present on Muaat as a member of the campus-colony administration, but rather as a private researcher. He would not want to divulge the location of his laboratory, even to fellow Hylar.

It was understandable, but it did nothing to ease Tol's concerns. She could gauge from the plunging sensation she felt within her suit that they were descending, though exactly where to she had no idea.

The journey continued for approximately twenty minutes, though time was difficult to gauge without her savant on. Her nerves were threatening to take over again, so she hyper-fixated on her initial findings with the zantu moss. Her hopes that it would contain cellular structures that might aid in the strengthening of silicate fiber-prosthetics seemed to be well founded, though more tests needed to be run. That probably meant another trip down to the Doolak Highlands. Next time she would be sure to leave well ahead of any rising firestorms.

The distraction techniques worked tolerably well until she felt the monoride easing to a halt. She unstrapped herself and rose just as the door slid open.

She had half expected Arr's familiar to lead her on another phase of the journey, but instead she found herself looking up at the doctor himself.

Arr was, like most Jol-born Hylar, much taller than Tol. His gray complexion and finless skull were a far cry from Tol's bright hues and frills, and even their enviro-suits seemed at odds – Arr's was pristine, medical white, while Tol's older, dark blue model was stuffed with the grime of the highlands and ash picked up while transferring from the shuttle to the monoride. For members of the same species, they could hardly have appeared more different.

If Arr felt any distaste at that difference, he didn't show it, at least not overtly.

"Harial Tol," he said, a statement rather than a question. Tol resisted the urge to offer the brief genuflection usually performed for senior members of the universities. Tol wasn't a student anymore, and Arr wasn't her lecturer.

"Doctor," she said, trying to sound confident. "I received your invite."

"Clearly," Arr said without inflection, causing Tol to cringe internally at her own words as he carried on. "You have made tolerable time. I trust your trip from the exosphere went without issue?"

Small talk. That was very unlike a Hylar academic, especially one from Jol. Tol played along while Arr began to walk, gesturing for her to follow.

"Yes, well, the orbital route took me past New Escha. It is a... fearsome sight."

She followed Arr, taking in her new surroundings as she went. They had alighted in a subterranean vehicle bay. The place appeared to have been tunneled out of the volcanic Muaat bedrock, and while it was still infernally hot, there was at least no sign of lava anywhere. Several other transport vehicles stood in a row, attended by familiar cleaning units that were scrubbing ash off the windshields and cleansing the engines.

"You are conversant in Jol-Nar military orbital installations?" Arr asked on the heels of Tol's comment about New Escha.

"Oh no, not at all," Tol replied hastily, not wanting to give the doctor an incorrect impression. "I'm entirely unfamiliar with the military activities of a campus-colony."

"Inexperience is often the cause of intrigue," Arr mused. "In truth I am thankful you are not of a militaristic persuasion. I have need of someone more familiar with biology than with armaments."

Tol resisted the urge to ask more about Arr's reasoning. They had reached an elevator platform that scanned Arr's biometrics before smoothly initiating. Tol had expected to go up, but the shaft took them further down, seemingly ever deeper into Muaat's depths.

"Tell me, Tol, just how is it that you came to be assigned to this campus-colony?" Arr asked as the descent continued. "Hylar of your young age rarely seek out your current level of isolation willingly."

It was a forthright question, but Tol was unsurprised. Jol-Nar rarely bothered with conversational niceties or politeness, which were usually disparaged as a waste of time and effort, a frivolity indulged in by less cerebrally gifted sentients. That was doubly true of university academics, past or present.

"I was sequestered here by order of the Pan University Council," Tol said, deciding it was best to be equally forthright.

"A body second only to the Circle of Regents and the headmaster himself," Arr mused. "As punishment?"

"Yes."

"Explain further."

"I wrote a series of publications the council deemed to be in violation of the best interests of the universities."

"A young Nar doctor writing seditious treatises," Arr summarized. "Quite intriguing. Continue."

The elevator came to a silent halt and its doors slid open. Beyond them lay a corridor of clean white plasticon tiling and stark, bright lumen strips. The air was cool and damp, only the faintest hum hinting at the plethora of systems working to maintain the precisely calibrated atmosphere. It looked and felt more like the inside of a Jol-Nar research ship than a facility buried in the bowels of an inimical volcano planet.

"I argued for the expedition of knowledge," Tol said. "Beyond the realm of the universities, or even the Hylar species."

"I see," Arr said, his tone giving no hint as to how he viewed her admission. They stepped out of the elevator and began to pass down the corridor.

"I made what I believe is a sound argument for the spreading of scientific knowledge," Tol went on unprompted, feeling now that she had to defend herself. "While the advancements of our species have been to the benefit of the entire galaxy, so much more could be achieved if we were willing to disseminate our knowledge to our fellow sentients."

"A radical concept," Arr said, beginning to show his hand. "What is it the humans say? Knowledge is power? As crude an axiom as their kind have ever come up with, but it has some merit. Knowledge is our gift to the galaxy. It is not the galaxy's right to take it."

"That is the received wisdom among the universities, yes," Tol said, wondering if she was really about to get into yet another argument with a doctor. Where could they possibly banish her to next?

"Our intelligence is what makes us the premier sentients in this galaxy," Arr continued, speaking matter-of-factly. "Were we to freely share said intelligence we would be providing the other great civilizations with an unfair advantage. What would they do with it? They are all, in their own unique ways, brutish, expansionist, shortsighted or degenerate. Imagine a galaxy where they enjoyed all the advancements of us Hylar, in medicine, in physics, in warfare, in technology, without the need to have said advancements maintained or operated by the oversight of the universities. It would lead to chaos, to devastation on a galactic scale. It would not only undermine the power of Jol-Nar, it would be morally unconscionable."

"I believe you have too low an opinion of our fellow sentients," Tol dared say.

"Then you have not recanted your thesis?" Arr asked. "You still believe that the universities should share their research?"

"It was sharing that first elevated the universities," Tol pointed out, using an argument she had utilized before. "Only with the Marn Tay's Informational Core and the free exchange of knowledge between the different academic bodies were we able to take the next step in our advancement."

"Knowledge between Hylar should be freely available, yes," Arr said. "But it is a grave mistake to imagine anyone not of our own kind would be able to comprehend the work we undertake, let alone put it to good use."

"Did the universities ask you to speak with me?" Tol asked, now driving at a point of her own.

"Not at all," Arr said. "Most of the universities are not even aware of my presence here on Muaat, and I hope to keep it that way."

There was a small concession. He had shared something with her that he didn't wish others to know. It should have been reassuring, in a way, but it only made her more determined to find the reason for her summons. Something felt wrong about the whole encounter, and her unease was building.

"Then can I ask for the purpose of this meeting?" Tol pressed on. "Unless the defense of my previous thesis has caused you to reconsider any future discussions?"

"It has not," Arr said. "The nature of your presence here indicated that you had done something to upset the hierarchy of the universities. If that had been a concern I would not have contacted you initially."

"And does your presence here indicate the same?" Tol asked.

"Only tangentially. Tell me, what is your opinion of the Sardakk N'orr?"

They had passed a number of doorways along the length of the corridor, all sealed. Now they were approaching the end of the passage, shielded by a military-grade blast door. Tol felt an abrupt resurgence of her earlier forebodings.

"I have no opinion of the Sardakk N'orr," she said truthfully. "I have never encountered one."

"You are aware of their… nature though," Arr said, stopping beside the door and entering a series of codes and bio-scans. "If you have any understanding of galactic history or the biology of the greater civilizations, you will know how they… infest."

"I suppose that is one way to describe them," Tol allowed. The Sardakk N'orr were indeed one of the most populous of the great civilizations. An insectile form of sentient, they hailed from the brutal world of Quinnara, and their tendency to spread and multiply was a point of some infamy across the galaxy, as was their ruthlessness on the battlefield. For those reasons they had long acted as auxiliary infantry for the Lazax.

Tol couldn't claim to know much of them, however, beyond the basics included in her studies, and she suspected they were heavily slanted by university bias.

"The N'orr have long been opponents of Hylar enlightenment," Arr said, finishing inputting the final code. "More than any other species, they are ignorant to the wonders of technology and indifferent to their proper place in the galaxy."

There was a whirring sound as the blast door's locking bolts retreated and the entrance concertinaed open. Arr stepped through, motioning for Tol to follow.

"I'm not sure there's such a thing as a 'proper place in the galaxy,' for anyone," Tol began to say, trailing off as she got a view of what waited beyond.

At a glance it looked akin to the medical lecture halls Tol had spent so much time in while at university on Jol. The operating room was circular, with a sunken center and a surrounding viewing platform. The middle, picked out by a harsh white spotlight, was dominated by a medi-array consisting of a surgery slab, quintisensor unit, and a bristling collection of injector racks and incision blades. Automeds, the robotic familiars dedicated to medical and surgical tasks, drifted languidly through the air, their anti-grav motors purring and chromatic shells gleaming.

None of that was unexpected. What Tol hadn't anticipated was that there would be a subject strapped on the slab.

It was, or had been, a Sardakk N'orr. The creature was larger than Tol had imagined, with multiple limbs and a rigid carapace. That carapace had been slit, its jagged, shorn edges gleaming and its inner organs exposed.

Tol also realized that the N'orr's limbs had been restrained with cuff clamps. Before its death, it had been struggling.

Arr was watching her. She forced herself to look away from the grisly specimen and face the doctor, the sense of revulsion she felt at the sight hardening her resolve. She would have answers.

"Tell me why I'm here," she said.

"You are here because I need assistance," he answered. "I am attempting to develop a pathogen linked to the biological composition of the Sardakk N'orr."

"But… why?" Tol asked, trying to process the situation properly. She was afraid she was misunderstanding, and making a terrible mistake.

"I am sure you know better than I that the creation of a virus is no easy feat, even for Hylar doctors such as ourselves," Arr said in a patient tone. "It requires balance. Too potent, and it will kill its subjects swiftly and fail to spread. Too mild and it will not kill enough."

"No I… I understand that. I mean, why are you trying to create such a virus?" Tol asked, her horror mounting.

Arr looked at her with only the slightest curl of a lip, bubbles popping up within his containment sphere.

"Because if we do not, the galaxy will be overrun," he said, tone changing. Now he sounded as though he were addressing a wayward spawnling on their first day of logic theorem. "I have run the algorithms, and I am not the only one. All projections agree. At their rate of reproduction, the Sardakk N'orr will begin overburdening the galaxy's basic resources within the next three centuries. Already their presence puts pressure on several of the other great civilizations, ourselves included.

"They are a plague, an insectoid infestation masquerading as a sentient civilization. And where there is plague, where there is infestation, then blight and famine surely follow. They are death, Under-Doctor Tol, death to us, and the rest of the galaxy."

"So, you propose to become death to them first," Tol surmised softly.

"Someone must. The only options for rapid and systemic population reduction are war and disease, and the former is considerably more costly, dangerous, and inefficient. The latter, however, offers cause for hope."

Tol looked once more around the operating room, ostensibly considering the doctor's words when in fact she was trying to compose herself enough to offer a coherent response. She had worried that there was some illicit component to whatever research Arr was conducting, hence his presence on a remote world like Muaat. The depths of his depravity though, and the brazen nature of it, were shocking. She had encountered numerous Jol academics who seemed to lack empathy or even a basic grasp of the concepts of mortality during her studies, but never had she seen those characteristics laid out with such chilling clarity.

As she paused, she realized too that the operating room was even more nightmarish than she had first noticed. The circular wall beyond the observation walkway held dozens of recesses, illuminated by the white glow of individual containment fields. Within each one was a N'orr's body part, dissected and put up on display. There were mandibles and limbs and carapace plates, even individual organs and a carefully bisected head. Tol felt her gills shiver with revulsion.

"I will not help you," she told Arr, her voice quiet but icier than Jol's most frigid depths. "I will do anything *but* help you. What you propose is utterly disgusting. I know that there is little love lost between the universities and the N'orr, but this… what you do down here brings disgrace upon all Hylar. I am ashamed to even share a home system with you, and all others who hold your views."

"How disappointing," Arr said. "I had hoped, regardless of the youthful foolishness that you have already espoused, that an enterprising under-doctor such as yourself might appreciate my vision. If you had any talent as a medical student you would be receptive to the great opportunity I am providing. Clearly, however, you are defective on numerous counts. I should have known as soon as I realized you were Nar-spawn."

"The only defective one here is you, doctor," Tol snapped. "I will not indulge your vileness a moment longer. In fact, I fully intend to report you."

Arr laughed, the mirthless sound scraping from his suit's vocalizer.

"I did not invite you here to be threatened, little stripe-fish. To what end would you report me? Do you believe my studies illicit, forbidden? You are naïve to a degree I find pitiful."

"You think the universities are the first and final authority, but how would those beyond Jol-Nar react if they discovered this kind of research was being undertaken?" Tol demanded. "What would the empire say? If you do not fear the Circle of Regents or the headmaster, maybe you fear the Lazax?"

Arr moved with surprising speed. Before she could respond, he had snatched Tol's wrist, the strength of the frame-enhanced grip digging into the cuff of her own enviro-suit.

"The empire would not dare interfere in the research of Jol-Nar," he hissed. "The Lazax need our technology, our intelligence, more than any others. Without the universities, there would be no empire."

"And yet you display discomfort at the suggestion," Tol said, forcing her voice to remain level and not show the pain she was experiencing at the Hylar's grip. "Curious."

Arr let go as abruptly as he had snatched her.

"Your intelligence is clearly far below what I would expect from a fellow Hylar, but I trust my point has been made," he said. "You will leave now. You may rest assured that I will be monitoring you closely. Any attempt to discuss the particulars of my research will meet with retribution. I hope that is clear, for your sake."

"Don't worry, I understand you perfectly," Tol said, turning her back on him with the full intent of causing the maximum degree of disrespect. "I hope I never set eyes on you, or this place, ever again."

CHAPTER SEVEN

QUANN,
SOL FEDERATION COLONY WORLD

The Phoenix Fleet of the Sol Federation arrived in the Quann system just short of a month after the first appearance of the Letnev fleet.

It was, all things considered, sooner than Zara had dared hope. While official directives from Jord were still thin on the ground, someone somewhere had clearly kickstarted the fleet mobilization.

Word of the development reached the planet surface not long after Zara arrived at the FedHub for the regular morning briefing update. It was met initially by quiet disbelief as everyone gathered around the viz projector and waited for the scans to complete their analysis, followed by whoops and cheers of joy when it became clear it wasn't an anomaly. Twenty-nine capital ships and carriers had just exited the wormhole, on the far side of the Letnev fleet. The barony's forces still had a numerical advantage, but the odds had been shortened at a stroke.

The Phoenix Fleet was led by Admiral Ular, an officer Zara recognized from her time back on Jord. He addressed the Quann administration via audio, the fleet too far out of range for a viz transmission and unable to get closer as the Letnev fleet assumed defensive stances of their own.

"Jord knows of your plight," the admiral said, voice chopped by static. "My orders are to bring this blockade to an end by whatever means necessary and restore trade through the Passage."

"Does that include the use of force?" Smyth asked sharply before Forebeck could speak, the governor throwing the delegate a furious glance.

"Yes, but I have been asked to take into consideration the mood of the Quann administration."

Those words gave Zara a little hope. She had felt the rush of elation when the fleet's presence had been confirmed, but it had quickly given way to fresh fears. If the Federation had responded in force, that would make Quann ground zero in any possible escalation of tensions. If war broke out, the colony would be devastated.

She was relieved when Forebeck voiced the same concerns.

We don't want a war," he told Admiral Ular. "We want the blockade broken. Those aren't the same things."

"Acknowledged," Ular said. "But one may lead to the other. We're in no position to negotiate with the Letnev. We're not the ones they're seeking redress with."

According to Ular the imperial ambassador on Jord had been working with the high minister and the Federation parties to decrease the possibility of armed conflict, but just what overall strategy the Lazax were adopting to deal with the crisis remained a mystery. Smyth had claimed repeatedly that Quann would have to look to itself first and foremost, a stance that even Zara struggled to disagree with. She had little knowledge of the inner workings of the empire. Given the emperor's reputation for indolence, she wouldn't be surprised if the blockade had barely registered at the heart of the imperium, on far-off Mecatol Rex.

The first few days after the arrival of the Phoenix Fleet were tense. Zara, already exhausted, pushed herself to the next level as the senior staffers maintained a continual state of readiness in case one side or the other went live with weapons systems. Throughout it all, she tried to reassure her family during the rare periods when she was at home and not asleep. She was terrified that she had brought them to their deaths.

"I hope there is a war," Macks said completely unbidden one evening, over dinner. Zara looked up sharply from the trigrain bread and tusker stew the household familiar had prepared for them, too shocked at first for words. Finding time to have dinner with Hiram and the children was a rare luxury, but she hadn't expected this.

"What do you mean, Macks?" Hiram asked, glancing from his son to his wife, his tone edged with warning.

"I want us to fight," Macks said, plowing on. "This is our world. If some other species wants to take it from us, we'll beat them!"

"Where did you get an idea like that?" Zara said sharply, fixing her son with a stern expression.

"Everyone's saying it," Macks shrugged. "And isn't it true? If something belongs to you and someone else tries to take it, shouldn't you fight them?"

"No," Zara said. "You should show them, and everyone else, that they're in the wrong."

"And what if they won't listen? What if nobody else cares?"

"It's these games he's been playing on that console," Zara said, turning her ire on Hiram rather than allow herself to be dragged down by the child's logic. "I knew they were too violent."

"Sometimes you have to fight, yes," Hiram said to Macks rather than answering Zara, speaking with a patience she couldn't currently find within herself. "But it should only ever be a last resort. The Federation didn't become great by fighting, except when it had to."

"How did it become great?" Elle piped up innocently, toying with her own tusker stew.

"Because of the hard work of people like your mother," Hiram said, nodding toward Zara. She met his gaze, and it took an effort to keep her emotions in check.

She couldn't admit that, right then, it felt like all the hard work was going to be in vain.

Then, five days after the arrival of the Phoenix Fleet, everything changed.

Traquay pinged Zara's savant in the dead of night, not long after she had gotten to bed. Her exhaustion was so severe that she considered ignoring the message, but even at the edge of endurance, the potent combination of duty and curiosity got the better of her. She rolled over in bed and checked the savant, flowing gently in its charging cradle.

The Letnev have been in touch. They're offering a way out.

Zara rubbed at her eyes, wondering if she was misreading the message. It remained unchanged. She snatched the savant from its cradle and slipped from between the sheets, padding out into the hallway and then on through to the kitchen so as not to wake Hiram or the kids.

She called Traquay.

"What have you heard?" she asked as soon as she picked up.

"Arrokan contacted Admiral Ular directly about an hour ago and told him that the colonial governor and his chief aides and advisors would be offered safe passage off Quann. They get to go home, to Jord."

"By the Maker. Does Forebeck know about the offer yet?"

"Yes."

"And? Is he taking it?"

"Not immediately. He has asked for clarification from Jord, via Ular. The situation is delicate. He told me he'll abide by whatever the parties and the high minister decide on."

"If they can decide on anything at all it'll be a miracle," Zara said caustically, letting her thoughts run. She could understand Forebeck's reticence. On the one hand, getting the most prominent officials offworld might help the Federation save face. If there was armed conflict, and the governor of Quann was killed, it would be almost impossible for Jord not to escalate to all-out war. On the other hand, the flight of senior administrators could be spun as an act of cowardice. If the public reacted badly to the mood, Forebeck would never hold another leadership post, and his staff would be similarly stigmatized. It would be the end of their careers.

Damned either way. Zara sympathized with Forebeck's dilemma.

"Why is Arrokan allowing this?" she asked Traquay. "Are the Letnev changing their tune?"

"We don't know if it's them, or if it's the Lazax pulling strings behind the scenes, trying to defuse the situation."

"Well, if it gives me a chance to get Hiram and the kids safely back through the Passage, I'll take it," Zara said, not ashamed to admit as much. There was a brief silence on the other end of the connection before Traquay spoke again.

"Arrokan's terms were clear. No families. Only the officials can pass through the blockade, on a Letnev ship."

Zara felt the embers of her hope being stamped brutally out. A clause forbidding the passage of the families of Quann's colonial administrators wouldn't be an especially contentious point, because hardly a single family had been brought to Quann. Even Forebeck's wife and children were still on Jord. Among the senior members of staff, only Zara actually had her loved ones with her currently.

She swore vehemently.

"I brought it up with Forebeck," Traquay said. "But he didn't have much to say."

Of course he didn't. He couldn't turn down negotiations based on the fact that his chief of staff had her husband and children with her in Aruzoe. Zara swore again. It was all utterly unfair. Despair gripped her.

"We'll see how it plays out," Traquay said weakly.

"Would you go?" Zara asked.

"Yes," Traquay said without much hesitation. "There's nothing we can do here. The fleet, the Letnev, the Lazax – they'll be the ones who decide Quann's fate, one way or another. But I understand your predicament."

That was an understatement. She stood staring out of the kitchen window at Aruzoe's night skyline, looking up at the twinkling stars spread above. The constellations of imminent war. How had it come to this?

"I'm going to stay," she told Traquay. "I have to, for my family, and for Quann."

"Your family I understand, but we can't help the people here any more than we already have."

"Maybe not. But it's my duty."

"Now you're making me feel bad."

"Don't. You have a duty to your own family. You need to make it back to Jord, for them. Especially if a war breaks out."

"It's difficult without them," Traquay admitted, causing Zara to consider the other side of her own predicament. "I hope they're safe."

"They will be. Go back, and be with them."

"We'll see what instructions Forebeck receives. We might be ordered to stay. Hopefully we'll know tomorrow."

"Yes. I'll report in at the usual time."

"Good night, Z."

Traquay broke the transmission. Zara remained standing in the dark.

This was all her fault. She should have been stronger. She should have left Hiram and the children back safely on Jord, where they couldn't be swept up in the dangers of frontier existence. She felt sick with worry and regret.

She tried to tell herself that there was nothing she could do about it now. It was all in the hands of the Maker. She turned, about to go back to bed. It was only then that she realized she wasn't alone.

At some point, silent as a ghost, Elle had entered the darkened kitchen. She was now perched on one of the high stools by the island work surface, her features pale in the light of the moons filtering in through the skylight, her eyes dark and somber.

"Why are you awake?" Zara demanded, startled by her daughter's silent presence.

"I miss home," Elle answered in a tiny voice. "Are we going home?"

"Yes," Zara said brusquely. "Now come on, get back to bed."

"When? Is it soon?"

"I don't know…" Zara trailed off. She realized she was too tired to lie. "Probably not soon."

Elle contemplated the admission in silence, then nodded, once. Then she slipped down off the stool and, without another word, began to pad silently back toward the room she shared with Macks. Zara stared after her then, on impulse, grabbed her and pulled her into a tight hug.

She thought she would lose it then, that she would feel the tears overflow and break down while holding her precious daughter. But instead she found her emotions held in check by a barrier of steel, an unyielding resolve she hadn't really realized was there until that moment.

"We're going to be okay," she told Elle, kissing her head, smelling her hair, and resolving, in that moment, to make sure that no harm could ever come to her. "I promise."

CHAPTER EIGHT

ARC PRIME,
HOMEWORLD OF THE BARONY OF LETNEV

Syd made a note of Zey's clothing as their shuttle began its final descent toward Arc Prime. Both Lazax were now dressed in formal white robes and gold data circlet headgear. Both also clutched their ambassadorial staffs, symbols of Lazax diplomacy. Syd hadn't held his for a few years now, since his promotion from the ambassadorial corps to the imperial council. Grasping its gene-reactive moontree wood felt at once strange yet reassuring.

To a casual observer, the two Lazax appeared almost identical in garb as they sat beside their respective Winnu in the shuttle's rattling confines, while Chel's rigid form stayed braced by the main hatch. Syd, however, had already noted a subtle difference. Zey's clothes weren't sitting quite right. The white robes had a slight stiffness to them, more so than might be explained by the application of excessive albionizer in their last wash – the product used by Lazax officials to keep their formal wear a uniform white.

"Expecting trouble?" Syd asked Zey. The younger ambassador looked at him without expression.

"Why do you ask?"

"You're wearing echo cloth."

Echo treatment could be applied to most garments easily enough. It coated whatever fabric it was used on with flexible polymers that bonded together to strengthen the molecular structure of a garment's fibers, toughening the material against blows or blasts. Usually, the only evidence of the echo process was a slight stiffness, which Syd had detected in Zey's white robes. It was a common precaution among ambassadors assigned to dangerous missions, especially since it was difficult to detect – attending a potentially hostile species wearing heavy protective gear rarely set a good example.

"A minor precaution," Zey said. "I always apply an echo treatment when traveling."

Syd offered no further comment. He had considered keeping his observation to himself, but had decided that making his realization known to Zey would serve him better. Everything was calibrated, everything weighed. It would have been exhausting, being aware of every word, considering every potential outcome, had Syd not trained his entire life around such a mindset.

The shuttle cleared the smog layer. Syd had only visited the Letnev homeworld a few times before, but he was not relishing the encounter. Arc Prime was unique among the planets of the greater civilizations in that it did not rotate around a star, but roamed freely through space, charting a random path across the cosmos. The Letnev claimed that rather than have a home system, all the galaxy was theirs, while everyone else joked that no star would want the abrasive, militaristic sentients.

Because of its nature, the surface of Arc Prime was perpetually dark and frigid, a cold sphere adrift in the depths of space. Syd had contemplated it as the sprinter arrived in orbit, the only lights that graced it the illumination of the many orbital stations and military docks around it, and the dull red glow of the megafactory vents that clustered like sores across the surface. Then the sprinter's shuttle had started its descent, plunging into the perpetual layer of ash and pollution that choked so much of the atmosphere.

Because of its frozen, dark nature, the Letnev lived within Arc Prime's lithosphere, in megalopolises sealed away from the inimical environment above. The only surface dwelling was the shuttle's current destination, Feruc. Syd caught sight of it through the prow viz monitor as the transport dropped down out of the ash layer.

It lay within the broad, shallow bowl of the Dunlain Crater, and looked to Syd as though the head of some great, spiked mace had come crashing into Arc Prime's surface, shattering the ice before being abandoned there. Letnev architecture was uniformly barbed and metallic, forming a great mass of wicked-looking towers turned black by a millennium of ash. Each structure was sealed, and passage between them relied on the equally airtight and heated traffic tubes that wound and twisted between and around the larger buildings.

As the city came into view the shuttle began to rattle. A moment later a warning alarm pinged, and the cabin lights turned red. Spiny ridges along Chel's back bristled as the hulking N'orr half turned.

Syd frowned and threw a look at Zey. The shuttle's sensors were reading surface-to-air fire. They were being shot at.

Zey seemed unperturbed, and Syd restrained himself from speaking until he offered up an explanation.

"Manufactory weapons testing," he said with a dismissive wave of a hand. "To ensure the latest batch of artillery pieces are properly calibrated and the shells are live. It happens intermittently. It also makes the skies above the crater dangerous to anyone not scheduled to fly."

"But we are scheduled to fly here."

"Which says much of what we might expect once we land."

There was no further rattling, and the alarm shut off, though the lighting remained crimson.

The reason for that quickly became apparent. The port and starboard viz monitors showed two aircraft pulling up alongside them, one on each side. Syd knew their distinctive, jagged outlines – they were Ashbringer-class fighters, some of the most infamous single-pilot warcraft in the galaxy.

"An escort," Zey noted.

Were the Ashbringers intended as a reassurance, or as intimidation? Syd assumed the latter. Certainly the sight of their wicked wings and glossy, opaque black cockpits brought little in the way of comfort.

"Going by the dagger-and-heart crest on the wings and tail, those are from Razor Squadron, part of the permanent Feruc garrison," Zey said. Now he was just showing off.

The shuttle banked lower, down among the upper points of the city's spear-spires. Syd could see their destination ahead now, a squat, out-of-place structure that was almost lost amidst the bristling knots of traffic tubes. Rather than cold Arc steel, it was built from unyielding blocks of permacore, imported from Mecatol Rex. Above its ramparts hung the red and gold of the imperial standard, frozen in Arc Prime's bitter grasp.

The building was the headquarters of the Lazax presence on-world. While the empire maintained embassies, consulates and missions throughout the galaxy, no other homeworld of one of the great civilizations held a permanent garrison consisting of both officials and military personnel. It was the price the Letnev were paying for two failed rebellions, and was now one of the sticking points of Baron Werqan's recent demands. Syd considered the presence of the garrison a mistake, a deliberate antagonism at a time when the empire should be looking to exert soft, rather than hard, power. Naturally, Zey thought the opposite – they had debated against each other in the Galactic Council on two previous occasions over whether the Lazax presence on Arc Prime should be either expanded or scaled back. On both occasions, the status quo had prevailed. Despite Syd's disagreement however, it was difficult not to feel a moment's relief at the sight of the imperial crest.

The Ashbringer escorts peeled away, allowing them to make the final approach to the Lazax base unmolested. A blast door in the structure's flank ground slowly open ahead, revealing a landing tube. Decelerating, the shuttle's automatic pilot slid the flier in and set it down.

Syd, Zey, and the Winnu unstrapped themselves and arose, while Chel primed the mesh blaster he was armed with, a precaution Syd thought highly unnecessary. The light above the disembarkation hatch remained red while the tube outside depressurized. Eventually it unlocked and levered down, accompanied by a blast of cold air.

After Chel, Syd made sure he was the first through the door and down the ramp. It was foolish, perhaps, but such things counted for something. He had no need of an echo garment.

While the landing tube had resealed and great electro-coils in the walls were glowing red-hot as they sought to bring the temperature back up, the space was still freezing. Ice, which had formed in the brief minutes the tube had been opened to the Arc elements, was starting to melt and run across the walls and deck, and had filled the air with clouds of chilly steam. Syd forced himself not to display any discomfort at the environment, instead focusing on the small delegation waiting for them, their breath frosting in billowing clouds.

The closest he recognized as Ambassador Kwarni, the empire's standing diplomat on Arc Prime. He was sallow-faced and tall, bore an ambassadorial staff like Syd and Zey, but had accentuated his white robes with an ankle-length thermo-coat. Beside him was another Lazax, shorter, her upper face hidden by a ferrium sallet helm, the rest of her body covered by an armor-plated greatcoat, trimmed with mottled white snowleaper fur. A little back from the pair were a duo of Lazax security troopers, dressed similarly to Kwarni's companion, but armed with shrouded beam rifles and batons. Syd felt their visors scan him as he descended the shuttle ramp, and could sense their dismay at the sight of the Tekklar Elite leading them out. There were no N'orr in the Arc Prime imperial garrison – all the on-site troops were Lazax.

"Eminent Councilor Ibna Vel Syd," Kwarni said over the whine of decelerating engines. "Welcome to Arc Prime."

"A pleasure, Ambassador Kwarni," Syd said with stiff formality. "But please, I am not here in my capacity as a member of the imperial council, but as a fellow diplomat of the empire. Allow me to introduce to you Ambassador Sorian Sai Zey."

"May the emperor's wisdom shine upon you, Ambassador Zey," Kwarni said. Syd noted that the formal greeting gave nothing away. During the voyage he had been wondering where Kwarni stood in the nebulous realm of Lazax politics. Did he favor Zey's overweening approach toward imperial affairs, or Syd's moderation? He was not aware of Kwarni making any public statements leaning one way or another, and the initial greeting had offered nothing to work with. Kwarni, it seemed, wasn't wholly incompetent when it came to the wiles of diplomacy.

"I wish I could say I am glad to be back on Arc Prime," Zey said. "But I see it is as frigid and cutting as ever."

"Hopefully I can help make your stay a little more comfortable," Kwarni said. "I have prepared quarters for you both here in the stronghold. You, and your Winnu. I was not aware there would be a Tekklar though."

"I need no accommodation," Chel said, his translation device turning his chittering into a dull univoca monotone. "I will set myself to guard the rooms of the delegates."

"As you wish," Kwarni said, glancing uneasily up at the soldier before presenting his ambassadorial staff. Syd and Zey did likewise with their own moontree poles, clacking them against one another. It was a traditional mode of greeting between Lazax, said to hark back to antiquity, though now it also served a practical purpose – upon contact with bonded moontree wood, the staffs carried out a data exchange linked back to the circlets worn by Lazax ambassadors. Kwarni had therefore transmitted a basic data package, Syd assumed information about their accommodation and the wider city, while he and Zey had in turn sent minimal information about their own visit, prepared in advance onboard the sprinter. Not, of course, that Syd was giving away anything vital to Kwarni.

"Allow me to also introduce Major Parax, commander of the garrison," Kwarni said, indicating the shorter, armored Lazax at his side. Parax crossed both sets of arms and clenched her upper fists, the Lazax military salute.

"I am honored to meet you, ambassadors, especially a member of the imperial council, Eminent Syd."

"The honor is all mine, major," Syd said, giving the two-handed version of the salute. That was more like it.

"Security is high, as you might imagine," Kwarni said almost apologetically. "I thought it would be good for you to meet Major Parax immediately. Her troopers will escort you and your N'orr to your rooms. Afterward I thought we might take supper together? The food here on Arc Prime is a long way from Mecatol in every sense, but I flatter myself that it's still better than sprinter rations!"

"I was rather hoping we could review the situation here on Arc as quickly as possible," Syd said, deciding to be as direct as was practical. "Without going into too much detail while we're out here in the cold, Zey and I are under instructions to speak with Baron Werqan as soon as we are able to attain an audience."

"That may be difficult," Kwarni admitted. "The baron refuses to see me, despite my entreaties. I'm not sure having three ambassadors rather than one will make a lot of difference.

We Lazax aren't exactly popular here at the best of times, and now…"

"With all due respect, Ambassador Kwarni, unless I am mistaken you have not held this post for long," Zey interjected. "You will not have full access to the personal contacts I maintain among the Letnev. An audience with the baron will be forthcoming."

"What a relief," Kwarni said, offering a smile as cold as the landing tube just after the blast door had shut – one that Syd couldn't help but notice, and that did nothing to make him feel more welcome. "Now, shall we head in, before we all freeze to death? I'm sure the Letnev would love it if that happened."

CHAPTER NINE

Muaat, Homeworld of the Gashlai, Campus-Colony of the Universities of Jol-Nar

"Are you sure you want to do this?" ZALLY asked Tol for the umpteenth time. She sighed, shooting the little floating familiar a look. It wasn't the bot's fault, she told herself. It was only obeying its preservation programming. Trying to preserve her, that was.

"No, I'm not sure," she snapped at the familiar. "Does that make you feel better?"

"I don't know, does it make you feel better?"

Tol felt her multi-hued frills shiver with frustration. She was sitting on the swivel-chair in the meager little pod that passed for Exosphere T19's control center. Her fingers hovered over the keypad of the station's primary computator. She had already fired up the comms array and typed out the report. All she had to do was send it.

Arch Doctor Atak Arr was conducting illegal experiments on live Sardakk N'orr. Doctor Atak Arr was torturing and murdering Sardakk N'orr. Doctor Atak Arr was a genocidal maniac apparently obsessed with the extermination of an entire group of sentients. The report made all of that clear. So why was she hesitating.

She asked ZALLY as much. Her answer was surprising.

"Because you don't have any evidence."

Tol had been worried that other considerations were undermining her. She feared that what Arr had said was true, that regardless of imperial edicts, the leaders of the Universities of Jol-Nar weren't concerned by minor irritations like morality. It was common enough knowledge among the students of the universities that, behind closed doors, senior academics were given free rein to pursue whatever research projects they desired. This, then, would come as no revelation to the Circle of Regents. All she was doing was making a nuisance of herself, and she had probably already done far too much of that.

But ZALLY had hit on a more salient point. Even if her claims were taken seriously and acted upon, she had no evidence to back up what she had seen and heard.

Was that just an excuse, she asked herself. Was she trying to sidestep the real problem – the soulless xenophobia so often displayed by the universities – by finding a fault in the practicalities of exposing it? It was a pretty big problem though. She was on thin enough ice without taking into account the lack of proof.

"Don't be a coward," she said out loud, trying to browbeat herself into action.

"Or, from another angle, don't be foolish," ZALLY said. Tol had heard that one before, a few times. She needed to tweak the familiar's programming.

The message appeared on the comms array's display,

warning her that without any activity the system would go into automatic shutdown. She blew bubbles, flexed her scales, hand hovering over the transmit button.

"Best not to overthink it," she told herself.

She pressed the button.

The communications array appended to Arr's laboratory chimed. The doctor glanced up irritably from the microscope he had been stooped over, causing the coupling lens that linked it with his containment sphere to come away.

It was rare for the array to receive anything. Arr's isolation was vital to his work, and few even knew of his presence on Muaat, let alone how to contact him.

Reluctantly, he moved away from the lab bench, eyes darting over the output monitor. He recognized the sender immediately.

It was a transmission, from an unmanned courier drone ship that had just arrived in orbit. The originator was Regent Pelem Shole, on Jol. Arr had many allies in positions of power throughout the universities – as well as many enemies – but none were as senior as Shole. As a member of the Circle of Regents, he had the ear of the headmaster himself, and was responsible for setting pan-university policy. He was also funding Arr's research, and backing his weapons development, both the mundane and the viral. He was one of the few beings in the galaxy that Arr would not ignore.

The message was a private missive from Shole himself, rather than his faculty office. Arr tapped the array's holo-buttons, projected into the air above the main transmission host. He opened the missive.

It was concise, as befitted a revered Hylar like Shole. An official of the Sol Federation had made contact with Wun-Escha. That in itself was not unusual. Due to the reliance of the great civilizations on Hylar technology, there was a near-constant dialogue between the technical experts of the universities and the various embassies and trade collectives of the galaxy's lesser sentients. What was unusual about this exchange, however, was that it had been made unofficially.

Arr felt his interest spike. The Sol official required the assistance of Jol-Nar outside of the usual parameters of Lazax-monitored trade and technological exchange. He was seeking Hylar expertise, but the requirements were very specific. He wanted weaponry. Weaponry on a large scale, sufficient for one of the great civilizations to wage war on another, and emerge victorious.

The doctor paused for analysis. He was, he realized, excited. This could mean only one thing. The rumors about a Letnev blockade of the Quann Passage were true. Furthermore, the humans were preparing to go to war. Arr had considered the possibility, but had dismissed it as a statistical outlier. The Letnev were as bullish as ever, but the current baron was not a firebrand, while the humans did not have the military capacity to fight a full-scale, symmetrical conflict with Arc Prime. Yet here they were, beginning a covert escalation.

It was brilliant. Arr felt the spiny scales protruding from his brow bristle with anticipation.

Shole had been right to come to him. The Hylar had other weapons experts and major manufacturing institutes within the hierarchy of the universities, but they all languished under at least nominal Lazax oversight. Jol-Nar could not sell armaments and the expertise to use them to another major power without imperial intervention. That did not, however, apply to someone now outside of the university hierarchy. Someone like Arr.

Conflicting emotions rose up within him, emotions he quickly suppressed. The pathogen still wasn't ready, and wouldn't be for some time. It wasn't for the humans, and it would do them no good in their feud with the Letnev, but Arr anticipated the Hylar's own need for it soon. In the meantime, the weapons caches he had been stockpiling beneath Muaat's surface would be put to good use, all for the glory of Jol-Nar, though the Federation might not yet have realized it.

He composed a reply to send to Shole via the courier ship, checking, out of curiosity, the name of the human who had first reached out to the Circle of Regents.

It was Hektor Smyth.

CHAPTER TEN

QUANN,
SOL FEDERATION COLONY WORLD

The first officially recorded deaths of the Quann blockade occurred six Jord days after the arrival of the Phoenix Fleet.

A Sol merchant ship belonging to LongHaul Logistics, a Federation-funded transportation firm, tried to make a break from Quann's high orbit, aiming for what appeared to be a gap in the Letnev cordon. The ship was designated E5-10/15 on the shipping manifestos and commanded by one Captain Jopp. In a later inquiry, the claim by LongHaul Logistics that Jopp had acted without orders was upheld, clearing the firm of any negligence. Jopp, it was believed, had personal investments in the cargo he was hauling, and the blockade was bankrupting him and half of his crew. Despite this, rumors persisted that what happened next had been privately sanctioned by firm leaders desperate to get at least some stock up and running between Quann and the rest of Federation space.

The supposed gap in the Letnev cordon wasn't really a gap at all. The zone was occupied by an Arc-class capital ship, the

Grand Sire, a behemoth of a war vessel that had been concealed by an advanced, Hylar-built cloaking field. By the time Jopp and E5-10/15 realized the mistake, it was far too late. One beam-broadside later, and the merchant ship had ceased to exist. Scans of the area of space it had previously occupied struggled to even find enough returns to be classified as debris.

E5-10/15's destruction occurred while Zara was in the FedHub control center in Aruzoe.

"The fleet is primed," Admiral Ular said over the visualization projector. "Shields up and weapons charged. Give the word, Governor Forebeck, and we strike."

Forebeck was standing clutching the projector's circumference rail, jaw clenched, his expression harried. He had lost a great deal of weight over the past month. His formal jacket now hung off him, his broad shoulders and square jaw gnawed away by the strain he had been under.

"Give the order," Smyth urged, standing next to the governor. "Those pallid monsters have just annihilated Sol citizens! This is an outrage!"

"It isn't your call to make," Zara said, fixing Smyth's gaze from the other side of the projector. "That merchant ship left orbit without authorization. We have to communicate that to the Letnev."

"Why do you always bow and scrape to them?" Smyth spat. "Are you a secret collaborator, or just a coward?"

"How dare you?" Zara replied with equal vehemence, quick to anger after weeks of similar clashes. Smyth's rhetoric had been becoming relentlessly more aggressive, and she was stretched to the breaking point by it. She worried night and day that he might do something stupid, or worse, convince

Forebeck to do it. "Your war-lust is a disgrace. We're on the frontline here. It's the people of Quann, not Jord, who will suffer if the Phoenix Fleet opens fire."

Throughout the exchange Forebeck had remained silent and tense, staring into the green glow of the projector. The words of the chief communications officer finally seemed to snap him from his trance, and he cut off Smyth and Zara.

"Governor, we've just received a communique packet from a courier vessel from Jord. It is from High Minister Hammid."

A hush fell over the control center as Forebeck strode over to the comms hub and reviewed the screen where the message was being displayed. Everyone had been waiting for a decision on the staff evacuation. This had to be it.

Forebeck seemed to take a long time reading the communique. Eventually he looked up, blinking, taking in the control room and its perspiring occupants as though he had just woken up.

"The Federation government wants us back," he said in a soft, rasping voice. "The king is in agreement. This is a formal recall of all the senior staff comprising the Quann colonial administration."

Silence returned in the wake of Forebeck's words. Zara bowed her head briefly, struggling with the proclamation, before looking around at her fellow administrators. She saw regret, concern, and relief warring on each face. One way or another, at least the uncertainty was now over.

"Admiral Ular, you will hold fire and maintain your position," Forebeck said to the viz projector. "I am going to speak directly to Admiral Arrokan again and ensure his offer of government evacuation still stands. If so, Jord wants everyone offworld within the next two day-cycles. Ular, you will need to provide transport through the Passage once the Letnev have brought us through the blockade."

Zara stood frozen, knowing what she wished to say but finding herself unable to say it. To her surprise, she heard Traquay speak up, uttering the words she needed.

"What about administration families?"

Forebeck paused, considering Traquay's words then, realizing their import, he found Zara in the crowd of staffers.

"I will speak to Arrokan," he told her. "But his initial terms were clear, and I fear he has no need to make concessions."

"I understand," Zara said. "But with respect, governor, I intend to stay regardless."

Those around her had started to speak in the wake of the governor's statement, but stopped and stared at her as she carried on.

"Please, take my family with you if you can. But whether they stay or go, I'll remain on Quann."

"That would be a violation of our orders," Forebeck pointed out. "The instructions specify a full evacuation."

"Then who's going to lead the people we leave behind?" Zara demanded. "They came here looking for a new life, and we are the custodians of that life. We cannot just abandon them. And besides, there's more at play here, and we all know it.

"Our departure sets the stage for outright war. I believe that is why the Letnev are allowing us to evacuate, and why the Federation wants our return. There will be no more restraining voice, and no reason for the Phoenix Fleet to hold back. Jord might not want to see its colonial government wiped out when the fighting starts, but it likely doesn't much care for the rest of the populace. Once we're gone, this world will become a war zone."

To his credit, Forebeck didn't try to disabuse Zara's logic. It was Traquay who spoke up.

"I'm staying too," she said, moving through the crowd and laying a hand on Zara's shoulder. "I'm not sure you can run the government of Quann alone, Z, but between us we'll have it covered."

"You can't," Zara said, feeling a moment's dismay at Traquay's intervention. "You said yourself, what about your family back on Jord?"

"Jord isn't where I'm meant to be right now," Traquay said firmly. "There are enough families here that need us."

"This is ridiculous," Smyth said. "Our orders are clear."

"I would urge you to reconsider, but I cannot seize you and force you both to come," Forebeck said, ignoring Smyth. "I understand your pain, Zara. This smacks of abandonment. I have always taken my duties as the custodian of Quann seriously. But I cannot disobey a direct order from Jord. If I did, what would be the consequences? Quann might be declared a rogue colony. We would be abandoned to the Letnev."

"We all must do what we think is right," Zara said. "But that means I'm staying."

Smyth accosted Zara as she left for her evening break, pulling her to one side beneath the scaffolding in the abandoned, half-completed central dome of the Federation Hub building.

"You're making a mistake," he told her. She nearly laughed in his face. She had grown to despise him – his arrogance, his apparent disregard for the dangers of the situation and the struggles that the people of Quann were facing all seemed to be born out of a personality that was disturbingly shallow and swimming with arrogance. She was also pretty sure he disliked her just as much.

"Please tell me how continuing to do my job protecting my family and the rest of Quann constitutes a mistake, delegate," she said.

"You can't protect them," Smyth replied. "You're deluded. The moment one side opens fire, your illusion of control will disappear."

"You say that like you're certain it's going to happen," Zara said, refusing to be cowed. "What are you doing out here anyway, Smyth? You seem to have very strong opinions about what the Sol response to this blockade should be. Interesting that you arrived only a month before it began."

"I'd think carefully about what you're trying to insinuate," Smyth said, his look turning even more poisonous.

"Maybe you could walk me through it then? This might be the frontier, but we know who you are, even out here. Why would an up-and-coming young delegate like you want to be assigned to audit a colony like Quann? I thought the stigma of your uncle had been left behind?"

"How dare you?" Smyth demanded, but Zara pressed on, letting her pent-up frustration vent in the face of the delegate.

"Your obsession with starting a war with the Letnev has been noted, Hektor, and not just by me. Do you really want to be thought of as a warmonger back home on Jord? Is that the direction the Smyths are headed in now, just when they've returned to the political scene?"

"It's not war I'm advocating, it's strength," Smyth said,

meeting her anger head on with his own. "You wouldn't be aware of it out here, but the galaxy is changing. The Lazax's grip is weakening, and when it finally breaks all the old certainties will be gone. I want to make sure humanity is ready when that happens."

"Sounds a bit like treason," Zara pointed out. "Maybe the public oaths your family reiterated to the empire after your uncle's execution weren't quite as sincere as they seemed at the time?"

"Be careful talking about treason, Zara," Smyth said, taking an unexpected step away. "There are two kinds of allegiance, to the Lazax, and to humankind. Be sure you know which one comes first. One day, they might be incompatible."

Zara said nothing more, and Smyth departed. She resisted the urge to shout after him, but waited until he was gone and called up a monoride.

Zara inserted new coordinates into the monoride's automated systems, having it take a more circuitous route back to her hab. Despite the fact she got precious little time at home as it was, she knew she needed to sit and blow off steam after the confrontation with Smyth. She brought enough anger and frustration back to her family as it was.

The ride took her out of the government quarter and along Star Trader Avenue and then down into the Slumps, the poorer quarter of Aruzoe. It was a place rarely visited by any of the colony's officials, and the sleek transporter drew looks from people as it thrummed by on its anti-grav plates.

Zara regretted the divide that was already so well entrenched between Quann's governors and the colonists that made up the body of the populace. Most of the administration considered it inevitable. Societies the galaxy over were rife with inequality, and Quann would naturally follow the example set by Jord. Zara wasn't convinced by that. A colony represented a new start, and there was no reason to emulate the worse elements of what had come before. In her time she had tried to champion bills that would enforce minimum payments for employees and provide financial safety nets for new arrivals and those who had left behind their trades on Quann. There was so much more to do though. Affordable housing within Aruzoe, rather than just in the outlying districts, the curbing of smuggling and artificial price inflation, the prosecution of people traffickers and the many criminal organizations that saw colonial outposts as rich pickings – all of that was only beginning to be addressed.

None of it was on the administration's urgent to-do list either. The government was more concerned with setting up new plasticon factories and getting the tyrellium mines up and running. Production was what Jord wanted, production and mercantilism, rather than a new, fairer society, and what Jord wanted from its colonies, it got.

The monoride looped through the Slumps and turned back up Star Trader Avenue. Before, it had been the heart of Jord's rapidly expanding commerce, a hub for both government-funded and independent firms as well as a forum for all manner of small-scale buyers and sellers. Now the broad, sloping street lay almost deserted, no more than a dozen small grav-stalls attempting to catch the attention of passersby. The blockade had changed everything.

Zara knew more needed to be done. The administration was

in crisis mode, living day to day as everyone anticipated the start of hostilities. But what if that didn't happen? Who knew how long the blockade might last for? Already pressure was mounting, not only on the trade consortium and the countless firms that relied on traffic back and forth along the Passage, but on law enforcement and the colony's basic healthcare system. Zara was afraid that soon, food and fresh water would start running low. She had sat through enough colonial modeling lectures during her early days of administrator training to know it was all downhill from there.

The monoride slid back into the docking strut at the base of her hab block. She disembarked and took the elevator to her unit. Hiram was serving up dinner – the housekeeping familiar had broken down, and the repair firm was closed indefinitely.

Zara took him aside while the kids ate.

"Jord has been in touch," she told him. "They want the officials offworld. Two days."

Hiram considered the news before replying. "Good."

"I'm not going with them," Zara went on. Hiram gave her a disapproving look.

"It's better that one of us gets out," Hiram said. "And maybe you can still negotiate to get the kids onboard?"

"I'm trying, but it's unlikely," Zara said. "I won't leave any of you behind. Besides, it's not just that. I can't abandon Quann."

"I'm not sure you can save Quann either," Hiram pointed out gently. "How much control does anyone on this world really have over the situation?"

"That's what others are saying, but I have to try. Traquay is staying too, Maker bless her. Together, with the lower-ranking administrators, I believe we can set up at least a temporary government. Offer some kind of leadership. Nobody's saying it, but Aruzoe is on the brink of collapse. We have to try to keep it running for as long as possible, for everybody's sake."

Hiram sighed, but smiled. "You're always thinking about other people, Z. You don't get enough credit for it."

"I'm just doing what needs to be done," she said then, on impulse, hugged him. It was difficult for her to articulate at that moment how important his acceptance of her was, how much she was silently leaning on him, even if he didn't fully realize. In a way it made her ashamed, but she was thankful he was here with her at that moment, and not back on Jord.

"Come on, let's eat," he urged her, prizing her off and smiling again. "If there's one service I can provide Quann, it's making sure the new acting governor is well fed."

CHAPTER ELEVEN

ARC PRIME,
HOMEWORLD OF THE BARONY OF LETNEV

There was, it seemed, little chance of an audience with Baron Werqan. After two days on Arc Prime, Syd and Zey's official approaches had yet to receive a response. On the third day, Zey departed the imperial garrison – alone, despite Chel's protests – to meet with private Letnev contacts. It was only then that Ambassador Kwarni gave Syd the news.

"There's a transmission for you from Eminent Councilor Atz," he told Syd after visiting his accommodation within the garrison building.

"Just arrived?" Syd asked, standing in the doorway.

"No. I received it via a courier sprinter two days before you reached Arc Prime."

The import of that was immediately clear to Syd. Kwarni had possessed a communique from Mecatol, but hadn't shared it when they first arrived. Even more importantly, it was a message that must have been dispatched by Atz *before* Syd had left the capital.

"Where is your comms array?" Syd said. Kwarni led him to it.

"You've read it?" Syd asked when they arrived, Kwarni dismissing the Lazax chief communications officer and showing him to the transmission monitor alone.

"No," Kwarni replied. "It remains sealed."

"But it came with instructions for you as well?"

"Indeed."

Kwarni was being coy. Syd suspected he was about to find out why. He assessed the digital transmission docket, noting that it was indeed still sealed – that could be tampered with though. He resisted the temptation to interrogate Kwarni further, and used his staff, linked to his circlet, to open it.

The message was indeed from Atz, and it was both brusque and chilling. Atz suspected Zey had been using imperial courier sprinters – which could be sealed on his diplomatic authority – to make covert communications with unknown figures on Arc Prime, an assessment Marchu agreed with. Atz had assigned him to Syd so that Syd could keep track of Zey while he was absent from Mecatol, which would give Atz and Marchu space to investigate within the imperial capital. Atz apologized for not being able to tell him while they were still on Mecatol – it was apparently too risky. He wanted Syd to monitor Zey's movements and activities and report anything suspect when practical. He offered no opinions regarding what it was exactly that Zey was doing.

Syd took a second to digest the message. He was angry with himself, he realized, angry that he had not sensed the ulterior motive for his assignment with Zey. He should have been watching the other Lazax more closely since setting out. But Zey… surely a member of the imperial household couldn't be involved in this? If he was, the ramifications were huge.

He made sure the message's gene signature really did belong to Atz before scrubbing away the transmission beamed from the courier ship. Then he looked at Kwarni, who had retreated a short distance to allow Syd to read the message in private.

"How much do you know?" he asked the ambassador bluntly.

"A little," Kwarni said.

"Now is not the time to be reticent."

"I know that in recent months there have been unidentified communications between Arc Prime and Mecatol. I know that Atz promised to investigate. Then you two arrived, and a message from Atz that was strictly for your eyes only."

"You've done the right thing. The empire is in danger."

"What more do you require from me?"

A dutiful response. Either Kwarni really was a dedicated servant of the emperor, or he knew more than he was letting on.

"I will let you know as soon as I have given the situation further thought," Syd said, not wanting to commit to anything with Kwarni just yet. "Thank you for your diligence, ambassador."

Syd returned to his chamber and explained the situation to Onni before questioning him about Zey's Winnu. Her name was Nauru, and seemingly she had been left behind by Zey while the ambassador met his Letnev contacts.

"Have you spoken to her before?" Syd asked.

"In passing, yes," Onni said. "During the voyage. She has not served Zey long."

"Do you think she would be amenable to assisting us?"

"Possibly," Onni said, his tone cautious. "It depends on the nature of Zey's infractions."

"Those are what we're trying to unearth," Syd said. "Go to Nauru now and see if you can gauge what she can do for us."

It was a gamble, Syd knew. A Winnu aide's loyalty to the official they were assigned to was borderline absolute – there was only one institution they would adhere to more fervently, and that was the empire itself. Enlisting the help of Nauru would depend on Onni's ability to cast Zey as a traitor, and that in itself was a grave risk.

"I can tell her about Atz's message?" Onni asked Syd.

"Yes," he replied. "Embellish it if you must. We have to act while Zey is absent. Who knows what he's really doing right now."

Privately he cursed himself for not taking a stronger stance on Zey at the beginning. He had known something was wrong. His failure to properly identify his duplicity was an embarrassment. How long had Atz known about the secret communications between Mecatol and Arc Prime? And just what did the transmissions contain? Was the blockade due to Zey conspiring with the likes of Arrokan? And what about the contact that had been made with the human colony on Quann?

Dark forces were at play, and Syd was determined to face them. That meant getting to the root of what Zey was really doing on the Letnev homeworld.

Onni departed to find Nauru. While he was gone Syd pondered possible strategies. With or without the help of Zey's Winnu, he couldn't confront Zey just yet, not while they were still on Arc Prime. He also couldn't give up on trying to bring an end to the blockade. There were now too many possibilities in play, too many threats.

Onni returned with Nauru. The smartly dressed young Winnu looked painfully nervous. She offered a short bow, which Syd returned with a nod.

"Onni has explained the current circumstances to you?" he asked.

"He has, sir," Nauru replied, not making eye contact. "It… is not a matter I take lightly. I would never betray the confidence of any Lazax, let alone an official I have been assigned to, unless…"

"Unless said official was working against the interests of the empire," Syd said curtly, trying to get a measure of Nauru. If she decided to report all of this back to Zey, the game would be up.

"Yes," Nauru said, briefly looking Syd in the eye. Despite her apparent subservience, there was steel there, determination.

"I have not been in Ambassador Zey's service for long, but there are other things that have given me pause," she continued. "I would not break his confidence on your word alone. The transmissions from Mecatol, however, I can confirm. I do not know their content or destination, but I know he frequently visited a remote communications array in the Lower Eastside of Marbur District. It was not one of the official arrays, but a private uplink that he used to transmit to a picket I've been unable to trace."

"That is valuable information," Syd said. "I will relay it to Atz to assist his investigation on Mecatol. In the meantime, Zey must not suspect anything is untoward. We cannot move against him while he is here on Arc. He has too many allies among the Letnev. I suspect he is with them presently."

"But why?" Nauru asked. "He is cousin to the emperor himself. Why would he betray his family, his species, the very empire itself?"

"I cannot claim to understand his thinking," Syd admitted. "I have been his rival since he became an imperial official. He is obsessed with strength, and the idea of Lazax primacy. If he is somehow involved in the blockade of Quann though, attempting to foment unrest within the empire, I shall ensure even his connections to Emperor Salai Sai Corian will not save him from justice. All I need is proof of his duplicity."

"I will do whatever you require, eminent councilor," Nauru said humbly. "For the good of the empire."

"Continue in your service to Zey for now," Syd said. "Onni will make covert contact with you as frequently as practical, so you can pass on anything more that you learn. Do not investigate on your own though. It could prove dangerous."

As Nauru agreed, Syd felt his savant buzz. He glanced down at it. A message from Zey had just come through.

Returning. Meeting with Chancellor Lamarque secured for tomorrow.

That changed things. Syd had feared it would be impossible to gain an audience with Baron Werqan – if indeed she hadn't authorized the deployment of the Letnev war fleet to Quann, the last thing she would want would be Lazax officials finding that out and exposing her weakness to her own people. Chancellor Lamarque was the second most powerful Letnev on Arc Prime, and a meeting with him was no mean thing. If, indeed, Zey really had secured one.

"Remember what I said," Syd informed Onni and Nauru. "Leave the investigating to me, and give nothing away."

Syd was concerned that he would struggle to maintain a reserved demeanor when he saw Zey again, but his instincts as a diplomat kicked in. He congratulated Zey on making the breakthrough with the chancellor and resisted the temptation to ask just how he had done it. The more secure Zey felt his secrets were, the less alert he would be.

The meeting with Lamarque was scheduled for midmorning the next day. It was relatively rare for a senior Letnev to be present in Feruc – the actual planetary capital was the city of Goz, buried far beneath the northern hemisphere, where Baron Werqan apparently spent most of her time. Lamarque was in Feruc reassuring offworld Letnev trade partners, according to Zey, and had been talked into a private discussion with the Lazax diplomats.

Syd wasn't sure what to make of it, but he couldn't completely give up on trying to resolve the Quann crisis while investigating Zey. At the very least, if he turned down the opportunity to speak to the second most powerful Letnev in the barony, Zey would know something was afoot.

The venue was to be Feruc's Manufactorum Primus, a location familiar to most visiting dignitaries, including Syd. It was a vast factory block, the size of a frontier world town. It squatted at the heart of the Dunlain Crater, a bitter mass of tower spikes, twisting traffic tubes, production belts, and hundreds of industrial vents, great and small, which perpetually churned out towering pillars of frozen ash and pollution. It forged all manner of goods for the Letnev, but the greater part of it was dedicated to the manufacturing of weapons and ordinance – everything from beam rifles, graviton pulse cannons, and evisceration shells to Dunlain Reaper battle-walkers and Ashbringer interceptors were churned out by the unceasing forges and assembly lines.

It was the last place most civilizations would have chosen as a regular venue for diplomatic talks, but Syd knew that it was a statement from the Letnev. Offworlder dignitaries would pass the rows of armaments, the manufactory wings, and experience the bitter bite of Arc Prime's eternal winter in the aftermath of the blast doors shutting. They would be overawed and discomfited, and the Letnev would show themselves as a species wedded to industry and war.

Neither Syd nor Zey was susceptible to such crude tricks. They took a rail runner from outside the Lazax garrison toward Manufactorum Primus, traveling through one of the pressurized traffic tubes. The private rail box, reserved for Lazax moving to and from the garrison, was uncomfortable bare metal, but that was the least of Syd's concerns.

How much of this was a legitimate conference with Chancellor Lamarque, and how much of it was a setup by Zey? He regretted not knowing the current state of Letnev politics – typically the chancellor was chosen by the baron, and was therefore closely supportive of them. If that was the case, Lamarque would be just as concerned about Admiral Arrokan's potentially rogue actions as the baron. That may give them something to work with.

Or they might not be going to meet Chancellor Lamarque at all. Even more so than before, Syd felt as though he was traveling into the unknown, into danger with nothing more than his ambassadorial staff as a weapon. It almost made him wish he had applied an echo treatment to his robes. At least they had Chel.

They hadn't gotten far when the thing Syd had feared began to happen. The box started to slow noticeably, gradually coming to a standstill. He looked at Onni, then Zey, his expression inscrutable. Nauru dared give a small shrug. There was a hum as Chel shifted and charged his mesh blaster.

"Trouble?" Syd asked aloud, feeling a sudden, deep sense of unease. As though in response, there was a thud, and what sounded like footsteps on the rail runner's roof, directly above them.

"Away from the windows," Chel snapped, extending two of his four upper limbs to push both Syd and Zey back in their seats a split second before there was a crash and a hail of glassplex.

It all happened so quickly. Syd was aware of a flare of actinic purple lights and the spitting hiss of beam weaponry as multiple shooters opened up from the right-hand side of the carriage, lacerating the wall, door, and windows with bolts of energy that left glowing red holes in their wake. Both Syd and Zey had triggered their ambassadorial staffs at the same time, electrostatic projectors providing a repelling field around the stave itself that could be used to punch away both hard projectiles and beams. Several of the shots hit Chel's hard carapace, scarring it with smoking black marks but not penetrating.

"Door," the N'orr snapped tersely, kicking open the left-hand entrance to the carriage. He grabbed Syd by the shoulder and practically flung him down into the traffic tube beyond after checking it was clear, before beginning to do the same with the others.

Syd regained his balance as Zey thumped down next to him. He half expected the fellow Lazax to lash out at him. What if he had planned this? What if he had worked out Syd's job was to monitor him? But the other ambassador looked just as shocked at what was happening, and made no aggressive moves.

Syd turned to help the Winnu, his heart racing, adrenaline kicking in. Nauru had been lightly clipped in the shoulder, her formal jacket smoldering, but the pair were otherwise unharmed.

The space between the tube's curving wall and the rail line was nothing more than a grimy, bare emergency walkway, only wide enough for one person to stand on. The bulk of the box was now off to one side, but it offered little in the way of protection – there was a shooter standing on top of the carriage, stooped beneath the curved ceiling of the tube. He was clearly Letnev, tall and white-haired, but his face was concealed behind the glowing lenses of an optical targeting mask. He was wearing a soot-grimed vibroplate cuirass and a spike pauldron over black leathers, and carrying what looked like a shotgun, which he now aimed down toward the delegation that had just come stumbling from the box.

Chel reacted before any of the Lazax or Winnu. Barreling out of the carriage after them, he fired his mesh blaster at the poised Letnev, launching his shredded remains back over the other side of the transport before he could discharge the shotgun. Even as he dispatched the assassin, the N'orr reached out with a free arm to stop Syd from tumbling off the narrow walkway space.

"Thank you," Syd gasped, still trying to catch up on everything that was happening.

Chel did not respond. The tube was ringing with more weapons fire, and a scattering of energy beams seared into the wall beside them. It turned out there were Letnev on the left side of the rail runner as well, just farther down, and they were now charging along the emergency walkway toward them. Acting on reflexes alone, Syd batted aside several beams using his electrostatic charged staff.

"Move," Chel said, motioning his charges past in the opposite direction from the oncoming assassins. "I'll keep them at bay."

CHAPTER TWELVE

ARC PRIME,
HOMEWORLD OF THE BARONY OF LETNEV

Chel stalled the Letnev charge. Syd was already hurrying in the opposite direction, Zey, Onni and Nauru in front of him. He half expected the other Lazax to try to impede them, and was hardly able to stop himself from attempting to strike and restrain his supposed fellow diplomat. This had to be his doing. He was trying to get them all killed!

"We need help from the garrison," Zey said. Syd checked his wrist-mounted savant as he went. Deep in the traffic tube, there was no sign of a transmission signal.

"Comms hub up ahead," Nauru shouted from the front. While most of the traffic tubes had little in the way of signal, there were hardwired emergency communicators at regular intervals.

Syd glanced back, experiencing a moment's relief as he saw Chel moving to catch up, carapace scarred by even more hits, but otherwise apparently unharmed. The Letnev pursuit had seemingly been stymied.

Not for long. They had reached the end of the rail runner

they had been on, which meant those on the other side of the transport would be able to get at them. Thankfully the tube was two-way, and a different runner was coming in the opposite direction, giving them a few moments more cover. Nauru tried to wave at it, but Syd knew it was hopeless. They were all automated, and most were only carrying raw materials or machinery.

The roaring passage of the runner engulfed them, the passing shock wave buffeting the delegation and almost knocking them from the walkway. Syd recovered, ears ringing, and hurried on, not wanting to let Zey reach the comms hub first. He didn't trust him to put the call through properly.

Thankfully it was Nauru who reached the handheld device first. She gave the code for an emergency to the garrison commander and identified the tube where they had been stranded.

"Support expected in four minutes," she shouted back to the two Lazax as they joined her.

"There's a curve in the tunnel up ahead that will give us some cover," Onni observed, panting with exertion.

"Keep moving," was Chel's only instruction.

With the other rail runner having passed, their Letnev pursuers now had a clear angle on them until they rounded the curve. At a glance, Syd counted seven of them, all masked up and kitted out similarly to the first one Chel had dispatched. They began to fire as they closed the distance again.

It wasn't all beam weaponry this time either. There was a blast of searing, intense heat, and a flare of blue light that momentarily blinded Syd. He stumbled, and it was only Chel's grasp that stopped him falling onto the rails.

"Plasma," the N'orr Tekklar Elite buzzed, the statement combined with the stink of vaporized concrete. Syd didn't get a chance to reply. A howling filled the tube, accompanied by a sudden, bitter gale.

"The wall's been breached!" Onni shouted over it. He was right. The Letnev's plasma blast had missed its mark, but had impacted the curving wall of the tube ahead. A molten hole had been bored in its infrastructure, breaking the traffic tube's sealed interior and exposing it to the nightmarish elements of Arc Prime's surface.

Syd felt his ears pop as the tunnel began to decompress. The bitter bite of the invasive chill took his breath away, and he instinctively wrapped his two sets of arms to his side, the icy gale now knifing down the tunnel tugging at his robes.

"We can't go forward," he was vaguely aware of Nauru shouting. If they did they would have to pass by the new hole blown in the tunnel, and that would freeze them to death in the space of a minute or two. Nor, however, could they go back. The Letnev assassins had momentarily stopped firing as they hurried to close the distance.

"Down onto the rails," Chel ordered. "I will hold them until relief arrives!"

Syd had been worried that the rail lines themselves were electrified or worse, but they didn't have much choice. He went first, dropping down into the curved, dead space that ran along the bottom of the circular tube, his relief as he brushed up against one of the metal bars without suffering any kind of shock lost amidst the freezing discomfort of the compromised atmosphere.

The others were down alongside him. Chel using the

curvature of one of the lines to brace his weapon and send a series of blasts down range, the reports echoing through the tunnel. It elicited another smattering of shots in reply. The Letnev were closing.

"Did you know this was going to happen?" Syd demanded of Zey. He would have snatched at him, but they had a rail bar between them.

"No," the ambassador exclaimed, looking suitably outraged. "Why in Mecatol's name would I have known about this?"

A beam seared into the rail bar between them, scorching the metal.

"Someone knew about our meeting with the chancellor," Syd said. "Someone who wants at least some of us dead!"

He knew he shouldn't be sharing such thoughts, but the strain of being under fire was fraying his diplomatic skills. In his long career he had been caught in two previous assassination attempts – none aimed directly at him, thankfully – as well as a number of riots and several scrapes with pirates. Nothing had ever been quite as frenetic as this though. Besides the gunfire, he was so cold he could hardly think.

"There's another rail runner coming," Nauru called urgently, words punctuated by a painful screech of brakes competing with the howling wind. Syd realized the rails around them had started to vibrate.

Nauru was right. The prow of another transport was surging round the bend in the traffic tube. Syd's relief at the sight of the Lazax crest on its front was tempered somewhat by the fact that they were currently beneath the rails carrying it.

In that moment their annihilation seemed certain. Either they were crushed and bisected by the runner's passage, or they scrambled up off the tracks and were gunned down by the oncoming Letnev.

Unless the runner stopped. Its brakes were already shrieking, sparks flying.

"Stay down!" Chel shouted. Syd fully faced the runner, fighting every instinct in order to stand still, his ambassadorial staff raised and electrostatic fully charged, as though the length of moontree wood would somehow stop seventy-five tons of steel and reinforced plasticon from reducing them to a crimson smear.

And yet, the runner continued to slow. It came to a leaden halt barely a dozen paces from Syd, the Lazax crest towering over him, so close to dashing him to pieces. That would have been ironic.

Even as it was stopping, figures leapt from the sides, half a dozen security troopers. One gestured urgently at them as the others began to lay down covering fire with shot rifles, the metallic, clanging discharge of the weapons' electromagnetic coil launchers running counterpoint to the spitting of the Letnev beam weapons, energy bolts warring with solid rounds.

Syd didn't need to give any more instructions. The others were already scrambling up out from among the rails and making for the runner. He tried to do likewise, but his body struggled to respond. He was frozen, numb, almost unable to breathe. His twin sets of arms trembled as he dragged himself up. Onni snatched at him, trying to help him, but he rasped at the faithful Winnu with what breath he could muster.

"Go! Stay with Zey!"

They couldn't afford to give him the opportunity to try

something now. Understanding, Onni turned toward where the other ambassador had made it up onto the walkway.

Syd's strength briefly failed him, until he found Chel assisting him once more, the N'orr clambering up out of the rails alongside while still firing toward the oncoming Letnev. Syd found his feet just as there was another blast of blinding heat and light. When it abated Syd realized, to his horror, that a molten hole had been bored clean through the middle of Chel's torso, another plasma shot, the stink of burned chitin overwhelming.

The big Tekklar quivered for a moment, limbs and antennae rigid, before collapsing back down onto the rails.

Ice was now slicking every surface, and frost bristled thickly along the runner lines. An alarm had started to ring, bouncing back and forth eerily through the tunnel. Syd stood stunned, overwhelmed by cold and shock, only vaguely aware of the nearest Lazax guards gesturing furiously at him to hurry. The Letnev were charging, yet another searing plasma shot hitting the rail runner's prow, leaving part of the Lazax crest twisted and molten.

This was the end, Syd realized. He would die here, caught up in a web of deadly intrigue. He had failed Atz, he had failed the emperor. Years of service for naught.

He half turned, deciding to take the fatal wound to his front. A Letnev scrambled over the icy walkway to him, target optics glowing a sickly green locked on to him. Syd could remember well enough the Rosharin, the defensive martial art taught to all Lazax ambassadors along with the Fifteen Miscu – or Truths – that formed much of Lazax philosophy, but he was too cold to even raise his staff in defense.

The Letnev didn't shoot him. To his surprise he snatched him roughly by the shoulder and rammed him against the tube's wall, before bringing up his beam rifle.

Syd realized that he had shoved him out of the way to clear a line of fire. He could have just killed him, but instead he opened up on the rest of the entourage. On Zey.

The ambassador was clambering up into the runner's first box, helped by one of the security troopers. The purple bolts slashed into the metalwork around him, before a pulse of blue energy engulfed him, dissipating a trio of shots that had been about to hit him. Syd realized that Zey didn't just have echo garbs on. He was carrying a shimmer shield device.

Another shot punched right through the sallet helm worn by the trooper helping Zey, dropping him like a lead weight.

The sight of Zey's survival helped Syd to finally recover from the shock and cold, enough to lash out at the Letnev standing right in front of him. Feet slipping on the ice, the assassin tumbled into one of the railings below with a yell.

"Sir," Onni shouted, again doubling back for Syd. He grabbed two of the Lazax's arms and hauled him the last few yards to the flank of the runner. Syd's limbs ached deeply, but they obeyed enough to get him up and into the transport with Onni's help.

"We're all on," the Winnu told the nearest security troopers, who snapped a string of instructions into his comm bead. Retiring in pairs, the Lazax boarded the runner, one hefting the body of their fallen comrade. Syd collapsed onto one of the seating bars, shaking uncontrollably.

"We're cranking up the heating," one of the troopers said as they sealed the transport's doors, the sounds of beam weaponry still ringing from the hull. "And rolling out of here. Just hold on."

Onni helped Syd fit the seating bar's restraining clamp. He flexed his fingers, trying to work feeling back into them, grimacing as he had to physically crack them free from around the haft of his staff. It was still difficult to breathe, and everything felt as though it had cramped up.

The Winnu dealt better with cold than the Lazax. Both aides seemed largely unscathed, though a medi-trooper was checking Nauru's shoulder graze. Syd found himself looking across at Zey, sitting opposite.

He was shaking too and almost white with heat loss. He was unharmed though, thanks to his shimmer shield, which was now as invisible as it had been before evaporating the incoming beam blasts.

"They shot you," Syd said, trying to force his mind to wake up just as he was doing to his body.

"They were shooting at all of us," Zey managed to reply.

"They weren't. They specifically didn't hit me. They were aiming for you."

Zey looked at Syd as coldly as the compromised interior of the traffic tube. Syd knew he shouldn't have admitted to what had just happened. It looked too suspicious, but it simply made no sense. He had been sure Zey was behind the hit. But there had been no hesitation in the Letnev who had shoved him aside, no uncertainty. He had aimed at Zey. His shots had hit him. Even if he had been informed about the shimmer shield beforehand, there was no guarantee it would have saved him.

"Do you want to explain why they left you alive?" Zey asked. Syd had no good answer.

"I don't know," he admitted. "But I'm going to find out. In the meantime, I think you had best inform Chancellor Lamarque that unless he wants to come to the garrison stronghold, our meeting is off."

The security troopers got Syd, Zey, and the Winnu back to the garrison safely. Kwarni and Major Parax met them as soon as they arrived. The place was abuzz, blast screens rolling down over slit windows and doorways, energy shields igniting with actinic cracks, the corridors echoing to the sounds of running boots as more troopers rushed by toward their stations.

"What happened?" Kwarni asked, gripping his ambassadorial staff. He had also ignited its electrostatic properties, its dull hum making the hairs along Syd's arms stand on end.

"A Letnev kill-squad just tried to murder me," Zey said with undisguised bitterness, glancing at Syd. "Me in particular."

"We were intercepted on the way to Manufactorum Primus," Syd elaborated, wanting to deflect from Zey's point about how the Letnev had spared him. "Hirelings, by the look of it, but well-armed. It was fortunate that your response was so prompt, major. They managed to kill our Tekklar Elite."

"We always have a platoon on standby, able to deploy with one minute's notice," Parax said. "I'm in touch with General Marne, Letnev commander of the Dunlain Crater. He has stood his forces to. Apparently the traffic tube you were using is now badly compromised. They've sealed it off. No word on your assailants."

"How about the rest of the imperial garrison?" Syd asked. "I fear we have to be ready for anything, major. For all we know, those could have been Letnev soldiers in disguise. Marne's mobilization could be a cover for a wider assault."

"The garrison has gone into lockdown, and our defensive measures are in place," Parax said. "Rest assured we are ready for anything, eminent councilor."

"I need to report back to Mecatol," Syd said pointedly to Kwarni.

"I suggest we both make our reports," Zey interjected. Syd realized Zey didn't trust him to mention the fact their attackers had spared him, but neither did he wish to allow Zey to make an unmonitored transmission from an imperial comms hub.

"We'll do it together," Syd said, knowing he couldn't use the opportunity to update Atz on the current efforts to expose Zey, but accepting the compromise. "The empire needs to know there's been an incident as soon as possible."

"An incident" felt like an understatement, but Syd had recovered from the worst of the shock, and the heat of the runner had banished Arc Prime's frigidity. Everything had started to escalate. It left him more concerned than ever, but also more determined. His actions would have direct consequences on the empire's future. He had to keep up with it, or risk being left behind again.

PART
TWO

CHAPTER THIRTEEN

MUAAT, HOMEWORLD OF THE GASHLAI, CAMPUS-COLONY OF THE UNIVERSITIES OF JOL-NAR

In the day-cycles following her message to Jol, Tol continued to monitor her comms almost obsessively. She didn't know what she expected, but it certainly wasn't the transmission she received several days after trying to warn the universities about the depths Doctor Arr had sunk to.

In fact, the message she received wasn't about Arr at all.

After calming down sufficiently to read it, she discovered it hadn't come from offworld, but had actually originated from the surface of Muaat, beneath her. It was from a station nearly as remote as hers, located high in the Doolaks, close to the tallest mountain in the entire range, KZ80. Tol was aware of the station's existence, albeit only as somewhere she tried to steer clear of whenever she ventured down into the highlands. She wasn't here to disturb other Hylar, and she didn't want to stumble into another disgraced scientist or doctor's secret lair. Officially, KZ80's listed purpose on the pan-university logs was an expeditionary force outpost responsible for meteorological monitoring and minor soil and mineral research, and that was good enough for Tol.

She had certainly not expected to be the recipient of a message from the outpost. Specifically, it was from a Stationmaster Joree, and it was so unexpected she had to read it twice to properly process it.

With typical Hylar brusqueness, Joree apologized for the unprompted contact, but explained that three days previously the outpost's only on-station medic, Wulen, had fallen badly ill. The cause of the sickness remained as yet unidentified. Normally it would have been a simple thing to request aid from the other Jol-Nar installations on-world, but a particularly potent firestorm had flared up around the base of the central Doolaks, rendering air travel to and from the mountain range practically impossible. Even advanced Hylar communications were being ruined by Muaat's environmental wrath.

Fortunately for KZ80, they had detected the orbital arc of Exosphere Station T19 passing directly above them, enabling them to bounce a signal up to her. Joree asked that she relay the signal herself to campus-colony headquarters in Mavgala, essentially acting as a satellite for the stranded station.

There was more. It seemed Joree had also done his reading on her. He asked that, once the message was sent, she come down to the surface and use her medical knowledge to treat the doctor. His condition was apparently critical, and could not wait on the abatement of the storm. She was his only real hope.

Even before completing her second reading, Tol felt conflicting emotions. She had been banished here, to the edge of nowhere, cast out of Hylar academic circles. In truth she had never cared for the stilted, backstabbing, egotistical environment the universities promoted. Her passions were her own research, and helping others. That was what she believed her purpose was. The Hylar had already proven they had the cerebral capacity to better the whole galaxy, but they so often seemed to give grudgingly. She wished she could change that. This was an opportunity to do just that, to help her fellow sentients. She was putting her beliefs into practice.

A fellow Hylar? She knew she shouldn't even have hesitated. The encounter with Arr had shaken her deeply though. What if KZ80 was serving a similar purpose? What if they were developing weapons, or conducting horrific experiments on the Gashlai? There was so little oversight on Muaat, it felt as though they could be doing anything, and the more remote the worse the odds.

"You have been reading that transmission for approximately ten minutes," ZALLY chimed in unhelpfully.

"I'm thinking," Tol responded.

"You do not believe you can assist the station's medic?"

"Are you reading it over my shoulder?"

"I have all your transmissions automatically downloaded," ZALLY said defensively. "That's how you programmed me, remember?"

Tol waved her away, refusing to let the familiar be her moral compass. She already knew what she had to do. The right thing.

She was going back down to Muaat. She tried not to think about the fact that, once there, she would be stranded until T19's orbital pathway brought it directly overhead again. She had carefully timed her previous trips to the highlands, but it was almost certain this one would require at least a full rotation, maybe more – that would be over forty-two hours GMT. That was without considering the fact she hardly knew what to expect from the mysterious station.

She would just have to find out what was down there waiting for her when she arrived.

Tol knew she had to be quick, before T19's orbit took her out from over the Doolaks. She fired up her old shuttle and brought ZALLY, permitting the familiar to remind her about all the pieces of kit she'd otherwise have forgotten.

Sterilization swabs, a small set of scalpels, an autosuture applicator, a canister of dermal sealer, multitablets, a sample pod, a few vials of antiviral cocktails and trexapine, and most importantly, her handheld quintisensor. She loaded most of it up on ZALLY's anti-grav beamer, transforming her into a small automed.

She was still nervous about descending into the unknown, but as she prepped she also realized she was excited. This was the real thing. She had always wanted to be a doctor, but besides the practical courses she had taken while at university, she had never actually gotten an opportunity to practice. She had been banished from Jol before receiving an appointment following her graduation. Fears that she would never fulfill her life's desires of helping sentients had reared their ugly heads. It was why she had thrown herself so determinedly into research on Muaat. If she couldn't treat the injured and the sick, she was going to make a breakthrough that would make a difference. Now, though, she was about to do what she had always dreamed of.

The flight was a brief one. As the shuttle descended she was afforded the spectacular view of a golden dawn over Muaat's rim combined with the wrathful fury of the firestorm that had surrounded KZ80 beneath her. The great mountain stood proud over it, its peak capped with snow turned golden by the rising light of Mashaak, while the world beneath broiled in fire-shot darkness, like an evil Mahact host besieging a proud Lazax keep in one of the stories she had been obsessed with as a young spawnling.

The shuttle locked onto the outpost's landing pad. It was a tiny installation, just two envirodomes and a hydro-dredger perched precariously on a small ledge on the mountain slope, its soaring bulk dwarfing it. The firestorm was visible as a layer of ash and flame below, raging against the lower reaches of the Doolaks but thankfully not climbing any higher.

There was no one to greet her on the pad. She disembarked with ZALLY. Joree had provided her with access codes, which she used to open the hatch in the larger of the two enviro-domes. As she did so she tried to master her resurgent nervousness, doing her best not to wonder what she would find on the other side.

The answer was a decompression box, which she triggered once the outer door was sealed again. Through another hatch, and she found herself face-to-face with a Hylar.

He was a fellow native of Nar, shorter and with neon-bright red and blue patterned scales and fins.

The two started, the other Hylar recovering first.

"Under-Doctor Tol?" he asked.

"Yes," Tol answered hastily, flaring her crest in a nervous greeting. "I'm here on the request of Stationmaster Joree? I received a communication from him at the start of the cycle."

"Yes, yes," the Hylar said, gesturing her fully into the dome. "I am Technician Kero. I am actually the one who sent the transmission, with Joree's permission. Since you received word from us things have… developed further."

"Developed further how?" Tol asked, looking around as she did so. The dome was typical of a surface-level Hylar installation. It was spartan, with plasticon-sheathed data modules capable of beaming out a variety of different systems for the dozen technicians and operators serving as staff. There was a comms hub and, along an upper walkway, mist bunks where Nar-born Hylar like Kero slept. The neighboring dome, Tol assumed, would be an aqua orb where the Jol Hylar would sleep and eat in full submersion.

"Stationmaster Joree is sick," Kero said. "Like Medic Wulen. He was showing symptoms but refused to accept it."

"Where are they both now?" Tol asked. "And the rest of the station staff?"

"I have ordered them confined to their bunks, to try to stop the spread of infection," Kero said. "The stationmaster and the doctor are both in the aqua dome. I… wasn't sure what else to do."

Tol realized that Kero was young, no older than her in fact, and very nervous. He was probably talented when it came to the station's surveying work, but these events had clearly thrown him.

"Do not worry, Kero," Tol told him. "You've done well. I will go and see them both, but I think you should remain here. Until we know what this is, we have to keep them as isolated as possible."

She paused to don an enviro-sphere that ZALLY had been

grav-lugging under her. She hadn't filled it with water, but she was hoping it could provide a modicum of protection against any potential pathogens. She didn't have a proper, sealed medical suit. She could only hope she wouldn't need one. All of this was far behind what she had anticipated, even in a worst-case scenario. She couldn't just leave them now though. They were clearly in desperate need.

"Once I'm inside, re-seal the hatch behind me," she instructed Kero, swallowing her fear. He dipped his crest in confirmation, clearly trying to master his own nerves. In truth Tol felt no better, but he was giving her a reason to stay strong.

The aqua dome was partially drained as she entered. A pair of plasticon tables stood near the center of what was essentially a small Jol habitation sphere, just below the surface of the chest-high water. Two Jol Hylar were laid out on them, unresponsive. The hatch thumped shut behind her and hissed as Kero sealed it.

She paused on the edge of the short flight of steps that led down into the water and uncoupled her quintisensor, using it to take a sample of the liquid within the dome. The last thing she wanted was to expose herself to a hydro-infection. At the same time ZALLY buzzed over to the two submerged Hylar and began scanning their vitals.

While Tol waited for the quintisensor to process its findings she identified which patient was which – both had been stripped down to their under-suits, which clung to their long, slender gray bodies. The suit of the nearest was dark blue, with the badge of the University of Interplanetary Environmental Studies on his chest, while the other's was white, with the red crest of the Pan University Medical Corps. That made the former Stationmaster Joree, and the latter Medic Wulen.

The quintisensor pinged up its findings. The water's hydric mix was not as ideally balanced as most Hylar liked it. It could do with at least a scrubbing, if not an outright flush, but the negative microbes present were not unusual or especially dangerous.

Tol stepped down into the water, feeling its welcome, soothing embrace. Nar Hylar may be better equipped for surviving terrestrial environments than their kin from Jol, but the water was still their home, and essential to their survival.

"How're they looking?" she asked ZALLY as she approached them.

"Suboptimal," the familiar replied as she continued scanning them. "Vital signs are being inhibited. Gross fluctuations in core temperature. They're in the throes of a potentially fatal infection."

That was just confirming Tol's fears. She slid through the water to Medic Wulen's side and, after running the quintisensor over him, gave him a small stab-injection of antiviral stimulants. She then did the same to Joree before taking samples of their plasma.

"We need to work out what this is," Tol said as she worked, finding herself slotting into the old routines she had become accustomed to while on secondment during her studies. "Diagnosis, then treatment."

"Stabilization, diagnosis, treatment," ZALLY corrected her. "They could both perish during this cycle. Medic Wulen in particular."

"Then I'd better work fast," Tol said.

ZALLY was right. Wulen looked close to termination. His

black eyes were staring through the water, his limbs rigid. Tol carefully inspected him from head to webbed feet, trying not to feel frantic as she ran through the possibilities. The doctor's gills were inflamed and raw-looking, while the scales around his eyes were filmed with a strange yellowish mucus. He was entirely unresponsive to any stimulus.

Joree wasn't as bad. His gills shivered as Tol gently probed at him, and he let out a moan, but his eyes failed to find focus. Tol resolved to question Kero more closely on the speed and symptoms of his decline.

The initial blood tests run via the quintisensor proved inconclusive. Tol carefully began to scrape a small amount of the mucus from around Medic Wulen's eyes, then recoiled when the contact caused his gills to jettison a slurry of vile yellow sludge. Tol hastily checked her revulsion and secured some of the effluvium in a sample vial.

"The antivirals have had some effect," ZALLY noted. "Both are reading as more stable, but I estimate it's merely an inhibition of the virus's progress, rather than a cure."

"Agreed," Tol said. At least they were slowing it down. Hopefully that would give her time to conduct further analysis.

She sat in one of the sterilization cradles that Jol Hylar used before entering the water, cleansing herself of any of the pathogens, before knocking on the hatch. Kero opened it, looking from her to his fellow station staff.

"Initial results are inconclusive," Tol admitted. "I'm going to return to my shuttle for the time being. From there I can uplink the samples to my orbital station, where my equipment can run more comprehensive scans. In the meantime my familiar will continue to monitor the patients."

"I will?" ZALLY asked from above the pair.

"Thank you for this," Kero said, giving a short, relieved bow. "And I am sorry for calling you down to the surface. I just didn't know what to do."

"I told you, you did the right thing," Tol said in what she hoped was a reassuring tone. "I will return by the end of the day-cycle. Until then maintain the quarantine, and I'm sure all will be well."

Tol withdrew to her shuttle, wondering just how much of a lie she had just spoken. A part of her was still thrilled to be here, doing what she had always strived for, but realities were now imposing themselves. She had rarely heard of a pathogen causing such a rapid deterioration in its victims, and never in a disease that affected the Hylar. Her initial hypothesis had been between one of three types of infection, but of the possibilities, Rashwater caused far greater degradation of its victim's scales, Gillworms didn't affect the eyes and Zemo's Disease had been wiped from the galaxy over three centuries previously. How could it have returned to an isolated outpost on Muaat? Comorbidity – the presence of simultaneous, separate infections – also seemed next to impossible given the speed of the spread and the near-identical symptoms being suffered by both. So what was it?

She fired up the shuttle's uplink and began to upload a scan of both the blood and the gill fluids. She had a more heavy-duty quintisensor diagnosticator onboard T19, though she would have to wait until the station had come back around on its orbital path before she was able to receive any results. If the firestorm continued, she would also be unable to return to the station until then. She just hoped the message from

KZ80 that she had forwarded on to Mavgala had made it through.

Muaat's diurnal cycle was relatively long for an inhabited world, forty-two hours Galactic Mean Time – or GMT – more than twice the length of the Mecatol day and night used by most sentients as a standard measurement. Without any spare bunks in the station, Tol slept in the shuttle with the mister on, secretly relieved to at least be out of the domes themselves. When she awoke the firestorm was still raging below – it was now night, and the fiery glow suffused the slopes around her, turning the sky orange and searing away the stars.

She returned to the main enviro-dome and asked further questions of Kero and the rest of the station staff. Most of the others were Jol Hylar, and reluctant to give much in the way of answers – being a young Nar under-doctor had that sort of effect.

"Had Medic Wulen left the station for any reason in the weeks prior to displaying symptoms?" she asked one, an unusually blubbery Jol by the name of Chem.

"No," the heavyset technician said with a dismissive tone. "He's the station medic, he is required to be here on a permanent basis."

The other Jol Hylar said the same, but Kero did not.

"He was absent from the station for a fifth of the Muaat cycle about two weeks ago," he claimed.

Tol paused in surprise, then asked him to elaborate. The technician looked awkward.

"I don't know why. The stationmaster approved it, so I assume he knew. It's unusual for the doctor to leave for any reason, especially with the spate of firestorms we've had of late."

Tol tried to contain herself. This was the sort of information she needed if she was going to find out exactly what sort of disease had gripped the station. She was so eager to find the source, she didn't even initially pause to wonder why the other Hylar had so stoically denied knowledge of Wulen's movements. "It's vital that we find out where he visited," she told Kero. "That way we can trace the source of the outbreak."

"The stationmaster probably logged it in the database," Kero said. "But I don't have the authority to review that."

"You probably also don't have the authority to send messages to orbital stations on Joree's behalf," Tol pointed out. "Whatever this infection is, it's deadly and virulent. It has to be dealt with, and I can't do that unless I know where it came from."

Kero looked unhappy, but he agreed. While the other Hylar were still in their mist bunks, he called up KZ80's records, beamed up from one of the plasticon modules. Tol watched, trying not to fidget as he waved his hand through the three-dimensional display, cycling through the logs.

"Here," he said. "There's a record of Medic Wulen's departure, but it doesn't say why or where. Only that he had scheduled a meeting with a Doctor Atak Arr."

The firestorm was beginning to abate. That at least was a blessing. Tol was struggling to contain her fear and anger, to maintain the reserved demeanor of a Jol-Nar medical expert.

Medic Wulen had visited Arr, not long after her own meeting with him. Tol had no doubt Arr had reached out to him. In all likelihood, Wulen was in a situation not dissimilar to Tol's, banished to some remote outpost for an infraction. Arr would surely have pitched his deranged ideas to him, seeking his medical assistance.

Whether or not Wulen had agreed was now unimportant. What mattered was that he had brought something back with him from Arr's laboratories. Infection. A virus. That was what Arr had been trying to develop. He had been searching for a plague to exterminate the Sardakk N'orr, but he was by his own admission not a virologist. Tol wasn't surprised that something in the morphological relations between the Hylar and the N'orr had caused it to transfer from one species to another. Galactic plagues did not discriminate.

Arr had infected Wulen. Whether he had done so knowingly or not remained unknown.

Tol hadn't told Kero of Arr's activities, or just how she thought Wulen had contracted the virus. She had to confront Arr first. She had to know more.

Before that, she forced herself to check in with the patients. ZALLY had been tracking worsening symptoms. Joree now looked as bad as Wulen had the cycle before, while Wulen's gills were so red and swollen Tol was forced to use a basic hydro pump to force water in via his mouth. One eye had also become completely crusted over, and the water around him was discolored. The only positive was none of the other station members were yet displaying symptoms.

She did what she could, administering the last of the antivirals she had. Privately, she feared all she could do for them was keep them stable until more help arrived. Tracing the source of the outbreak, however, was another matter.

She sent a viz transmission request to Arr via her shuttle. It went unresponded-to. She was about to send a second when the shuttle's systems read an incoming download.

T19 was once more passing overhead, and as it did so it automatically sent the analysis results to Tol's uplink. She read them with racing heart and flared fins, trying to assess just how bad things were.

It seemed like her worst fears were being confirmed. Analysis of the blood had found traces of Zemo's Disease. Its makeup wasn't identical however, and it didn't match the last recorded version of that particular pathogen. It had been spliced with something else to make it barely recognizable.

On the third transmission request, Arr answered. The small viz projector mounted on the shuttle's main control board flickered into life. The firestorm was still disrupting communications, and both the image and the words that emanated from the speakers were chopped and distorted, but it was legible enough.

"Under-doctor," Arr said. "I was not expecting to hear from you again."

"Have you been using Zemo's Disease in your experiments?" Tol demanded, with no regard for even the scant pleasantries a Hylar like Arr offered.

"I do not see why that concerns you," Arr answered. "After all, you have already turned down my request for aid."

"And did Medic Wulen?" Tol said. "You made the same proposal to him, didn't you?"

"I do not know who you are referring to."

"Don't lie, Arr. This is serious. More serious than your twisted ambitions. Wulen is sick. It's Zemo's, but it's something more as well. He's already infected another member of the station where he's posted."

Arr was silent for a while before answering, both tone and expression as emotionless as ever. "I do not know of a Medic Wulen. Your communications array is suboptimal at the moment. I am cutting the transmission."

Before Tol could respond, the distorted viz display cut out.

Tol cursed vehemently and at length. When she had composed herself, she left the shuttle and returned to the enviro-dome.

"I need to return to orbit while my station is passing overhead," she told Kero, before pausing. She had noticed his sheepish expression and then, moments later, his gills. It was difficult to tell because of his brightly patterned scales, but at a glance it looked as though they bore the first hints of an inflammation.

"When did you notice that?" she asked him.

"Just at the start of the new cycle. Is it…" he trailed off miserably.

"I'm going to get more supplies," Tol said, trying not to ponder the very real, creeping possibility that she too had been infected. That wouldn't help anyone right now. "While I'm up there I'll check for responses to the message I forwarded to Mavgala. As you said, the storm is starting to pass, so we should be able to receive assistance within the next few hours."

"Did you find any results?" Kero asked. "Do you know what it is?"

"I have some theories," she said, doing her best to appear even remotely upbeat. "I'll be working with whoever they send from Mavgala to find a cure to this as quickly as possible.

Remain here, and I'll return within the next two hours. ZALLY will assist you if there's an emergency."

Tol returned to Exosphere Station T19. She was just finishing closer analysis of the mucus sample taken from Wulen's gills when an alert from the station's proximity sensors popped up.

She assessed it, feeling a sense of disbelief as she read back the readings of a quick zonal scan.

A Jol-Nar military frigate had drawn into hailing range of T19. What's more, it had just launched a small vessel. While T19's crude sensors weren't capable of identifying it, Tol could only assume it was a boarding craft.

Hastily, she locked onto the frigate and sent a communications request. The red icon on the display monitor continued to pulse, unanswered. She sent a message transmission instead, asking the vessel to identify itself.

Likewise, nothing. The boarding craft was drawing so close now that she could see it on the external recorders. It was definitely Jol-Nar, and definitely military.

She tried and failed not to panic. Why was she about to be boarded? What did they want with her? Hastily, she sent a message spike down to KZ80. Her station had already passed over it, so it likely wouldn't get through, unless the firestorm had now died down. All she could hope was that it would.

I've been waylaid. Whatever you do, don't leave KZ80. Don't let it spread.

She sent it. There was no indication as to whether it had been received or not.

There was a clanging impact that made her cringe, rattling

the metal framework around her. A single transmission popped up on her display. She had hoped it was Kero, but it was an anonymous order from whoever commanded the boarding craft.

Open the lock, or the hatch will be destroyed.

Tol considered leaving it in an effort to slow them down, but there was nothing more she could do anyway. She went and undid the autoclamps on the main docking hatch. There were further thumps from beyond, and a hiss as the boarder's prow compartment and the external dock clamp of the station stabilized.

Then the hatch banged open. Pan University Military boarding tyros, the void marine forces of the Jol-Nar war fleet, came barging in. They were fully kitted out, with armored vibrosteel chestplates, beam carbines and plated containment spheres that left only a slit for their glaring eyes.

"Hands up," the first one in barked, fins and gills inscrutable behind the grim metal visor. "Now!"

"I've done nothing wrong," Tol shouted as she complied, glaring at the invaders. "Why are you here?"

"Under-Doctor Harial Tol, you are under arrest for academic slander and the disruption of research attempts," the leader responded as another Hylar moved behind her and roughly clamped her wrists with magnetic cuffs.

"I've only told the truth," she shouted, unable to keep her composure in the face of such aggression. "There's been an infectious outbreak on the surface! KZ80! They need help! They're dying!"

"Bring her," the leader snapped, gesturing toward the hatch. Tol began to resist, fighting to unclamp her hands.

"You have to believe me! We're all in danger! Just check the samples! Check the quintisensor findings! It's Zemo's Disease, but worse!"

The tyros ignored her. Still shouting and struggling, she was hauled into the Jol-Nar vessel.

CHAPTER FOURTEEN

ARC PRIME,
HOMEWORLD OF THE BARONY OF LETNEV

The Reaper Hall was vast, its ceiling lost in darkness while its walls were obscured by the objects filling it, dimly illuminated out-of-hours by the low-energy floor lighting strips that ran between the storage rows.

The Reaper Halls, as a term, could be used to refer to the hundreds of vast manufactories in Feruc that turned raw materials into the Letnev weapons of war, but officially they were the hangars that adjoined such centers of industry. Here the Letnev collected the largest of their planet-bound weapons of destruction.

There were Ashbringer escorts, Razor interceptors and the great Widowcrusher bomber fortresses, their jagged wings pinioned in, crouched like gigantic, deadly bats in the half-dark. Alongside them sat row after row of Skullmaker grav-tanks and Swiftstrike armored troop transports, along with file after file of the infamous Dunlain Reapers, the war-walkers ranging in size from a little larger than an average sentient to towering Devastation-class mechanoids so tall their heads and shoulders were lost in the darkness of the overhead vaults, their hulking, armor-plated bodies bristling with weapons systems. Nor was it just vehicles – everything from racks of beam rifles and their charge packs to antistarfighter armaments, intercontinental missiles, and shells for orbital defense cannons sat ranked precisely up, one after the other, stretching off seemingly into infinity.

The hall was one of a dozen similar structures in Feruc, a hub of Letnev weaponry that, unlike anything maintained in the subterranean megalopolises, could easily be transported into orbit and onward to any war zone of the baron's pleasing.

Normally the Reaper Halls were heavy with security even during the dead of night, but on this particular evening one section of the building was unguarded. Shadon Reyna had made sure of that. She was a senior Letnev weapons logistician, responsible for equipping and supplying the barony's grand army and fleet, and she had the authority necessary to ensure no one witnessed who she brought into the hall at such a late hour.

Syd was still in the Lazax garrison, on the other side of the crater, but thanks to the Hylar-made oculus lenses and comms piece Onni was wearing, it was as though he was present in person. It was common knowledge that all regular comms channels used by the Lazax were monitored, and after the assassination attempt in the traffic tube the day before it was impossible for anyone to leave the garrison unnoticed, but the same could not be said of the Winnu. Onni had therefore slipped out and was acting on Syd's behalf.

He did not have the sorts of contacts Zey possessed on Arc Prime, but nor was he wholly without. He had deliberately allowed the ambassador to think he was more unfamiliar and adrift among the Letnev than he really was. In truth, Syd did have a few old acquaintances he could reach out to in case of an emergency. Unfortunately, the attack on the rail runner had propelled the situation into emergency territory.

Shadon Reyna was an old friend. Every sentient grouping had their associated tropes, be it the wily Hacan trader or the slow, wise old Xxcha, but Syd had seen enough of the galaxy to know that stereotypes were for fools. The Letnev might be more aloof and more militarized than most other civilizations, but not every Letnev was an arrogant warmonger.

During Syd's first visit to Arc Prime he had encountered Reyna as a recent graduate from the Logistics Sub-College in Agiz and a rising star in the barony's civil service. She had been a part of the demilitarization campaign following the last Letnev uprising, and had found herself in favor with the gradualists. Things hadn't gone so well for her lately though, given the rising prominence of the warmongering Resurgentists. She had lost her position as a policy maker and been shifted to military logistics, an irony given the fact that, for a Letnev, she was practically a pacifist. She was still senior enough to have an insight into what was happening at the barony's higher levels though, and when Syd had reached out she had agreed to meet.

"This will do," Syd heard her say as she and Onni stopped in the shadows beneath one of the huge Dunlain Reapers, shielded from most of the rest of the hangar by one massive, armored leg.

"You may trigger the mask, Onni," Syd told the Winnu. He was sitting in his chamber in the garrison building, with a viz reader set up opposite him, locked onto his features. Onni, meanwhile, as well as the lenses and earpiece, was wearing a beam-mask. Deactivated, it looked like a plate of white plasticon, featureless apart from the eye slits and the small projection nodes that studded it. When activated however, those same nodes projected a three-dimensional holographic faceplate, an exact rendering of whoever was locked onto the mask remotely via transmitter. Besides making remote interactions more natural, Reyna could be sure it was really him she was conversing with.

"Thank you for agreeing to this," Syd said as the visualization transmitter came on, his face now appearing over Onni's mask. "In truth there's no one else on this world I trust right now."

"I understand how you feel," Reyna said without humor. "Things have been deteriorating for some time."

"So it seems. Onni has told you the basics of why I wish to speak to you?"

"He has, and it was clear enough anyway. The traffic tube incident is having major short-term repercussions, though the baron is trying to keep it all under wraps."

"Do you know who ordered it?"

"Not for sure, no. But a lot of sources are suggesting the same thing. It was Baron Werqan herself."

"Dazie Allic Werqan," Syd repeated, thoughts turning. He had considered the possibility, but it only opened up further questions.

"The baron has all the resources she could possibly need to kill both myself and my fellow ambassador, Zey," Syd said aloud. "She could have had that traffic tube destroyed, for example. Guaranteed both our deaths. Why use a small hit-team instead?"

"Perhaps she wanted more precision," Reyna suggested. "Confirmed kills. Regardless, it seems as though Chancellor Lamarque was ordered to arrange a meeting with you to draw you out from the Lazax garrison."

"He didn't arrange it with me though, he arranged it with Zey," Syd said, finding several possibilities aligning. The assassin's shots at Zey, the fact that the chancellor had agreed to meet Zey specifically in the first place, the use of gunslingers instead of explosives, to hit a specific target rather than cause unnecessary collateral – in this case, perhaps that collateral included accidentally killing Syd as well. He hadn't been the target, nor had Lazax authority in general. Zey had been the only one the baron was trying to take out.

Why? Syd didn't intend to share his instructions from Atz or his suspicions about Zey with Rayna. It was clear though that Baron Werqan was working toward an objective that Syd didn't yet fully appreciate. Why specifically target just Zey? Did Werqan know about a connection between Zey and Arrokan? That would add up. Werqan, privately furious and concerned about the rogue Arrokan undermining her authority and leading the Letnev to the brink of war, was trying to resolve the Quann crisis and sever Arrokan's co-conspirator, Zey, without the ignominy of admitting she had lost control of the situation.

"Your ambassador seems to have made the baron his enemy," Reyna said, echoing Syd's thoughts. "Be thankful she isn't targeting all the Lazax here."

"Is there appetite for another rebellion?" Syd asked, fearing the answer. Reyna looked conflicted, giving a tense shrug.

"Among the usual quarters, of course. The Resurgentists are

in the ascendancy, and their hardline views are spreading. Most of the military is behind them. They *are* most of the military. But the general public aren't there yet. We're standing on the precipice, deciding if we'd rather fall or jump."

"Things are in motion to pull you back," Syd said, trying to sound reassuring. Reyna scoffed.

"The thing you Lazax consider to be motion is usually a slug's pace," she said. "How long before a formal imperial response from Mecatol? Something more helpful than your cloaks and daggers?"

"We're working on it," Syd said, knowing how weak he sounded, but able to offer nothing more. In truth, he knew he was getting out of his depth. He didn't have the authority to act unilaterally in negotiations with the Letnev. He just had to trust that his suggestions would be backed by Atz when the time came, back on Mecatol.

"I'm going to report back to my contact on the imperial council once we're finished here," he said, trying to buttress Reyna's confidence. "You will see measures taking effect in the coming weeks."

"We may only have days," Reyna pointed out. "It all depends on what happens on Quann."

"Agreed," Syd said. "For the time being, we can only hope rationality prevails there."

Syd dispatched one of Kwarni's sprinters to Mecatol, the transmission locked to Atz's personal receiver. In it, he explained his theory that Zey and Arrokan were conspiring to force Baron Werqan to start a war, and Werqan was working to end their threat without it becoming public knowledge.

When it came, it was the last thing he either hoped for or expected.

The courier picket bringing messages from Mecatol had not been dispatched directly by Atz, but by the emperor himself, via the imperial council. It seemed the formal deliberations of what to do about what it called "the Quann misunderstanding" were now complete, and the emperor's will was known. Discourse was necessary between both Quann and Arc Prime. To that end, Syd had been ordered to the former, while Zey remained on the latter. They would coordinate their efforts and bring a peaceful resolution to the "misunderstanding."

Syd experienced a moment of potent, crushing despair. The last thing he wanted was to be separated from Zey. Without him present, who knew what the ambassador might do on Arc Prime? Syd was already certain that the so-called contacts he had been using were radical members of the Resurgentists, working together to ramp up the calls for war. The orders from Mecatol were unambiguous though. It was an imperial decree.

A private communique from Atz came with the same courier. He apologized for the orders, and swore he had done all in his power to stop the council from separating Syd and Zey. It was impossible to convey the gravity of the situation to the council, however, without indicating that Zey was under suspicion, and that was unacceptable. He had too many allies, as well as the favor of the emperor himself. The entire investigation would collapse. Atz would do what he could on Mecatol, but in the meantime, Syd would have to obey the edict and travel to Quann.

It made Syd want to weep with rage. Instead, he composed himself, destroyed Atz's message as instructed, and met with

Zey to discuss their official instructions from the council. Zey showed no hint of happiness that he and Syd were to be separated, and merely said that he would continue to pursue leads on Arc Prime while staying in contact.

There was nothing more to it. Feeling as though he was being dragged away from the investigation when it was at its most crucial stage, he chartered one of the garrison's faster vessels for passage to Quann.

Only one thing remained to do before departing. While Zey was absent he took Onni and spoke once more with Nauru.

"It is vital you try to monitor Zey's movements, who he sees," he told the Winnu aide. "I know he does not take you into his confidence, but you are the closest loyal servant of the empire to him, and the best remaining hope for catching his misdeeds. Tracking him will be vital."

"I understand, sir," Nauru said earnestly.

"Take this and keep it on your person," Syd carried on, placing an object in Nauru's hand. It was roughly spherical, like a metallic egg, unadorned but for two dimples on opposite sides. Depressing one made the object vibrate briefly.

"It's a locator beacon," Syd explained as Nauru examined it with a frown. "An advanced piece of Hylar technology. It will ping your position to the nearest orbital datacache in the system, which will then be transmitted to the next courier picket. If you remain with Zey, I will be able to track you as each picket reaches Quann. I have already requisitioned a trio to perform a journey on rotation. I doubt you will be able to use a communications hub regularly to send your own messages via the courier, but with this I will at least be able to monitor where you – and Zey – are remotely."

Nauru accepted the device.

"Remain as close to him as possible, but do not put yourself in unnecessary danger," Syd urged her. "You are currently one of the empire's most valuable agents."

"When will I be relieved of it?" Nauru asked, unable to fully mask her apprehension.

"As soon as we have Zey back in a space where we can properly monitor him," Syd replied. "I have already dispatched word with the last picket to leave to my associate on Mecatol; he will ensure that if Zey is recalled there or given another posting someone will complete a handover with you."

"I understand," Nauru said. Onni gave her wrist a squeeze.

"You are doing a great service not only for the empire, but for all Winnu," he said.

"Indeed," Syd added, trying to build Nauru's confidence. She was currently his only hope of even partly monitoring Zey. "Once all this is over, I will make sure your invaluable contribution is acknowledged."

"There is no need for that, sir," Nauru said. "As long as the empire prospers. Pax Magnifica."

CHAPTER FIFTEEN

Governor Forebeck called Zara into his office on the morning he left Quann.

The strain recent times had put him under was clear. The broad, straight shoulders had become lean and rounded, the square-jawed face gaunt, the silver-streaked hair now patched with white. He looked like a broken man. Zara supposed in a way he was.

He apologized for leaving. She told him not to. He had his orders. In truth, she didn't begrudge him. Living under the constant threat of war was no life at all.

"I'm making you acting governor in my absence," he told her from behind his desk.

"Sir, I'm hardly qualified to–" she began to say, but he cut her off.

"You're absolutely qualified. More so than me. I just give good speeches. You're the one who's been running this damned place for years now. You and the rest of the staff."

"Wouldn't Jord have to ratify it?"

"I think they've got more important things on their mind at the moment," Forebeck said with the merest ghost of humor. "If I declare it, it stands until they say otherwise."

Zara didn't really want to accept, but it was something she had already largely come to terms with. As the most senior member of the administration left behind, she would become governor in all but name anyway. At some point she was going to have to embrace the weight of that responsibility.

"I'll try to make you proud, sir," she told Forebeck. He stood slowly and walked round the desk to shake her hand.

"I think pride is one of the reasons we're in this mess," he said. "I know you'll do everything you can to stop this becoming any more disastrous. And you won't be alone. We're all going to fight in your corner back on Jord. Well, maybe apart from Smyth."

"I'm just glad I don't have to put up with him anymore," Zara said. "At this point I'd rather face the Letnev firebombs."

Later that day, Zara and Traquay bade farewell to the rest of the colony's leadership, who were boarding a shuttle on the edge of Aruzoe Prime Gateway. The shuttle would take them to the Letnev ship in orbit scheduled to see them through the blockade. Afterward, Zara and Traquay returned to the Federation Hub's control center. Zara had ordered the entirety of the remaining government staff to gather there. While the leadership of Quann might have departed, the dozens of lower-level administrators that made up the main body of the colony's governing apparatus hadn't been authorized to depart. They were Zara's colleagues, the real vehicle of colonial rule. The sight of them looking toward her as she entered the control room was equal parts reassuring and intimidating. She was no longer another cog in the machine. Now she was expected to direct it.

She was glad she still had Traquay. There was guilt too, but she no longer had time to wallow in that. If she was going to maintain Quann's government and avoid a descent into anarchy, she would need all the help she could get, and she knew Traquay well enough to appreciate her technocratic instincts.

She paused as the muted conversations among the rest of the staff died down. There was one more moment of nervousness, of uncertainty, of wondering how it had come to this, how she was possibly supposed to meet her new expectations. Then she began to speak, and everything else vanished.

"Governor Forebeck and his entourage are now offworld. As per his decree, I am acting governor of Quann, assuming all the authority that entails, as well as all the responsibility. My first act is to promote Traquay to the rank of chief of staff.

"Regardless of Forebeck's departure, the situation we find ourselves in remains unchanged. The Letnev are showing no sign of lifting the blockade. Hostilities could escalate at any given moment. I have been reassured that work is being done to end this crisis. The Federation has not abandoned us. Nevertheless, we must look to ourselves now more than ever.

"The simple fact is that Quann was not ready for any of this, and it remains unprepared. For too long this administration has been paralyzed by fear and lack of direction. We are going to change that, starting today.

"We are under siege, and it's time we started acting like it.

One of my first acts will be to introduce a rationing system in Aruzoe. We already know that we cannot sustain Quann's population without food shipments from Jord – that must change, and quickly. This blockade could last for many months. Unless something is done, famine is as much a threat as the Letnev fleet.

"I am also in discussions with Captain Ruko and Colonel Patel about improving our defensive capabilities. I'm aware that military measures have been forestalled by a desire to avoid panic in the populace, but we are well past that point now. There is little we can do if the Letnev employ an orbital bombardment against us, but with the Phoenix Fleet now on-station that danger is much reduced. We can prepare for a ground invasion. Conscription will be authorized and Aruzoe will be turned into a fortress. There is no good reason why we should not be prepared to fight to the last, regardless of the odds.

"I will be announcing all of these measures in my first public speech later today. I know I am asking a lot, but none of you accepted a colonial posting thinking your tasks were going to be easy. If you had wanted careers as pen-pushers you could have stayed on Jord. Traquay will give you your group designates and individual assignments by the end of the day.

"I have no doubt that many of you likely wish you weren't here anymore. Some of you would probably have left with Forebeck if you were able. Maker knows, for a while I wanted to as well. Some of you have families back on Jord, and many of you, like me, have families here. Either way, this is our home now. Not Jord. The people out there, in the streets of

Aruzoe and in the other settlements across this world, are our family. We were adopted into it when we came here, to build a new, better life. That's the life we must now defend, to the last.

"Dismissed."

She expected the gathering to dissolve into chatter and motion. Instead, everyone remained still and silent, staring at her. She wondered briefly if she had gone too far, if the determination she was trying to harness had tipped them into rebellion.

Then someone, in amongst the rest, began to clap. The applause spread, filling the control room. Zara stood rooted to the spot, disbelieving, then trying to cover her embarrassment – and her relief – as she looked at Traquay. She was applauding too, and smiling.

"As good as Forebeck in his prime," she said over the acclaim. "Sounds like it's finally time to get to work."

"What are they saying?" Zara asked Hiram when she got home, uncertain as to whether or not she really wanted him to answer.

She had paraphrased her speech to the administration in her first live viz address. It had felt more stilted and unnatural than when she had delivered it in person, but initially she was just glad it was done. Now, however, she was beset by doubts. What if she caused a panic? Those in government had always known that the colonial infrastructure would struggle to deal with a major incident, be that a pandemic, natural disaster, or uprising. If there was unrest, everything could degenerate into chaos overnight.

"There seems to be a lot of chatter," Hiram said. "It's mixed. There are complaints about conscription."

"Maybe that's a good thing," Zara said, hoping her husband wasn't gilding the truth for her. While it would be a dereliction not to finally put Quann on a defensive footing, she still wanted to avoid conflict at all cost. If the Letnev did invade, there would only be one winner. It was just a question of how long they could hold out for.

"It'll take a few days for things to settle," Hiram went on. "At the very least, you've made a statement. You sounded good. The Letnev know we won't be bullied any more, and the Federation know we plan on holding out. That might focus some minds, on both sides."

"I hope so," Zara said, clutching Hiram's hand and squeezing it tight. "Thank you for backing me on this. I didn't really have a choice. Forebeck thrust it on me, and I couldn't exactly turn him down."

"There's no one better for this than you, Z," Hiram said, leaning in to kiss her lightly on the brow. "Quann's lucky to have you, and so am I."

It was Traquay who noticed Zara's stalker. Despite the fact that an initial data docket was transmitted to Zara's savant every morning on her way to the FedHub, she insisted on meeting Zara on the front steps and briefing her on the latest progress as they walked to the control room. One morning, however, she greeted Zara with silence, standing looking past her.

"What is it?" Zara asked, nonplussed.

"That mono has been following you for the last three days,"

Traquay said. Zara followed her gaze, and spotted a nondescript ride gliding away past the FedHub building before turning right onto Sol Street and disappearing.

"Same one," Traquay continued. "It shadows you here and then leaves. Probably does the same on the way back."

Sudden unease gripped Zara. Several staffers had advised her to move into the now-vacant governor's suite and take on his security detail, but she had so far refused. The last thing she wanted for either herself or her family was further disruption. Now though, it didn't seem like such an outlandish suggestion. She was the governor of a colony world in the midst of a crisis. Who knew what sort of attention that might attract? What if Hiram and the kids were in danger?

She reported it to Captain Ruko. The next day, they laid a trap. To her relief, the person following her was apprehended, his monoride hemmed in by the sudden appearance of several heavy-duty Federation Guard transporters.

It turned out to be a human. He was frogmarched to the FedHub's holding bay, where Zara insisted on being present while Ruko led the interrogation. The man was resistant.

"He'll break if you let me get physical," Ruko told her during an interlude, standing in the observation unit adjoining the bay.

Zara had little doubt that was true – while stubborn, the man didn't exactly look like much of a fighter. Ruko, meanwhile, did. She resisted the impulse.

"We're doing this legitimately," she said. "Wear him down. No violence, at least not physical."

In the end Ruko didn't need to break him. It was Traquay who made the breakthrough.

"I recognize him," she told Zara outside the control room. "I thought he seemed familiar when I saw Ruko bringing him in. I did some digging. He's one of Smyth's aides, or at least he was. Name's Challum."

Zara frowned, trying to make sense of the accusation. "I thought his assistants went with him offworld?" she pointed out. "Why was one left behind? And why would he be following me?"

She put those same questions to Challum in person.

"I don't know what you're talking about," he responded, his tone surly. Privately, Zara agreed with Traquay – she now recognized him as one of Smyth's entourage, despite the straggly beard he had attempted to grow.

"If Smyth wanted to stay in contact, he could have done it legitimately, instead of giving me a tail," Zara said, letting some of her anger show through. "Are you just reporting back to him? He would have to still be in-system for that, assuming you don't have a way of circumventing the wormhole blockade."

"Sixty-six hours," Challum said impassively.

"Excuse me?"

"You've got sixty-six hours left," he elaborated. "I've been here five already. Seventy-two hours is the length of time a prisoner can legally be held on a colony world. After that, charges have to be brought, or he has to be released."

"Well, you can look forward to the worst sixty-six hours of your life if that's the case," Zara said, knowing he was right. "Captain Ruko is a far less delicate interrogator than I am."

She turned to leave, deciding to end it on an ominous note, but to her surprise Challum spoke up.

"That wouldn't be the case if you instituted martial law."

She looked back sharply as he continued.

"If a colony is declared to be under full military jurisdiction, prisoner rights are waived. You would be able to detain me indefinitely."

Zara felt her anger spike. Was Smyth really this bold? Was he actively trying to start a war? What would he have to gain from that, besides the certain devastation of Quann? She strode back toward where Challum was seated, wrists chained to the table in front of him.

"Is that what this is about?" she snapped. "Did Smyth leave you behind to keep trying to press me into starting a conflict?"

As she spoke she continued to turn possibilities over in her head, trying to find the angle Smyth was viewing all of this from. "It would definitely be easier for some of the parties back home if some unknown colonial official authorized firing the first shots."

"You're failing Jord," Challum snarled, meeting her anger with his own. "People are starting to starve. You might not have realized it yet in here with all your aides and guards, but it's happening."

"Don't try to use my compassion against me, you worm," Zara hissed. "The suffering of this world will be far beyond its current state if we end up in the middle of a war."

She felt her savant buzz, and made herself glance down at the screen. An urgent message from the control center. Vermillion, as per the standard imperial priority system.

"Enjoy your sixty-six hours," she told Challum before turning and leaving.

"We've got possible orbital entry," Traquay said when Zara

joined her in the control center. The viz projector was on, beaming up a rotating, static-fuzzed representation of Quann, complete with the vast array of the two war fleets spread around it.

"Here," another staffer, DelVay, said, highlighting one particular ship. It was Letnev, and had dropped below the exosphere. It was on the other side of the planet from Aruzoe, above the as-yet uninhabited tropical zone known as Zaztak.

"A landing?" Zara wondered aloud.

"Unclear," DelVay said. "Our scanners aren't strong enough to detect sub-orbital craft there."

"Right in our blind spot," Traquay observed.

As they watched, the sharp crimson triangle representing the invasive Letnev ship began to move, to rise up and away from Quann.

"It's leaving," Traquay said.

"But what was it doing?" Zara said.

"It must be a troop landing. What else could it be?"

"But with one ship?"

"A scouting force. Letnev special forces."

Zara gripped the projector's rail and tried to consider other possibilities. She tried to think of a way she could stop this from escalating any further.

"There's another ship approaching," DelVay said, breaking her concentration. At first Zara couldn't see what the aide meant, until the highlight switched to the vessel in question. It was far out, having just left the wormhole, a single ship making a heading for the densest contraction of Letnev and opposing human vessels.

"Scan it," Zara said.

It felt like an age before the results pinged up. When they did, it was the last thing she expected. She stared in shock, trying to process what its appearance might mean.

It was an imperial vessel, a Lazax diplomatic sprinter.

"It's hailing us," DelVay said.

CHAPTER SIXTEEN

MUAAT, HOMEWORLD OF THE GASHLAI, CAMPUS-COLONY OF THE UNIVERSITIES OF JOL-NAR

The Hylar Adjudicator's name was Enro. He sat across from Tol in the brig where she had been confined since being seized from her orbital station and taken to a Jol-Nar war frigate, perhaps a cycle earlier.

"Have you sent medical teams to KZ80?" Tol asked him. It was the fifth or sixth time she had mentioned the question.

"I am not here to discuss matters with you," he said, an identical answer to all the last ones. "I am here to inform you of your sentence."

He had already done as much. According to Enro, the Pan University Council had made a unanimous decision to revoke her doctorate. Furthermore, she had been banished from Jol-Nar space, indefinitely and without chance of repeal.

Tol had demanded to know whether the decision was based on the message she had sent to the Circle of Regents concerning Doctor Arr, or whether it was because of the unfolding incident at KZ80. The adjudicator had refused to answer.

"You have no right of repeal," he had simply repeated.

"I am not asking for a repeal," Tol replied, forcing herself to match the cold, firm tone of the Jol Hylar. "I am asking you to consider my findings and act on them. Because of Doctor Arr's research there has been a serious viral outbreak on Muaat, at Station KZ80 and possibly elsewhere. If it is not contained, I fear it will spread. It will become a pandemic."

"Considering your conviction as a slanderer and defamer, these claims are not wholly unexpected," Enro said.

Tol slammed her hand into the table before her, knowing she had nothing left now but her frustration. "You are an idiot! You and all your obsessive, misguided kind! Hundreds of thousands, perhaps millions, will die if this outbreak is not dealt with! The very future of our species may be at risk! I am begging you, take what I have found and show your superiors. If not, this will all be on you!"

"It is disappointing that you think so little of the universities," Enro said, showing a flash of anger in return. "If, as you claim, there has been an infectious outbreak in the Doolaks, Jol-Nar will be more than capable of producing and disseminating a vaccine, if not an outright cure. You claimed earlier that its root is Zemo's Disease?"

"Yes."

"An infector we all but eradicated centuries ago. It will be a simple matter to finish the job."

"Are you a medical practitioner, Enro?" Tol demanded.

"No, I am an adjudicator–"

"Then show good scholarly practice, and do not make assumptions about a field in which you have no expertise!"

"I will not take lectures from an under-doctor," Enro said,

rising to his full, imposing height. "Apologies, I misspoke. Former under-doctor. You will be granted a transport docket to take you to the nearest inhabited system outside of the boundaries of the sub-sector campus. From there you are on your own. Unauthorized access to any university planet or property will result in your arrest and termination."

As he spoke, tyro guards entered, pulling her up.

"Please, tell the universities about KZ80," Tol begged as she was marched to the brig's hatch. "Tell someone! Anyone!"

Enro said nothing, merely watched her being escorted out. She shouted back at him, a last, desperate venting of her rage and frustration.

"You've doomed us all!"

Rarely did Doctor Arr feel intimidated, but there was no other word to describe his emotions as he stood upon the viz scanner platform, facing the holographic projection of Pelem Shole.

"What became of the infected?" the regent asked coldly.

"They were terminated," Arr responded, keeping his answers concise.

"And the facility itself?"

"Destroyed."

"I hope so. I am currently having KZ80 wiped from all records. You should be thankful your disease only spread to an isolated outpost."

The fact that Shole had come all the way to Muaat spoke volumes about the seriousness of the situation. He had accompanied a force from Jol-Nar intent on, as he called it, fixing the problems created by Arr. He was now transmitting directly from the expedition's flagship, in orbit above.

"Indeed," Arr said. "I am confident it won't have spread further."

He had already decided not to mention the fact that the meddling little spawnling Tol had visited KZ80 at the time of its infection. He knew that troops had been dispatched to remove her from her own orbital outpost and banish her, following her outrageous claims about his experiments. Privately he had been surprised she had the courage. The younger generations really were misguided fools. Given that she had already been dealt with however, it seemed... unnecessary to bring it up.

"Perhaps you should focus your research on a pathogen that targets the Sardakk N'orr, rather than fellow Hylar," Shole continued, clearly not done with his chastisement. "The patience of your investors grows thin, especially now that matters are accelerating. We expect the Quann crisis to deepen very soon."

"My facilities here are suboptimal," Arr began, but Shole's projection cut him off.

"Excuses! I thought better of you, doctor. Were it not for the weapons systems you have successfully supplied to the Sol Federation, your competence would now be in doubt."

Arr would have bristled at such a statement, but he held his tongue as Shole went on.

"I believe it is time we focused your attention on a matter better suited to your talents. New Escha is nearing completion, and its production yards are able to run at maximum capacity. I have plans for them, plans you can assist with. One of my peers in Mavgala has been working on schematics for a new project. I am transmitting them to you now."

Arr waited and the projection of Shole distorted and

disappeared, replaced by a rotating set of plans. The doctor sealed his gills in concentration as he began to analyze them.

"This is... vast," he said, his scientific demeanor momentarily breaking down while he tried to fathom the display.

"It is, and with New Escha's facilities fueled by Muaat's raw materials, we have everything necessary to undertake its construction. I wish for you to oversee it. More traditional weapons manufacture, rather than viral biology, is where you excel. I am giving you an opportunity to make up for your more recent failures."

Usually Arr would have contested the comment about failure, but he was too awestruck by what he was looking at. Its potential was simply magnificent. The proportions of it, the destructive potential – a vessel of its sort had never been seen before, he was certain.

"I shall begin immediately," he said. "Though I will need more contacts at Mavgala and New Escha if this project is to become viable."

"I shall supply them," Shole's voice declared. "Do not make me regret choosing you to oversee this."

"You will not, regent," Arr said, the troubles of viral coding and disease outbreaks and former Under-Doctor Tol all forgotten. "With a weapon such as this, Jol-Nar will finally be ready to take its rightful place – as rulers of this galaxy."

CHAPTER SEVENTEEN

QUANN,
SOL FEDERATION COLONY WORLD

Arrokan had agreed to speak. After the past few weeks, that alone seemed like a minor miracle. A part of Syd was convinced as soon as his ship came into range of the Letnev fleet, they would obliterate him. Thankfully, though, the scans showed that while their shields were up and their weapons out, there was no telltale spike of energy that would indicate a beam lance or void cannon about to discharge.

"On this course, how long until we're within docking range of the *Magnificatum*?" he asked the sprinter's captain, Foli.

"At current rate of deceleration, an hour and a half GMT," he replied, glancing up from the ship's systems display. "Also, the humans have accepted your transmission request. They are ready to connect."

"Put them on," Syd said, taking his post atop the bridge's small visualization plate. The plate directly opposite him activated as well, flickering before stabilizing.

He found himself looking at a human woman, younger than he expected, dressed in the suit of a Sol Federation official.

From what he knew of human tells, she looked tired and somewhat flustered.

"Good morning," Syd said, noting the current time on Quann and giving a small nod, a typical Sol form of greeting. "I am Eminent Councilor Ibna Vel Syd. I have been sent here by Mecatol to help resolve the current blockade crisis."

"Eminent councilor," the woman replied, making the Lazax gesture of greeting as best she could, with only one pair of arms. "I am Acting Governor Zara Hail. I currently head the Federation government of Quann Colony in the absence of Governor Forebeck."

"Is Governor Forebeck ill?" Syd asked, wondering what developments he had missed while in transit. He knew little about the colonial ruler of Quann besides his identity, and nothing of his administration.

"Departed," Zara clarified. "Less than a week ago. He was recalled to Jord along with other senior administrators."

Syd paused to assess this information. If the Federation were withdrawing their senior members of government, were they planning a military strike? Would the absence of Sol politicians encourage the Letnev to mount an invasion of their own, knowing the repercussions would be less severe? Was that the reason the Letnev would let the likes of the planetary governor depart in the first place, or were there other motives?

Those didn't seem like questions Zara would know the answer to. He decided to press on.

"I am this moment on my way to speak in person with Admiral Arrokan," he said. "Rest assured I am going to do all I can to stop this aggression toward Quann."

"The situation here is extremely serious, sir," Zara said

hastily. "Food and medicine are being rationed. There is unrest among the populace. I have taken emergency measures, and have been considering introducing martial law–"

"I would avoid that if at all possible," Syd said. "At least until I have spoken with Arrokan. Escalation is a road Quann cannot afford to take."

"I understand that, but so is idleness. You are the first senior Lazax official either myself or Governor Forebeck have spoken to. In truth, our own government has hardly been more forthcoming. We feel… abandoned."

"And for that I apologize, on behalf of the emperor," Syd said, but Zara carried on.

"It's like the empire doesn't care. As though war could break out between two major civilizations, and the Lazax would hardly notice. As long as Mecatol remained untouched."

"That is not the reality of the situation," Syd responded, suppressing a moment's frustration at Zara's assumption. "Myself and numerous other senior officials are doing our very best to end this. The lives of the people of Quann are not the only ones that have been put in danger recently."

"Arrokan refuses to speak with us," Zara said. "I fear he has no interest in actually ending the blockade."

"That is what I intend to ascertain. I will let you know as soon as our talks are concluded, but I must urge you again not to escalate. I'm sure you appreciate how delicate the situation is. We are on the brink."

"I understand, eminent councilor," Zara said. "We shall await your word."

The transmission ended. Syd addressed Captain Foli. "Have a boarding shuttle prepared. I will be in my cabin."

"Yes, sir," Foli replied.

Syd withdrew from the cutter's bridge, trying to master his unease. It was bad enough that the presence of the Federation's Phoenix Fleet opposing the blockade indicated that the humans were prepared to fight. Now Quann itself was close to taking up arms. It all pointed toward a tipping point.

It was just another thing to add to his troubles. The journey from Arc Prime had not been a tranquil one. While passage through the Quann wormhole had made it briefer than it otherwise might have been, the whole time his mind was fraught with what he was leaving behind, and what might be awaiting him. What evils was Zey concocting with his Letnev allies on Arc Prime, and how was that affecting matters on Quann? Would he exit the wormhole to find the system in the grips of an intergalactic war?

The latter at least hadn't yet come to pass. His signal and, by extension, his status as a Lazax diplomat had been acknowledged by both the Letnev Grand Fleet and the Sol Federation Phoenix Fleet. Their course took them between the vast warships. Syd could keenly feel their vulnerability, but knew also that, bar his inability to monitor Zey, he was in the right place. Here, at the point of greatest tension, to ease the pressure and potentially stop the empire from snapping in two.

More concerning now was the fact that he was unable to detect the signal of the tracking beacon he had given Nauru. Was it simply not working? Or had Zey already discovered the duplicity? Syd had experienced a moment's pang for Nauru herself, but he refused to dwell on that aspect – he had no choice other than to use the Winnu, for the good of the empire.

With Onni's assistance, Syd dressed in his formal white robes and datarecorder circlet, then proceeded to the sprinter's docking shuttle. He realized that a part of him was looking forward to this. At last he was going to look one of the sentients most responsible for this crisis in the eye, and enter into negotiations.

The passage between the sprinter and the Grand Fleet's flagship was a brief one. As the landing hatch hissed open and its ramp descended amidst a burst of hydraulic steam, Syd got his first view of the interior of the *Magnificatum*.

The shuttle had been directed by the docking coordinates to alight in a launch bay. Letnev starfighters filled most of it, crouched on their service platforms, their wicked outlines gleaming beneath the harsh white light that illuminated the space. Directly beneath the shuttle's lowered ramp, a platoon of Letnev marines in full combat gear came sharply to attention, the stamp of grav-clamp boots and the scrape of boarding armor echoing through the bay. A single figure stood between them, gazing up with ill-disguised disdain at the shuttle's open hatch – a Letnev fleet officer dressed in blue and silver. His high black boots shone as immaculately as the scrubbed deck underfoot.

"Ambassador Syd," he said, making no show of deference and getting Syd's rank wrong, presumably on purpose. It was, he was sure, just another attempt at unsettling him, part of the wider show of force that might win them concessions. "I am First Lieutenant Bullow of the *Magnificatum*. I have been instructed to take you immediately to the bridge."

Syd thanked him, and followed him to a transport tube. Akin to smaller versions of the traffic tubes used in Feruc, the rail pod was used on the largest Letnev ships to transport important personnel to wherever they needed to be on the vessel hastily. During the ride Bullow sat in silence, ignoring his guests, a decision that suited Syd just fine. He was marshaling his thoughts for the task ahead.

They alighted from the tube outside the flagship's bridge, shielded from the annex by a huge set of reinforced blast doors. They began to roll heavily open, revealing the core of the Barony of Letnev's Grand Fleet.

The bridge was circular and tiered, rings of monitor displays and computator platforms encircling the pinnacle, where a command throne sat surrounded by gilt-edged personal system output displays and high-function, Hylar-made fixed savants. The heat generated by the huge array of technical machinery was offset by massive, humming coolant stacks that ribbed the chamber's walls, rising up to a central point in the domed arch above. They kept the air cold and brisk, the way the Letnev liked it. The far end of the bridge, on the other side of the command dais, was a huge, horizontal viz display board.

No mere frigate or minor capital ship, the *Magnificatum*'s nerve center was also replete with classical Letnev military grandiosity. Holo-busts of famous barony admirals glared down on the scene from niches in the walls, while the spaces between the coolant stacks higher up were covered in a panoply of banners – black and purple and blue and white, each one representing an individual ship of the Grand Fleet and its battle honors, lists of engagement victories woven in finest silver and gold silkcrawler thread. Largest of all was the standard that hung immediately behind the throne itself, the heraldic crest of the barony and the Grand Fleet intertwined.

Syd took it all in alongside the figures filling the space. The *Magnificatum's* bridge crew looked to number at least a hundred Letnev, all immaculately uniformed, long hair powdered white and tied back, boots and buttons shining and brocade brushed. They occupied the data-pits and communications banks, the shield array and the weapons input and output systems. Others paced between the various tiers, junior officers overseeing their ratings and midshipmen, while still more stood around the edge of the busy chamber, armed and armored marines from the fleet security detail. Nor were the Letnev themselves the only beings busily overseeing the running of both their ship and the wider blockade – chromatic familiars hovered between sections on thrumming grav motors, delivering in-person data updates or monitoring the remote hardware. Syd also noticed three Hylar in the uniforms of the Fleet Attachment Division, working at the most advanced stations, the engine core monitors, FTL drive units, and shield array.

The place was abuzz with activity, and seemed to take no notice of Syd's arrival. He suspected that in itself had been rehearsed, as had what came next.

"The admiral has seen fit to speak with you, ambassador, but your servant does not have permission to come aboard the bridge," the sallow-faced Bullow said before stepping through the open blast doors. Syd met his gaze unflinchingly.

"Where I go, Onni goes as well," he said. "Do you not know, first lieutenant, that a Lazax and a Winnu share a bond that trumps any of your baronial military hierarchies?"

"I have my orders," Bullow began to say, but Syd cut him off.

"Your orders, I'm sure, are to see me to the bridge. I will not enter it without Onni."

He was taking a risk, he knew. Letnev were prickly at the best of times, even more so when it came to dealing with the Lazax. The fact that he had to assume all of Arrokan's crew were hardline Resurgentists made things even more fraught. Still, he had no doubt this was a test. They wanted to see how easily he made concessions.

"Very well," Bullow said tersely. "But if he strays, he will be terminated. Follow."

Syd exchanged a quick glance with Onni as the Letnev turned and paced away, giving him a reassuring nod. They stepped onto the bridge.

Bullow led them round to a cleared deck space directly beneath the command throne. It was made from raw purple saimoc crystal, a precious mineral native to Arc Prime and an iconic piece of Letnev culture. Its jagged flanks and hard, laser-cut edges gleamed at the heart of the bridge, like a jewel atop a high crown.

In the middle of it sat a particularly tall and well-built looking Letnev. His hair, a perfect snowy white, had been bound back in a queue, the temples curled into small, precise ringlets. He looked relatively young, but his scarring left no doubt as to his experience – jagged welts marred the left side of his face, and his eye had been replaced by the purple glow of a cybernetic optic sphere, wired directly into his skull. He wore the uniform of a Grand Fleet admiral, purple with gold trim and epaulets, chest heavy with medals, white pants, flared above the knee, and high black boots. A straight-edged broadsword with a vibro-edge and a gene-reader grip sat propped, point-down against the edge of the sparkling throne.

Syd recognized him as Admiral Arrokan, victor of the Battle

of the Star Shoals, the youngest ever Letnev officer to hold the rank of admiral. He made no effort to stand or greet Syd as he and Onni stopped beneath the dais.

"Well met, Grand Admiral Daz Arrokan," Syd said, using a traditional Letnev opening. "May the stars shine bright on your endeavors."

"Ambassador," Arrokan said coldly, not even naming Syd in response. "What brings you to my bridge?"

"I suspect you have some inkling already," Syd responded. Right from the start, he intended to make it clear he wasn't here to play games.

Rather than reply immediately, Arrokan made a terse chopping gesture toward a grizzled-looking Letnev officer standing just down from the throne. The woman activated a throat piece she was wearing and made a booming declaration that was amplified via speakers throughout the room.

"Bridge, attention!"

There was an echoing crash as, like automata, every Letnev not already standing leapt to their feet and brought a heel slamming down. Even the familiars came to a halt in midair. Every eye turned on Syd and Arrokan, every voice silenced, only the thrum of the systems and air recyc continuing.

Despite all his experience, Syd almost quailed. It felt as though he had walked into a nest of cold, dead-eyed redfang vipers. He tightened his grip fractionally on his ambassadorial staff and focused his attention on Arrokan and Arrokan alone, refusing to be further intimidated.

"Your blockade of Quann must end," he said.

Arrokan laughed, a chilling sound that quickly faded. "Why?"

"It is a violation of the Pax Magnifica and the statutes of the empire. It is stifling commerce, disrupting peace, and bringing fear and suffering not only to the planet below us, but to the humans, your fellow Letnev, and every other civilization, great and small, that treasures the peace we Lazax have built."

"I could tell you what I and my people think of your so-called Pax Magnifica," Arrokan said. "You are a member of the imperial council, so you will have been educated in the classics. You're aware, I'm sure, that the empire's motto isn't simply 'Pax Magnifica.' There is also Bellum Gloriosum. Glorious war. The empire was founded on war, on a righteous struggle. Without it, it has grown fat and indolent."

"You speak of the war of liberation against the Mahact Gene Sorcerers," Syd countered. "Tyrants whom we Lazax overthrew for the good of all sentients."

"So you constantly remind us. Tell me, do you think the Mahact saw themselves as tyrants? Do you think they believed their own imperium despotic, or enlightened?"

"The rule of the Mahact kings was one of galaxy-spanning slavery, genocide, and twisted experimentation," Syd said, working hard to check his anger. "There was no peace, and certainly not the democratic advantages civilizations great and small currently enjoy thanks to the likes of the Galactic Council. You argue in bad faith, but I did not come here to debate the tenets of empire. I came here to ask you to reconsider your demands."

"Those demands cut to the core of your 'tenets of empire,'" Arrokan said brusquely, offering Syd an unfriendly smile. He was enjoying this, Syd realized. Putting on a show in front of his subordinates. Humbling the proud, hated Lazax.

"But why here?" Syd asked. "Why antagonize the Federation? There have never been tangible disputes between human and Letnev, so why pick them to suffer?"

"We are merely giving the rest of the galaxy a taste of the injustices Arc Prime suffers every day. The empire unfairly sanctions us and strangles our economy. Now, with the Quann wormhole shut off, others will know what we endure. With time we will tithe passage through the wormhole, and make up for all the losses the empire has inflicted on us. Besides, Quann was first discovered by we Letnev. It is we who should have been given colonization rights, not the humans."

"There are ways to settle matters like that without resorting to piracy and bringing the galaxy to the edge of war," Syd said. Arrokan sneered.

"We know those ways well enough. The veneer of Lazax democracy. The price of the last two rebellions has been too high to trust your 'ways.' If there was a third rising, the imperial fleets would scour the surface of Arc Prime and fill our subterranean cities with fire."

"And you think we won't if you begin a war with another part of the empire, rather than the Lazax directly?"

"I think it makes that choice a lot more difficult for your emperor."

"He's your emperor too. And what about your baron? You can drop the charade that she approves of all this. You'll never be able to return to Arc Prime while she is in power, not after you've stolen the Letnev fleet to try to instigate a war."

"Maybe," Arrokan said, looking surprisingly thoughtful for a moment. Syd sensed an admittance of guilt, but was chilled by the fact that Arrokan seemed willing to lay it out. It showed him that they had reached the end, and there was little more he could do. He suppressed his fear, about to speak again, but Arrokan carried on.

"But we all have to make sacrifices. That's something you Lazax wouldn't understand. You rule, and expect others to obey. To sacrifice. Even now, do you think the emperor really cares about the humans? About Quann, and the blockade? I doubt he's even considered the tragedy unfolding here. But we'll put on a show he can't ignore."

Syd sighed, bowing his head briefly. He could see no way out. Arrokan had not agreed to this because he wanted to negotiate. He had agreed because he wanted to make a point before his followers. He was having Syd play a role as the arrogant imperial envoy. It was only making things worse.

"Things will not go the way you think they will, Admiral Arrokan," he said eventually, fixing the Letnev with a deathly glare.

"Oh really? I did not know the emperor had sent a seer as well as a diplomat."

"You are arrogant and mocking, as befits the worst of your kind. But I know that not all are like that. The Letnev are a proud people, but they are not warmongers. They do not seek conflict. Most of them are content to live their lives, and let others do the same. No matter what occurs here, I will not let that be forgotten. I will not let you and the Resurgentists speak for all Letnev."

He felt the savant on his wrist vibrate, and glanced briefly down. A moment's elation was replaced by horror. The locator beacon he had given Nauru had just abruptly reactivated. But it wasn't the data package he expected, a transmission from a remote courier showing Nauru – and, presumably by extension, Zey – as being on Arc Prime any longer. It was coming to him directly from the *Magnificatum*. From the same ship Syd was currently standing on.

That meant Zey was here, in the midst of it all. Whatever plot he was carrying out, it was still ongoing, and Syd was in no position to stop him.

"Do you have more important duties you need to attend to, ambassador?" Arrokan demanded. Syd struggled to redirect his focus to the admiral. He was in shock.

"You have agreed to speak to me here in bad faith," he managed to say. "I will return and talk to you when you are ready to negotiate. Maybe then we can make some headway."

"So much for imperial diplomacy," Arrokan said scornfully. "First Lieutenant Bullow, get this pair of lickspittles off my bridge."

CHAPTER EIGHTEEN

QUANN, SOL
FEDERATION COLONY WORLD

Syd sent a quick message ping to Onni's savant as they were escorted from the bridge.

Zey onboard. Be ready.

Bullow took them back to the rail pod without further comment. Syd noted the destination he punched into its input panel next to the doors. It was in the Letnev's native language, but Syd had a basic enough grasp of it to be able to read it. All imperial ambassadors were expected to be at least conversant in the foremost language of each of the great civilizations, though it had been a while since Syd had spoken much beyond univoca and the slow ticking of the Xxcha tongue.

As expected, they were headed back toward the launch bay. Syd made a point of sitting opposite Bullow, his ambassadorial staff clutched between his thighs, Onni beside him. He abruptly found himself missing Chel for the first time since the N'orr's death.

The rail pod had just started to move when Syd spoke.

"Does Arrokan really intend to start a war, then?" he asked Bullow. He was sure he knew the answer already, but that didn't matter – he just wanted to leave the Letnev officer unfocused for a moment.

Bullow was halfway through a snide answer about any potential conflict really being the Lazax's fault when Syd hit him in the crotch with the base of his staff. The first lieutenant's scornful tone abruptly became a squeal akin to a Jordian pig being slaughtered. He lurched forward in pain, the motion coinciding with the upward swing of the ambassadorial staff as Syd followed through, cracking the haft off the Letnev's pale, slender jaw. Bullow was slammed back, the rear of his head connecting hard with the wall of the thrumming pod. He went limp, slumping in his chair.

"Not bad, sir," Onni said as he rose and went immediately to the input panel. "Now, where to?"

Syd consulted his savant, locking into the locator beacon.

"It's coming from the ship's prow," he said by way of explanation. "It just reactivated while we were putting up with Arrokan."

"You think Zey is really here? He would have had to follow us straight through the Passage? Or even overtaken us on a faster ship?"

"I don't know, but we have to find out," Syd said urgently. "There can be no more doubt he's working with Arrokan. In fact, I suspect the Letnev admiral is an Accelerationist, just like Zey. Certainly the Accelerationist way of thinking would fit well with the Letnev Resurgentists. They're working towards the same goal. Set the galaxy alight, and rebuild from the ground up."

"If we catch Zey onboard the Letnev flagship, Atz will be able to go before the emperor and the imperial council, and the Accelerationists will be unmasked,'" Onni mused.

"Exactly," Syd agreed. "This would unmask Arrokan too. It would show he's working with the hated Lazax, and allow the baron to finally disown him. Letnev bringing their own war fleet to heel might just avert all this. That's why we must hurry."

He instructed Onni which location to enter into the input panel, redirecting their pod to the *Magnificatum*'s prow berths.

"One other question, sir," Onni said as he looked across the pod at Syd. "If we do manage to corner Zey, what next?"

"I can ping the evidence of his direct presence to the Quann orbital relay, it will be picked up immediately by the closest courier picket," Syd said, thoughts racing.

"Yes sir, but… what happens to us? I suspect our Letnev hosts won't be too happy about what we're doing, and they'll surely realize soon."

"That's the one part I haven't accounted for," Syd admitted, feeling a fierce upwelling of determination at the prospect of finally cornering and confronting his old rival. "I'm afraid you're just going to have to trust me. Even here on the edge, they wouldn't dare harm a member of the imperial council."

Syd feared resistance the moment they disembarked from the rail pod, so he was relieved to find himself in an empty corridor. The area around the bridge was more grandiose, with purple rugs, bronze or silver-edged input nodes, and displays of saimoc crystal, but down here at the prow things were more utilitarian – a simple metal walkway lit by wall lumination strips.

Syd consulted his savant again. He was afraid the locator would cut off once more and leave them stranded, but it was still sending. They were close.

They rounded a corner and almost collided with a Letnev junior crew member coming the other way. Syd reacted quicker, cracking the tip of his staff over his head and pitching him against the wall.

The problem was, the crew member wasn't alone. Two marines were walking just behind him, conversing. They were in off-duty slacks, but as per Letnev fleet regulations they still had their sidearms strapped to their thighs.

Onni charged past Syd as he dispatched the crew member. In their arrogance the Letnev hadn't confiscated his snub-nose, but nor had he drawn it – instead he caught one of the marines sharply on the jaw, half spinning him around.

The other marine was caught cold between reaching for her own pistol and tackling Onni. Syd stepped past the downed crew member and, to his surprise, she went for him, presumably identifying a Lazax as the more important target.

She was fast. She got one hand up to grip Syd's staff before he could get a blow in, while the other went for her holster. Syd lashed out in turn with a left hand rather than trying to force through his staff in his right, knocking aside the beam pistol as she drew it. There was a loud *t-zaap* as it discharged point-blank into the wall, fusing one of the strip luminators.

Syd realized immediately that the Letnev was stronger than him. But she was still at a disadvantage – she only had two arms. Syd had four.

He delivered a one-two to her toned midriff with his free arms, neither blow with much power or finesse, but enough to drive her back. She managed to rip her sidearm free a split second after Syd had torn back his staff and triggered its electrostatic field.

A spray of purple beam shots earthed themselves into the staff, so close that sparks flew. Syd delivered a textbook Rosharin jab with the staff's head to her throat and, as she dropped, gasping for air, delivered the knockout blow to the back of her head.

There was no time to take stock. Onni was grappling desperately with the other marine, and was losing, pinned up against the opposite wall. Syd weighed in, staff thrumming, and put the last Letnev down. Onni pulled himself free from his grip. They were both panting and flushed.

"Thank you, sir," the Winnu said.

"We have to keep going," Syd responded, already heading off down the corridor. It couldn't be long now before the whole ship was alerted to the fact that they had gone rogue.

The corridor opened out into a control bay. It was thankfully deserted, but as they arrived the lighting turned abruptly red, and an alarm began to wail.

"He's just ahead," Syd shouted over it, holding the savant on his wrist. The locator beacon was pinging in what appeared to be a set of bunk berths on the opposite side of the bay, off to the right.

As Syd hurried forward figures clattered into view between them and the doors, the red light gleaming from their armor. More Letnev marines, these ones fully equipped.

For a wild second, Syd considered trusting his staff's electrostatic field and charging them. Onni's hand on his shoulder combined with the loud whine of beam rifles reaching full charge dissuaded him.

"Left," the Winnu shouted, tugging Syd toward a door in the side of the control bay and punching the access plate.

It hissed open to reveal more Letnev.

One cracked the butt of a beam rifle into Onni's face, sending him reeling back into Syd. He brought up his staff defensively, then half turned as he heard more boots beating off the deck the way they had come – yet more Letnev. The bay was now full of them, the air pulsing with charged weaponry.

With a sickening sensation, Syd realized that it was over. They had been trapped, caught. He looked down at his savant in pure frustration, seeing the locator beam transmitting from just round the corner.

The Letnev swept in from all sides. Hands clutched at him, ripping the staff from his grip and forcing him down on his knees.

"I am an imperial councilor," he shouted in what he hopped was his best Letnev tongue. "If you strike me or the Winnu, you strike the empire itself!"

He wasn't sure an appeal to imperial authority was the best idea surrounded by furious Letnev marines, but he was trusting them to be grunts accustomed to following orders. As he had hoped, after disarming and pushing Syd and Onni down, they stood over them, weapons leveled, but didn't strike either of them.

"There has been a misunderstanding," Syd began to say, knowing that at this stage there was no reason not to try everything. "We were only trying to make it back to our boarding shuttle."

"Say nothing," one of the Letnev snarled, her rifle muzzle almost in Syd's face. "Remain still."

He realized his staff had been snapped in two, the broken halves lying split beneath Letnev boots. He tried to ignore the shame and anger, tried to think ahead to what happened next. He had spoken confidently to Onni earlier about the inviolability of Lazax authority, but he had misjudged just how absolute the defection of the Letnev was. Not reaching Zey only made it worse.

He glanced briefly at Onni. The Winnu's nose was bleeding, maybe broken, but he seemed otherwise unharmed. He met Syd's gaze and gave a terse but reassuring nod.

They had been in scrapes before. They would get out of it together.

As Syd had feared, the marines were holding them for Admiral Arrokan. He arrived with a clack of polished military boots, his face like thunder. He said nothing to either of them. Syd noted his hand was resting on his ornate holster.

"This is all a mistake," Syd told him. "You know I am a senior member of the imperial council. I will overlook the physical violence shown to myself and my aide if we are expedited immediately to our shuttle."

It was all untrue of course, but that was all they had left. It should be enough. Even Arrokan knew the empire could only be pushed that far – that was why he was blockading Quann and the Federation, rather than striking a blow against the Lazax themselves.

"Is the Winnu an imperial councilor too?" Arrokan asked, the question catching Syd by surprise. He glanced again at Onni, starting to speak.

"Well, no, but–"

Arrokan drew his long-barreled silver beam pistol and shot

Onni through the heart. The Winnu slumped against Syd, dead.

Syd just stared, words frozen, half-formed, on his lips.

"Dump the body out of an airlock," Arrokan ordered his marines icily. "And get this Lazax scum off my ship. Properly, this time."

Hands grasped roughly at Syd, dragging him to his feet. He was barely aware of them. He stared at Onni, that brave, loyal, hard-working, talented Winnu, suddenly slack and lifeless, like a discarded doll.

Finally, Syd began to struggle, to cry out, to shout and rage, but it was pointless, impotent.

He had failed, failed utterly. Failed not only his emperor, the empire, and all those species holding out for peace, but most of all, failed Onni.

Syd knew, from that moment, his life would never be the same again.

Zey had a beam pistol raised but lowered it when Admiral Arrokan stepped into the ship's berth.

"What's happening?" the ambassador snapped.

"It's Syd," Arrokan replied darkly. "He was trying to reach you."

Of course he was. The fool was only just beginning to realize how badly he had lost. But it left one thing unexplained. Zey looked from Arrokan to Nauru, who was sitting on one of the two cot beds that folded down from the berth's walls.

"How did he know I was here?" he demanded. "Did one of your crew tell him?"

"Of course not," Arrokan said.

"We only docked while you were speaking to him," Zey said slowly, working it through. "Even if someone told him I was onboard, how could he have known where I was, down to the exact bunk room? The only ones who would have known that were you and the two officers who conducted us here."

"And the two of you," Arrokan said.

Zey frowned for a moment, realization dawning. He turned to Nauru.

"Give me it," he said.

"Sir?" Nauru asked, looking up, nonplussed.

"Whatever tracking device Syd gave you before he left Arc Prime."

"Sir, I don't have a tracking device! Why would I– "

"You should know better than to mock me like this," Zey said, his tone taking on a deadly edge. He had made a mistake, and that was something he wasn't accustomed to. "The Letnev sprinter we took through the Passage was running a Hylar scrambling matrix as part of its cloaking shield. Any tracker wouldn't have worked. But the *Magnificatum* is too large for that, so it would have started beaming its signal again as soon as we boarded from the sprinter. Now don't play me for a fool any longer, Nauru. Give it up now and I'll be lenient."

Nauru's face had gone ashen. After a moment, with trembling fingers, she removed a spherical, metallic object from her travel case and handed it to Zey.

The Lazax grunted as he held it up, examining it for a moment. He turned it off, then back on again.

"Unusually duplicitous for Syd," he said. "It only confirms what I have suspected. He is, at the very least, suspicious of me."

"How much does he know?" Arrokan asked.

"You're the one holding him, you ask him."

"Not anymore. He's being returned to his ship as we speak, minus his aide. It's a bad day to be a Winnu."

"You're letting him go?" Zey demanded, his anger flaring. The Letnev were such blunt instruments, it privately amazed him that everything had gone according to plan, so far.

"What else would you suggest? Detain an imperial councilor? Worse? He is no mere ambassador. The whole reason for this stultifying blockade was to avoid a confrontation with the Lazax directly. As long as the emperor and his cronies aren't in harm's way, their response will be slow and disjointed. That changes if we harm a high-ranking Lazax official."

Zey sighed, weary of the points Arrokan was making. He had heard similar before. Clearly a more direct form of instruction was required.

"You must do exactly what I say, right now," he told Arrokan. "Destroy Quann's orbital relay."

Arrokan, already bristling from the brusqueness of the Lazax's tone, shook his head. "That could start the war. The Phoenix Fleet might take it as a final act of provocation."

"And you aren't ready for that?" Zey demanded. "I came here to oversee the final steps in person. It will begin soon. Isn't that what you want?"

Arrokan was silent, before eventually saying, "It is."

"Destroy the relay, and quickly," Zey repeated. "We need to stop Syd getting word to Mecatol. Even if he doesn't have any good evidence of my presence onboard a Letnev flagship, we can be certain he will now do everything in his power to uncover our alliance. Hit the relay, and it will buy us the time we need."

"Time for what, exactly?" Arrokan asked.

"To start the war your people so richly deserve," Zey said. He gave back the locator beacon to Nauru.

"It's still on," Arrokan observed.

"I know," Zey replied. "That won't matter where she's going."

CHAPTER NINETEEN

QUANN, SOL FEDERATION COLONY WORLD

The orbital relay anchored in high orbit, the transmission beacon that allowed courier pickets to transmit and receive messages from the system's far edge, had just gone offline. Scans indicated weapons fire from the closest Letnev frigate.

"This has to be the start of it," Captain Ruko said as the administration gathered in the control room, staring at the representation of Quann on the viz projector.

"Order the garrison fleet not to return fire," Zara told the chief comms officer firmly, trying to appear clear and commanding when in fact her thoughts were racing, close to panic. She felt helpless, but she couldn't let that show.

"Should we send out an emergency broadcast?" Traquay asked. "Get the people into the shelters and alert the Phoenix Fleet?"

"Not yet."

"But if we don't it will be too late! If the Letnev open fire on the surface…"

"The ambassador was clear," Zara said, trying to keep her voice level. "We can't escalate. We wait for his word."

It felt like a long time before it arrived, and when it did, it wasn't what Zara had been expecting. In truth, Syd had been unexpected in every way. He had appeared abruptly, unannounced, and seemingly with the authority to bring Arrokan to the table. She didn't dare put too much faith in him.

Was he the same Lazax who had spoken out against a sentence of execution during the trial of Smyth's uncle? They shared a name, but then so did many imperial officials, drawn seemingly from the same sprawling families. It had been some years ago, but most of the great civilizations outlived humanity in terms of natural lifespan. She supposed it wasn't so farfetched. But could he deliver what he had promised during their brief discussion? The destruction of the relay made that seem unlikely, but Zara refused to abandon hope.

In the end, he didn't even send a viz transmission request, only a message.

Arrokan will not end the blockade.

That was all. Zara felt a surge of frustration and disappointment. She quelled it. She had known the Lazax couldn't be trusted to make a difference. They were too indolent, too far removed from the struggles of anyone within the empire who wasn't a member of their own species.

"Should we reply?" Traquay wondered.

"I don't see any reason to," Zara pointed out. "There's nothing more he can do for us."

"I'm not sure that's true. He said he wasn't the only one. That there's a response…"

"Do you believe that?" Zara asked, looking at Traquay fiercely. A sudden tiredness gripped her, born of despair. She wanted to turn away, to simply leave the chamber and go home, but she knew she couldn't. Traquay didn't give an answer. She didn't even meet Zara's eye.

"The bill for the introduction of martial law is ready," DelVay said, moving through her fellow administrators to join them. "It can be implemented immediately. It might still make the Letnev think twice about an invasion."

"No," Zara said, gazing at the circling holographic of Quann on the viz projector. The word surprised even her, but she had been thinking about Syd's last words to her before he had attempted to speak with Arrokan, and they had twinned with her exhaustion to bring about a cold sense of fatalism.

"No?" DelVay echoed uncertainly. Ruko in particular looked shocked.

"You heard the Lazax. We cannot escalate."

"With respect, that was before talks broke down."

"But that doesn't mean he isn't still right. Perhaps it was a mistake to even institute emergency measures. It's caused nothing but worry and unrest in Aruzoe."

"It would have been negligent not to do something," Ruko said sharply. "Cowardly even."

"There is no cowardice in choosing not to fight when everyone else is clamoring for it," Zara replied, letting her despair feed her determination. It didn't matter what they did now, didn't matter what she said to the others. "I think that's been my mistake. I've been arguing against the likes of Smyth for weeks, saying we need to show restraint, that if there's a war, no matter who wins it, Quann will lose. But when Forebeck and the others left, I felt as though I had to make a show of strength. I had to prove myself worthy to lead."

"You've done that," Traquay said. "The administration is behind you, at least what's left of it."

"But what about everyone else?" Zara asked. "There's an anti-conscription rally being held along Star Trader Avenue in just a few hours. It looks like it'll be well attended. When Smyth was arguing in favor of conscription a few weeks ago, I spoke out against it. I've allowed the situation to turn me into a hypocrite."

"Things have changed," Ruko said. "The Lazax negotiators have failed. Just earlier we had a Letnev ship in low orbit. There could be baronial troops on-world right now! As the captain of the Federation Guard, it's my duty to urge you to take defensive measures."

"What difference are they going to make?" Zara asked. "How are we going to resist them? If the Letnev strike from orbit, there's nothing we can do. If they mount a planetside invasion, we're hardly in a better position. I've seen Colonel Patel's projections. One week holdout time in our current state, eleven days maximum with conscription, and that's assuming another month to actually call up recruits and give them the most basic equipment and training!

"The reality is the emergency measures were to give us something to focus on, so we could tell ourselves we had done all we could. They were never going to save us. They could still doom us though."

"It may be too late already," DelVay admitted. "If the Lazax has failed, what else is there left to stop the Letnev from opening fire? Arrokan doesn't seem to want to negotiate. He wants confrontation."

"Which is why we're not giving it to him," Zara said, making up her mind. "I'm going to speak at that rally tonight, and use it to address Arrokan, the Letnev, and the Federation publicly. None of them can avoid that. I'm going to tell them that there will be no more special measures, no conscription. That Quann does not desire war, and will not participate in it. That if there is a war, the peoples of this world will be not held responsible for starting it. We have no stake in the great galactic game. We don't care for quarrels between the Letnev and the Lazax, or jockeying for position and power within the imperium. We are ordinary sentients trying to eke out a new life far from home. A better life, we had hoped. This is a new world, and we won't fall into old quarrels."

Traquay and DelVay exchanged a glance. Ruko just glared at her, seemingly furious. Zara welcomed it. She didn't care what any of them thought of her anymore.

"It's good, but will it really make a difference?" Traquay wondered.

"What about security as well?" Ruko demanded. "There's no way I can make that rally safe for you to appear at. Not if there's a possibility Letnev infiltrators have just touched down."

"If they've dropped from that ship, they're still on the other side of the planet," Zara said. "It's just a risk I have to take. It's the only play we've got left."

Zara had made her point. It felt good, she realized, to have settled on a course of action, no matter how desperate. Her conscience had been struggling, and she had only just realized how much. Now, no matter what happened, she believed she was doing the right thing. She would force Arrokan and all the others to listen, whether they wanted to or not.

•••

"You aren't going to ask me to reconsider?" Zara asked Hiram later, in the privacy of their hab. She had returned home for a few hours to finish drafting her speech and get changed. Ruko had eventually, reluctantly, agreed to do a sweep of Star Trader Avenue in an attempt to get things locked down before escorting her there. She knew it was a security risk, but time was now of the essence. She half expected to hear at any moment from Traquay, saying that the Phoenix Fleet had responded to the destruction of the orbital relay by opening fire on the Letnev.

"I know when you've made your mind up," Hiram replied to her, smiling despite his obvious worry. "And, for the record, I think you're doing the right thing. Someone has to speak truth to this foolishness. Someone has to make a stand."

"I doubt anyone from either side will listen," Zara admitted, indulging her fears for a moment. "If even the Lazax can't make the Letnev stand down, then what chance do I have?"

"The Letnev are only here because they hate the Lazax, but fear striking against them directly," Hiram pointed out. "A different voice might be just what's needed."

Zara hugged him tight, murmuring to him as she abandoned her resolute mindset for a moment. "I'm sorry it's coming to this. I'm sorry I brought you all here."

"For the last time, it isn't your fault," Hiram said. "We wanted to be here. None of us could have known this would happen. And we're so proud of you. I always knew you were a leader, but you've shown it now more than ever. I'm the luckiest man in the galaxy to be able to call you my wife."

Zey stepped onto the bridge of Admiral Ular's flagship,

Stalwart, flanked on either side by a cohort of Sol Federation space corps troopers. The bridge was centered on a massive tactical visualization projector around which ship's officers and senior fleet staff were gathered. All eyes turned to the Lazax as he entered.

"Ambassador," Ular said, stepping forward. "I trust your journey from Arc Prime was not overly taxing?"

"Allow a diplomat to give a diplomatic answer," Zey said, affecting a smile, like a human. "I am not overly sorry to be gone. Letnev hospitality is as chilly as their homeworld."

There was some laughter. Ular gestured to another human, this one in Federation politico garb rather than a military uniform.

"Allow me to introduce Sol Delegate Hektor Smyth," Ular said. Zey locked eyes with Smyth, neither of them indicating they were already well known to one another. It was strange, Zey mused, meeting him in person for the first time. They had only communicated via scrambled viz-transmissions that then required decoding. Zey hadn't anticipated how tall he would be, nor how cold and hard his gray eyes were, almost as pale as a Letnev's.

"Smyth was present on Quann when the blockade started," Ular elaborated, oblivious to how much Zey already knew. "But we were able to evacuate him alongside the other senior administrators. He has remained with the fleet to provide liaison back to Jord."

"It is good to see the Lazax responding to this crisis in person," Smyth said. "There is an old Jord joke about two carrums arriving at the same time – now we have two ambassadors where there were none."

"My colleague from the imperial council has made contact, I take it?" Zey asked, still feigning innocence. Syd's release still angered him, but he forced himself to focus on the present. He could only work with what was to hand.

"Only in passing," Ular admitted. "He informed us he had an audience arranged with the Letnev. That was before they fired on the orbital array. He didn't mention you would be joining us."

"Eminent Councilor Syd is to speak with Grand Admiral Arrokan while I work with you, Admiral Ular," Zey said smoothly. "Though I fear the fact that the Letnev have struck at Quann's relay system bodes ill for Syd's efforts. You are not authorized to respond with force now that the Letnev fleet has fired on Sol property?"

"I have been urging an armed response for some time," Smyth said, meeting Zey's gaze once more.

"The relay is unmanned, and I am waiting for confirmation from either Jord or Quann regarding a response," Ular said, tone growing a little defensive.

"Quann?" Zey queried, feeling a moment's unaccustomed surprise.

"Governor Forebeck's former chief of staff is acting governor there, and has expressly forbidden opening fire unless our own ships or planetside population centers are fired on," Ular said. "Jord can override her of course, but the parties and the king are split on the level of our response."

"It is foolishness to bring the *Stalwart* and the Phoenix Fleet all this way only to then sit and watch as the noose is drawn tighter," Smyth complained. He was blunt to the point of foolishness, Zey thought, but right now perhaps that was what they needed.

"So you have said, delegate," Ular replied. "But forgive me for not wishing to be the one to fire the first shot in what would surely be the deadliest war in human history."

"I took you for a man of action," Smyth said bitterly.

"I am a soldier, and I follow orders," Ular replied. Zey had to mask his annoyance with the admiral's stoicism, feeling for a different, more effective route. They couldn't fail, not now, not when it was all so desperately close.

"Are there not reports that Letnev soldiers have made planetfall on Quann?" he asked, hoping to prompt Smyth without looking like he supported his warmongering.

"Unconfirmed," Ular said. "I await more news from the surface. I believe Acting Governor Hail is set to give a live address in a matter of hours. When we last spoke she was still championing a peaceful resolution."

"Then I will assist her by whatever means possible," Zey said, deciding to make a show of humility. "Regardless of Eminent Councilor Syd's difficulties with the Letnev, I know humanity will only strike the first blow if they are left with no other choice."

CHAPTER TWENTY

QUANN,
SOL FEDERATION COLONY WORLD

It was time. An armored multiride in Federation livery picked Zara up from her habitation unit as the Quannarian star began to set, drenching everything in a bloody red glow. She glanced briefly up at the hab she had lived in since arriving on Quann, then embraced Hiram, Elle, and Macks, and kissed them goodbye.

"Watch for me on the viz," she told them, trying to seem more confident than nervous. "And I'll see you afterward."

Captain Ruko was sharing the multiride with her, while two escort skimmers dropped in front and behind, gliding along the aerial route to Star Trader Avenue.

"Are we all set?" Zara asked the captain of the guard. He offered a shrug.

"It's not ideal. We don't even really know who organized this rally. We've tried to clear the area where you're set to speak from, and I've got marksmen in position, but beyond that we're winging it. I've brought you an anti-beam vest to wear under your suit, you can put it on when we arrive."

Previously, Zara might have considered turning it down, wanting to appear brave and unconcerned. Right then, however, she felt anything but. She tried to busy herself by tapping her savant and calling up the speech she had quickly written with some help from Hiram. She had poured her emotions into it, believing at this point that there was no reason to hold back. The blockade had to be ended, for the good of everyone.

The first explosion threw her so hard to the side she thought she had dislocated her shoulder, and likely would have, were it not for the seat restraint. Pain still bit into her side, and her vision blurred and grayed for a moment.

Before she could recover, she experienced a plunging sensation, and then a terrible impact that sawed her even more violently against the restraints. Her vision swam, and she thought she was going to be sick.

An alarm in the mulitrider was pinging. Smoke was filling the transport compartment, along with the glare of street luminators through the shattered and crumpled door beside her. Coughing, disorientated, she managed to pop the restraints and scramble up and out of the vehicle.

As she did so, a second explosion rocked the street. Smoke and grit hit her as she crouched down, rattling off the buckled vehicle beside her. Her ears ringing, she struggled to rise, struggled to grasp the enormity of what was happening.

A hand grabbed her shoulder and hauled her through the smoke. She stumbled, but the figure kept her up. It was only when they cleared the worst of the wreckage that Zara realized it was Ruko.

The relief she felt was short lived, quashed by the captain of the guard's grim expression as he helped her lean back against a wall in the alleyway they had made it to.

"It's them," she panted, trying to rationalize what was happening. "It's the Letnev."

"No," Ruko said. "It's us."

Zara didn't understand, so Ruko continued. "We have to be ready for this. Conscription, fortifying Aruzoe, it's our only hope."

A cold, horrifying realization began to dawn on Zara. She stared at him.

"You... these bombs are yours? Have you taken leave of your senses?"

"It's realism," Ruko growled. "We've been abandoned by Governor Forebeck, by our other leaders. Someone had to do something. I hoped it would be you, but that hope was misplaced."

"You're going to start a war," Zara shouted, trying to snatch Ruko by the collar, but he shoved her back and, to her dismay, drew his beam pistol.

"It's starting anyway," he said. "There's too much in motion. Too much momentum."

"You would betray the Federation?"

"No. I'm preserving it. You can't stop this. Nobody can, not anymore. All we can do is be ready. That's the last hope for Quann. For my family, and yours."

"You're with Smyth too, aren't you?" Zara asked bitterly. Ruko nodded.

"Challum delivered his instructions," he said. "He was supposed to remove you, but he didn't have the guts or the skill, so it's fallen to me."

"Get it over with then," she said, turning around. There was no fear, only rage, more potent and bitter than anything she had ever known. Damn Ruko, and the Federation, and this whole cruel, treacherous galaxy. "You can shoot me in the back, like the coward you are."

"You're brave," Ruko admitted. "And you'll be remembered as such. A martyr in Quann's struggle for freedom."

Zara had no more words. She spat, tense, placing her hands against the cold, harsh brickwork. She thought of Hiram, and Elle, and Macks, the only things in her life that had turned out to be worth anything. She prayed that, against all odds, they would be safe.

It seemed to take a long time. Then, the discharge, a searing pain beyond anything she had ever known, driving out everything – her hopes, her fears, her anger and despair.

Then, nothing.

"It's confirmed, sir," Zey overheard communications Lieutenant Stevard say to Admiral Ular as he looked up from the transmission bank. "Multiple detonations in Aruzoe, as well as gunshots. Acting Governor Zara Hail's body has been recovered. She was killed after her transporter was hit. The captain of the Federation Guard believes Letnev infiltrators are responsible."

A deathly silence fell over the bridge of the *Stalwart*. Ular stood quiet and still, his expression guarded, staring at the holographic of Quann and the surrounding ship dispositions. Zey didn't dare say anything. He realized his heart was racing. It was strange and uncomfortable, feeling suddenly powerless.

Predictably, it was Smyth who spoke first.

"It was the Letnev. It has to be. This is an act of war, nothing less."

Ular still said nothing. Zey watched Smyth carefully and silently as the other human approached the admiral, raising his voice.

"Admiral, you must act. The governor of Quann has just been assassinated, and we cannot possibly wait for word from Jord. If we don't retaliate now, we might as well turn this fleet around and withdraw through the Passage. Leave Quann to the barony."

Still, Ular said nothing. Zey battled to stay silent, not wanting to make his hand even vaguely apparent. It was tempting to overcommit now, but that would be a mistake. He had more work to do after this, much more.

Then, as though waking from a trance, Ular looked around the bridge, finding the eyes of every officer on him. He took a slow breath, then finally spoke, his voice hard.

"Lieutenant Stevard, vermillion priority signal to all ships, as well as to Commodore Yarrow and the Quann garrison fleet. Raise shields to maximum, prime beam lances and target-lock priority vessels in the Letnev fleet. Captains are to fire on the mark set by the *Stalwart*. End signal. Acknowledge."

"Aye-aye, admiral," Stevard responded. "Transmitting!"

Zey used every ounce of experience to keep his expression grave, a counterpoint to the surge of exhilaration he felt. He refused to even meet Smyth's eye, no matter how briefly.

"Second Lieutenant Horat," Ular continued, the bridge now stirring around him, nerves and fear giving way to training. "Transmission to prow gunnery sections. Lock onto the Letnev flagship *Magnificatum* and prepare to fire on my mark. Maximum damage output. End transmission. Acknowledge."

"Aye-aye, admiral," Horat barked. Ular turned his attention back to Stevard as the bridge now exploded into activity, systems coming fully online and officers and technicians scrambling to their stations.

"Second vermillion priority signal to all ships, as well as the garrison fleet," Ular told Stevard. "The Sol Federation is now in a state of open war with the Barony of Letnev. Today we will destroy the Grand Fleet and liberate the people of Quann. May the Maker be with us all. End signal. All hands, acknowledge."

"Aye-aye, sir!"

For a long time after returning to the sprinter, Syd remained in his cabin, enduring the cold silence alone.

He expected anger to take hold at some point, the anger he had finally felt as he was forcibly removed from the *Magnificatum*. It eluded him though. All he could do was struggle against the silence, and the frigid desolation of his own thoughts.

He had failed. Failed the empire. Failed Onni. He had gotten his faithful friend killed, all because of his arrogance.

Why had he accepted the assignment in the first place? The seriousness of the Quann crisis had been clear from the beginning, even if Zey's involvement in it had not been. He felt hatred for Zey, for that vile traitor, but it was an impotent emotion, hollow. There was nothing he could do now to stop him. In truth he should have realized that far sooner. If he had, Onni would still be alive.

He had sent a short message to the acting governor on Quann, unable to even admit the extent of his failure. His last hope, that he could get word of it all – of Onni's murder, of Zey's betrayal, of Arrokan's determination to start a war – back to Mecatol in time to make a difference had been dashed. The Letnev had destroyed Quann's orbital relay. The blockade meant courier ships would be unable to easily make it in-system, helping ensure it would be weeks at best before Atz or anyone else in the imperial capital heard about what had transpired.

Or what was about to transpire. The sprinter had drawn out of high orbit and away from Quann, Captain Foli anticipating orders to return through the Passage. It took them away from the rival fleets as they faced one another above the colony world. Such a worthless place, Syd thought, his bitterness rising. A mere outpost, populated by a smattering of grubby humans. Nothing worth fighting a war over. But the implications of that war would be so much bigger.

Foli's voice clicked over the cabin intercom, making Syd look up from where he had slumped against his travel cot, opposite Onni's now-unoccupied bed.

"Sir, I think you better come to the bridge. We're reading massive energy spikes across the Sol fleet, and the Letnev are responding in kind."

They both knew what that meant. The Federation was about to open fire. Zey, Arrokan, the Resurgentists, and every other barbaric warmonger was about to get their fervent wish. They were welcome to it. Let them slaughter each other. Let them see how little the Lazax really cared.

A part of him was tempted to remain in his cabin, cut off from all reality, refusing to partake in the absurdity any longer, but he was drawn to the bridge. He supposed it was morbid curiosity, or the same reasoning that drew theatergoers to watch tragedies. He certainly had a front-row seat.

Foli had the external viz monitors on full magnification, as well as a small holographic representation up and running on the cutter's control panel.

When it happened, the projector picked it up before the screens. Abrupt lines and arcs imposed themselves between the ships around Quann, jagged red and orange. Syd noted the first to have appeared, between the Sol flagship *Stalwart* and Arrokan's *Magnificatum*.

He looked from the projection to the monitors, and saw the beginning of the end. Quann, a perfect sphere of blues and whites and mottled greens, was marred first by a single red line. It was joined by another, then another, then a dozen, then a hundred. Beam weapons, hard shot ordinance, vast arrays of energy and tons upon tons of explosives, launched into the void between the ships that hung in orbit. They were followed by bursts of light and flares of pearlescent illumination as attack met defense, shields struggling to hold the barrage at bay, forming half-seen cocoons around each vessel.

Almost immediately, the Letnev returned the salvo. Now Quann was imprisoned, locked in a cage of fire and light, the eerily silent display only hinting at the carnage being unleashed. Sentients were dying. Syd knew that countless more would follow.

He felt sick. Without meaning to, he found himself turning away, unable to watch any longer. That dread curiosity had given away to revulsion, and a plunging sense of despair deeper and more terrible than anything else he had ever known.

"Set a course for Mecatol Rex," he told Foli quietly, heading back toward his cabin. "It's over."

PART THREE

CHAPTER TWENTY-ONE

"Wait for it," Marlo rasped in a low, dry voice. His words were almost eclipsed by the grating of gears and the thudding impacts of the nearby mechanoid, its passage causing the surrounding rubble filling the building's wrecked shell to shudder and vibrate rhythmically.

"Wait," Marlo repeated.

"I am waiting, damn it," came a hissed reply over the comm bead. Marlo chided himself. Zit didn't need instructions. They had done this all before, enough times to know the angle they needed to take out a Dunlain Reaper.

The Letnev war machine stomped past the ruins the pair of armor-hunters had taken position in. Normally the wrecked street would have offered little in the way of protection from the Letnev's sensors, but that didn't matter as much as usual, as this particular reaper was half-blind. At some point someone from the Eighth Army, or maybe even one of the Combat Wings battling for the skies overhead, had scored a half-decent hit on the walker's sensor array, a cluster of optics and scanners that lay nestled between its broad, weapon-laden shoulders. It could still see in a rudimentary way, as it had viz detectors in its torso and limbs, but its more advanced senses were offline. The best option would be for one of the crew members to pop the hatch and scan the old-fashioned way, but experiences with Eighth Army snipers meant the baronial lapdogs weren't going to be doing that anytime soon.

Which, when coupled with the lack of infantry support, left the big war engine particularly vulnerable. That was where Marlo and Zit came in. Since deploying to Quann two year-cycles before with the rest of the Eighth, the duo had tagged three other reapers, eleven grav tanks of various sizes, and more light vehicles and scout mechanoids than they could count. They were the most effective armor-hunters on the planet's surface, and Marlo was sure they were about to add another ring to the barrel of their sliver rocket launcher.

The reaper lumbered past Marlo's position, and he kept still. Up close he could see just how scarred and battered this particular reaper was, riddled with old bullet dents and the scorch marks of beam weaponry, some of it heavy-duty. Its gears didn't sound up to much either. The fact it had been thrust out to the perimeter of the Letnev's defensive cordon, wounded and unsupported, said a lot about the state of the war on Quann.

The Sol Federation was winning.

Time to continue that trend. As spotter, Marlo was in a prime position to observe the reaper's passage, and he could also see that Zit now had the best possible angle from the half-buried basement she had concealed herself in. He keyed his comm bead.

"Stab it."

Zit let her sliver answer for her. Marlo heard the familiar *whump* of the tube's discharge, followed by the whirr of the gravitic engine coupled to the needle missile's rear tripping as it left the barrel. The rocket locked onto the lower back of the reaper. Zero-point-seven-five seconds after launch, the overpowered granitic engine in the missile's rear went into overdrive, blazing itself out in a burst of flame and punching the missile's warhead, a needle of synthetic diamond, into the reaper at hypersonic speeds. The sound of the overdrive came with a ferocious, echoing roar, followed almost immediately by an almighty clang as the diamond was driven like a lance into the machine.

It made Marlo's ears ache, and caused him to smile. It was the sound he had come to associate with victory.

The needle drilled straight through the reaper and whipped out the other side, ricocheting off into the rubble. It left in its wake a perfectly spherical hole, right through the reaper's heart.

The Letnev war machine tottered for a moment, and then, with a crash that shook stones from the few remaining walls still standing, it fell.

"Target down, target down," Marlo said into his comm bead. He could already see the Third Platoon bursting from cover and descending on the reaper, the dust-caked infantry grunts ripping open hatches and filling them with beam shots or grenades. There were crunches and screams as they made sure of the kill.

"Nice one, sis," Marlo told Zit in person. "Clean as you like."

"It's getting too easy," Zit said with a modest shrug of her slim shoulders. "They should really just give up."

"That'll be the day," Marlo said darkly. If there was one thing they had learned in their years of fighting, it was that Letnev didn't like to lose.

The pair sat on the ruins of a low wall as they waited for Third Platoon to finish their grisly work. Zit had pulled off her helmet and targeter and was scratching at her short, mousy hair while Marlo unwound his smog shroud from around his own lean jaw and pulled out a ration bar. He halved it, and passed one end to Zit. He was six years the elder, and accustomed to sharing.

"Think they'll send out more before it gets dark?" she wondered, looking toward the dead reaper and the Federation infantry swarming it like N'orr hatchlings.

"Hope not, we've only got one needle left," he said, swinging his satchel off one shoulder to show Zit how empty it was. As he did so, something below caught his eye. He stuffed the ration bar in his mouth and hopped down off the wall, using his boot to scuff aside rubble and detritus until he could stoop and pick up what he had seen.

It was a metal street sign in the style common to Jord. It had been bent out of shape and scarred almost to illegibility, but Marlo blew dust off it and held it up for both himself and his sister to decipher.

"Star Trader Ave.," she read slowly, then shrugged. "Guess that was what this place was called."

"Been a long time since it saw much trade, unless it's trading beam shots and hard rounds," Marlo commented dryly, looking around. Like the rest of Aruzoe, it was a desolate wasteland, all form and structure reduced to mounds of rubble and the skeletal remains of broken walls. What had once been a city now bore no closer resemblance to a place of habitation than the surface of a barren moon.

If Marlo knew his war history – and he did, because the Sol military drummed it into all their grunts – this was the third campaign for Quann. It was ground zero for the conflict that had been raging between the Sol Federation and the Barony of Letnev for nearly three quarters of a century. It had been lost to the Letnev, reconquered, lost again, reconquered again – what had once, according to the records, been a promising colony world had been scarred and scoured down to the bone. It was now hard to imagine it would ever be anything other than a place of ruins and trench lines and craters and wrecks, as much a broken corpse as the destroyed Dunlain Reaper occupying the center of what, seemingly, had once been a place call Star Trader Avenue.

"Looks like they're done," Zit said, finishing her half of the ration bar. Marlo looked up and realized Third Platoon had re-formed and were headed their way. He tossed the bent old sign back into the detritus.

"Good kill," Lieutenant Xhi, the platoon's commander, said. "And well timed too. I've just had word from command. There's someone back there who wants to see you. Someone important."

"Who?" Marlo asked, feeling suddenly uneasy. What would "someone important" want with a grunt like him?

"Captain didn't say," Xhi said. "Just that I should get you both back in one piece. Let's hope we don't run into any more walkers or grav-tanks on the way."

"It'll be their loss if we do," Zit said.

Xhi had been right when he had said someone important was waiting to see them.

"By the Maker, it's the general," Zit hissed as they stood outside the sector command post. They had both just gotten a glimpse of Master-General Holborn inside the post, conversing with their captain.

"What did you do?" Marlo demanded of Zit as they both struggled to pull their kit into some semblance of order and beat the dust from their fatigues and armor. He was only half joking. Marlo found he was desperately wondering if one of the Federation's most senior officers would really come to the front to discipline two grunts.

"Just don't tell her I've been hoarding ration bars," he told Zit, trying to alleviate some of the sudden tension. Holborn was a famed disciplinarian. Neither of them had ever encountered her in person, but she was known to everyone. She was, after all, second only to Field Marshal Pratz and the High Minister in terms of the Federation's command structure.

"Inside," snapped Sergeant Rollins, who had been waiting just past the command post's entrance. Marlo and Zit came to attention and marched sharply past him, into the presence of the captain and Holborn.

"Corporal Marlo Nozwo, ident number five-seven-five-eight-two," Marlo said loudly as he came to a halt.

"Lance Corporal Zita Nozwo, ident number five-seven-five-eight-three," Zit said as she came into line next to Marlo. Holborn looked at them both for a moment before speaking.

"Stand easy, corporals."

Marlo relaxed his posture, if not his thoughts. He dared glance at the general, rather than straight ahead. She was aging, but as straight-backed and rigid as a battle walker. Her hair was silver, pulled back sharply and tied up in a bun. Her face had a dangerous leanness to it, and her eyes were cold and gray, like a winter ocean. She wore the combat kit of the Federation as naturally as she appeared to wear the dress uniforms Marlo had seen her in on the viz screens.

"I suppose you're wondering why I've requested your presence here," she asked. "Requested" seemed to Marlo like a very nice word for "ordered." He stayed silent, and cursed inwardly when Zit spoke.

"I'm not sure if it's because we're good at killing barony armor, sir, or if it's because of who our grandma is."

Holborn grunted, seemingly unconcerned by the borderline insolence.

"Mostly the latter, but the former helps," she said. "You are the granddaughter and grandson of Governor Zara Hail, correct?"

"Correct," Zit said, Marlo remaining silent. "Our mother is Elle, Zara's daughter."

"Well, you have certainly done your family name proud, and gone some way toward avenging your loss," Holborn said. "One of my staff officers informed me of your presence in the Eighth Army. It is some irony that the tides of war have led you to fight for the same world your grandmother died protecting."

"Tides is one word," Marlo said, cutting in this time before Zit could speak. "We're just grunts, general. We go where we're ordered."

"Good," Holborn said. "Then I'm ordering you to be seconded to my honor guard for the foreseeable future."

Both of the corporals stared at the general. Zit was the first to manage to put her thoughts into words.

"With respect, sir, I think we'll be more use to the Federation here on the front, popping barony clankers, than with you… wherever it is you're going."

"On the contrary," Holborn said. "Do you know who I am?"

That sounded an awful lot like a trick question, so both the corporals stayed silent.

"My name is Maria Eliza Holborn, because I took the name of my husband, Minister Cedric Holborn, when we were married. Before that, however, I was called Maria Eliza Smyth. My father was Hektor Smyth, former Federation delegate and chancellor. He knew your mother, when the Quann crisis first erupted."

All of this was news to Marlo. He snatched a sideways glance at Zit, and saw her look of consternation. Now wasn't the time to ask why though.

"The precise reason I am requisitioning you both will become more obvious soon," Holborn said. "Until then, go and clear out your bivouac sections and report back here. And rest assured, what you're going to be doing is as important as… 'popping barony clankers.' We're going to end this war."

CHAPTER TWENTY-TWO

ARCHON REN,
TWIN-HOMEWORLD OF THE XXCHA

The war had reached the Xxcha Kingdom.

It was visible from the surface of Archon Ren. The blues, blacks, and reds of the evening sky were shot through with a thousand flares of light and beams of brilliance, a crisscross display that could have been considered beautiful had it not marked the deaths of thousands.

In high orbit, the war ships of the Sol Federation were once again locked in a battle of annihilation with elements of the Barony of Letnev's Grand Fleet. Federation dreadnoughts and baronial capital ships exchanged body blows, while the carriers of both sides disgorged swarms of bombers, shield-breakers, and interceptor starfighters, the pilots locked in a deadly dance around the great hulks. They fought on amidst the wreckage of previous engagements, damaged ships venting plumes of frozen oxygen and blue-tinged flames, ejected life-shuttles lost amidst the chaos. It was slaughter, it was devastation on a vast scale, and it had been raging furiously across the Xxlak system for almost two years.

Ibna Vel Syd ignored all of it, focusing instead on his game of escar. It would soon be over. Three more moves, and the mechafamiliar unit he was playing against would be outmaneuvered and forced to concede.

There was a creak and the clacking of a cane as someone approached him across the timber platform he had laid the board out on. He didn't look back, even when he sensed Tutur looming over his shoulder, peering misty-eyed at the game's progress.

"Close one," the Xxcha commented after a while, voice a low croak.

Syd felt a moment's surprise pierce his moroseness.

"I'm moments from victory," he said.

Tutur gave out the grunting sound old Xxcha made when they wished to be dismissive.

"Are you sure?" he said as he hobbled around the board and slowly lowered himself into the cradle strung between two branches off to one side. "Look at your friend's flanking piece, there on your right."

"It's isolated," Syd claimed, trying to spot what he had missed. "My holding piece has it pinned in place. It is no threat."

"Not in its current state," Tutur allowed. "But if that reserve piece was to use its double move, your holder would be overwhelmed. There is nothing more maintaining that flank. It could very easily collapse."

Syd had missed the potential for the double move. It was indeed a threat.

"Well, I'm glad this familiar can't learn by listening to you," he said to Tutur.

"Actually I can, or at least you programmed me to," the

familiar buzzed unexpectedly. Tutur chuckled while Syd let out a sigh.

"Devious mechanical device," he said to the small bot. Normally its function was little more than a mobile savant, able to provide regular data and situational updates and beam long-range messages from across Archon Ren, but Syd had indeed spent some time tinkering with its programming. He had made it able to play escar, for a start. Too well, apparently.

"I fold," he told the familiar bitterly, ordering it not to mock him. That, at least, he still had control over.

"Don't you think it's a little ironic, playing that Letnev war game while a real Letnev fleet is in action above us?" Tutur asked from his cradle.

Syd supposed he was right, but then he had stopped paying much attention to irony a long time before.

"It keeps my mind agile," he said defensively.

"You speak as though you are an old Xxcha, my friend," Tutur said with a crackling laugh. "But you are not old, not truly so."

"I feel it."

"That is because you are here, rotting beneath the boughs of the Q'waar, when you should be out there."

"Not another lecture, please. This isn't one of your Ssaalel debating halls."

Tutur couldn't argue about that at least. He lapsed into silence while Syd packed away the board, a gust of warm wind making the leaves surrounding them rustle.

Syd had taken to climbing into the upper platforms of one of the great Q'waar trees that surrounded the Ssaalel in the center of Klaak. The village was a humble Xxcha arboreal settlement – a ttillon, in the local tongue – located well outside of the planetary capital of Kklaj. It was isolated, which made it perfect for Syd. It was also the home of his oldest friend, Venerable Tutur, a retired diplomat.

The Xxcha snapped off a small branch hanging just above him and began to chew on its large, thick, green leaves meditatively, watching Syd. The skin about his neck hung slack, his scales rough beneath his deep yellow robes, his slow-blinking eyes rheumy. He exuded warmth and benevolent wisdom, and never failed to find an angle Syd had not considered or a perspective he had not appreciated whenever he brought his troubles to him.

Syd supposed Tutur was right, once again. He was rotting in Klaak, on Archon Ren, pretending a war wasn't happening even as it played out across the heavens above him. He had come to the homeworld of the Xxcha almost a decade earlier, resigning his post on the imperial council and doing what he believed he should have done over seventy years before – withdrawing from public life, accepting that he had failed the empire, and taking an early retirement while doing his best to ignore the fact that everything he had once held dear was falling to pieces.

It had all started on Quann. He had made mistake after mistake, and it had resulted in a war. Even at the beginning, he hadn't appreciated quite how ferocious the human-Letnev conflict would become. It had spread over almost a third of the galaxy, and the Lazax's halfhearted attempts at containing it had done little. And, of course, the Jol-Nar had used the chaos and confusion to almost immediately declare war on their great rivals, the N'orr, seemingly convinced that their highly evolved cerebrums and the insectoid nature of their enemies would make it more of an extermination than a military conflict. That too had proved wholly incorrect, and half the systems not hosting Sol-Barony battles became warzones for the Hylar and the N'orr instead.

It was a nightmare, and it had utterly eroded imperial authority everywhere. Pirates now roved unchecked along shipping lanes, while smaller civilizations and outlying systems were declaring their independence, seeing that the imperium had neither the will nor the manpower to stop them. The vast bureaucratic machinery of the Lazax was beginning to break down as taxes stopped coming through, communications were cut off, and the sentients supposedly under their suzerainty stopped working together.

At first, Syd had tried to stop it. He had fought against the Maandu Edict, which had been issued not long after the start of the conflict in a failed attempt to put all war ships across the galaxy under imperial control. It had only deepened the rift between the Lazax and their subjects. Next, Syd had attempted to petition the emperor himself in front of the imperial council, convincing him to abandon the outer territories. He had been shouted down by his fellow councilors, who had started calling him the "Doomsayer" and the "Fearmonger."

Despairing, he had eventually recused himself from it all, maintaining his title but retiring from official duties. There was no more point, he had decided, in trying to stop the inevitable. It was like trying to kick against a rising tide. There were too few Lazax in positions of authority who cared. Most only wanted to keep the peace on their own petty fiefdoms, or guarantee their own jobs and standing within the imperial hierarchy. So what, they asked, if humans and Letnev, Jol-Nar and N'orr were at each other's throats? They were waging war amongst themselves, not against the empire.

Whoever won, the Lazax would still rule. No need to further upset an already turbulent situation. The wars had been dragging on for the better part of a century now. No need to add further kindling to the flame.

That, ironically, was not the view of Eminent Councilor Sorian Sai Zey. The treacherous Lazax was now a member of the emperor's inner circle, his crimes and treasonous politicking still unexposed. Over the years, and especially in the last decade, the Accelerationist faction within imperial court politics had grown ever-more powerful.

Unlike the anti-interventionists, who were happy to let the empire slowly collapse under its own weight, the Accelerationists were now actively campaigning for more aggressive imperial policies. Higher taxes, tighter regulations, and most of all, a direct intervention in the wars of the other great civilizations. In the past few years there had been several bills passed that dramatically increased the size and capabilities of the Lazax imperial armed forces.

Syd took no part in it. The realization that the empire was now on a collision course with its wayward subjects filled him with such despair that he no longer knew how to process it, beyond leaving it all behind. He had withdrawn to Archon Ren. The war, however, had followed him. The Letnev Grand Fleet had entered the Archon system not long after he had settled on the Xxcha homeworld, and had threatened it with occupation. The Xxcha, considered by most to be the oldest sentients in the entire galaxy, had no means of waging war, and no ability to resist besides their prodigious diplomatic skills. Tutur had come out of retirement and, along with a cadre of his people's best negotiators, had convinced the Letnev to only occupy Archon Ren's mineral-rich sister world, Archon Tau.

It had bought the Xxcha time, time enough to make a secret pact with the Federation and bring their Phoenix Fleet to the Archon system. For two years both forces had battled in orbit above Archon Ren and across the surface of Archon Tau, which had now by all reports been reduced to a blasted wasteland by the devastating weaponry of both sides, its once-verdant forests burned to cinders, its azure lakes broiled away or poisoned by chemicals, its mineral deposits stripped bare, and its atmosphere tainted by the hideous, corrosive effects of total war.

Syd had feared, when the Letnev had first arrived, that he would be seized or forced offworld, but the Xxcha's negotiating had ensured no Letnev had set foot on Archon Ren itself. So he had stayed, in this isolated little ttillon, only occasionally venturing into Kklaj to listen to the weekly philosophical debates or visit the great library of Xuun. Occasionally, he almost managed to convince himself it was an honest retirement, and not a self-imposed exile born out of shame and failure.

"Have you heard about the action at Saudor?" Tutur asked him as he finished dismantling the escar board and sat back in his bough-chair. He could sense the Xxcha still wanted to upbraid him about his refusal to leave Archon Ren, but also did not wish to drive him away.

"I did not," he replied, refusing to be drawn. "Isn't that on the Hylar N'orr frontline?"

"Not anymore," Tutur said, plucking another leaf from above him and beginning to chew again. "The Jol-Nar war fleet met the N'orr swarm-ships and annihilated them. They employed a new weapon they're calling the war sun. It is a ship beyond any form of classification, vast, with weapons capable of razing a planet. Apparently, it is only one of a number they are looking to produce from their docks above Muaat."

Syd gave a noncommittal grunt, a habit he realized he had picked up from Xxcha debaters.

"Jol-Nar needed a victory," he said. "Between the plague and the constant N'orr advances, their war effort has been on the brink of collapse."

"Much like the Letnev here," Tutur said, gazing up slowly at the battle still playing out in orbit, the sky now almost dark but for the violent flashes that ripped and slashed across it.

"You outplayed them," Syd said, thinking back to the escar game. "You held them in place long enough to bring reinforcements to bear. Because the Xxcha have no armies, the Letnev underestimated you. The barony respects only hard power."

"It was all done at a cost," Tutur said. "Archon Tau is no more."

Syd sensed the genuine sorrow in his voice, and experienced a moment's regret of his own.

"Has that been confirmed?" he asked. Tutur clacked his beak in affirmation.

"The Letnev were heavily entrenched, and neither they nor the Federation truly cared what became of the planet. It has been scoured. No Xxcha will ever inhabit it again, at least not for many millennia. And who knows if our peoples will endure for that long?"

"I am sorry for your loss," Syd said. "I know that Archon Tau was as much a home to your peoples as Archon Ren. I count myself fortunate to have beheld its beauty myself, before the war."

"We did what we had to do," Tutur said. Syd suspected he wanted to carry on and tell him "now you must do what you have to as well," but again he checked himself. Syd was thankful for that. He did not wish to have that conversation.

The familiar, which had been floating beside Syd on standby – presumably silently reveling in its victory – pinged abruptly with an update.

"Erial would like to know your current location; she has a data packet for you," it buzzed.

Erial was Syd's Winnu assistant. She received semi-regular news updates from Mecatol Rex, and insisted on bringing them to Syd, hoping the effort of doing so rather than just transmitting them to his familiar or savant would guilt him into reading them. Sometimes it worked, but usually he just ignored them. He felt the urge to do so now, but hoped it might distract Tutur from his slowly unfolding angle of attack.

Erial appeared, clambering unsteadily up onto the platform set atop one of the Q'waar tree's vast boughs.

"The latest package from the courier ship, sir," she said, presenting the files in hard copy.

"Thank you," Syd made himself say as he took them.

For a Winnu assistant, Erial was young. She had been with Syd for almost seven years, but it felt as though he had barely learned her name and was still forgetting her mannerisms – down the decades he had been through more Winnu than he could count. None of them had been able to replace Onni.

Even all this time later, he still felt a stab of regret every time he remembered what had happened above Quann. Most Winnu didn't want to endure his ill moods or the fact that he had practically banished himself – they almost always resigned after a few years. Erial had been the longest-serving yet.

He knew he could never replace Onni, and even trying felt like sacrilege. What did he need an aide for now anyway? Perhaps, as he limped into old age, a carer would be more appropriate.

"There's one more thing not included, sir," Erial said as he began to leaf through the packet. "An open text communication from Eminent Councilor Atz, on Mecatol."

Syd experienced a moment's concern, bordering on shame. He had not spoken to Atz for many years, not since he had petitioned the emperor to withdraw the Lazax fleets and consolidate power around Mecatol Rex, in a desperate attempt to return the initiative to the empire.

"What does it say?" he asked. Erial read the printed-out message chit.

"It… Eminent Council Atz says he is dying, sir. He… apologizes for reaching out to you once again, but he does not have long left, and he requests you return to Mecatol Rex one more time, before the end."

Atz, dying? For some reason Syd had thought the ancient Xxcha would always be there, always striving to end the empire's indolence and corruption. If he was gone, it truly was over.

"Should I compose a response, sir?" Erial asked. "I can say the current fleet action above Archon Ren makes it impossible to–"

"No," Syd said, surprising himself. "Don't lie, not to Atz. I will go. I have to see him before the end. I have to… let him know I'm sorry."

"Take my regards to Atz, and tell him of his homeworld," Tutur said, the Xxcha showing no visible happiness that Syd had finally chosen to return to the imperial capital. "You may find it is not an end at all, but a renewal. A renewal of yourself. A renewal of purpose. You could never hope to find that here."

"I don't hope for anything anymore," Syd declared bitterly. "I only wish to see an old friend, one last time."

CHAPTER TWENTY-THREE

The battle station lay in near darkness, only its low-level emergency lighting offering any sort of illumination. Silence had settled, a silence that should not have existed in such a place. Even in the quiet watches of the night cycle, there was the hum of the life support systems, the hydro pumps and recyc units, the chitter-chatter of mechafamiliars, and the pinging of control panel updates. All of that was gone. This was the silence reserved for death.

Eventually, something dared to disturb it. There was a thump that reverberated through the station. It was followed by a whining sound, rising to a shriek, as though the phantoms of those already dead had returned to claim those few still gripping tenuously onto life. The whine rose to an unbearable pitch, before cutting off as quickly as it had started.

Another thump, shorn magnetic clamps and vacuum seals falling away. The main hatch to the station swung ponderously open, accompanied by a swirl of decompressed steam.

The first figure stepped through, a human, though it was

difficult to tell. He was wrapped up in the rubberized yellow layers of a grade-one medical environmental suit, head shielded by a glassy containment orb, a medicum kit and an oxygen tank strapped to his back. The gear wasn't just for protection against disease – there were no guarantees about the integrity of the station's interior, whether the air was still breathable or whether the non-aquatic sections had become flooded.

He was accompanied by an automed, thrumming softly on its grav plates, swinging from left to right as the optic nodes that comprised its head did a scan of its new environment.

"Oxygen levels, acceptable," the familiar droned. "Pressure levels, acceptable. Air microbe levels, unacceptable. Removal of protective gear; still inadvisable."

"You can say that again buddy," the human murmured, doing a scan of his own with his flashlight. The beam picked out the cold, clean lines of a Jol-Nar military space installation, and something rather more ominous – there was a body lying on the deck at the far end of the access chamber.

The human strode forward quickly, followed by the automed. As he went, he uncoupled a quintisensor and activated it, before kneeling beside the body.

It was a Hylar, one of the Nar subspecies, her once brightly colored and patterned scales turned dull and scabrous. The human let the automed's stab-beam illuminate her while he ran the quintisensor, lips pursed.

She was alive, just. Her scales were bone-dry. That, ironically, was probably what had saved her. Against a waterborne pathogen, the Hylar were extraordinarily vulnerable, but tests had shown that many of the Nar, who were less wholly reliant on hydro-equilibrium, had a better chance of surviving long enough for their antibodies to begin fighting back. Ironically, less water was good. Only up to a certain point though.

If the Doolak Plague didn't kill this one, the dehydration would.

"We're all clear inside," the human said into his containment sphere's comm bead. "I've found our first patient. She's alive."

"So, this wasn't a wasted trip after all," replied the smooth, rich purr of a Rokha.

"It's never wasted," said another. "We're coming aboard, Malik."

The human, Malik, prepared the unconscious Hylar for transportation. As he did so, he heard the heavy clump of environmental suit boots on the decking plates. He half turned and saw his Rokha colleague, Pata, ducking in through the hatch, her feline features underlit by the small lumen strip at the base of her containment sphere. She was followed into the station by a second figure, equally suited up, a Nor Hylar, not dissimilar to the one Malik was about to start treating. Harial Tol.

"Have you scanned the rest of the station?" Tol asked Malik as she looked over the quintisensor readings of the first patient.

"No, Scales, we're just through the hatch," he replied.

"Get this one back to the ship then, and I'll carry on with Click," Tol said. "On an installation this big, if there's one survivor, there'll be more."

"Are Mox and Terrin going to deign to join us?" Malik asked.

"They're just finishing suiting up. I'm leaving the others onboard the *Renewal*. We'll need to start treatments as soon as we have each patient in containment."

"Agreed," Malik said. "You don't want someone to come with you? We don't know what's in here."

"A lot of dead and dying Hylar," Tol said. "I'll be fine."

She sensed Malik wanted to reach out to squeeze her hand, or just lightly knock his containment sphere against hers, a strange form of reassurance the couple had developed over the last few years, but he resisted the urge. They were in the midst of it now, and contamination protocols had to be obeyed. One slip-up, one moment of laxity, and years of work would be in vain.

"Stay in touch," he said simply.

"I will," Tol replied, and beckoning to the automed, Click, she moved toward the hatchway that led into the body of the station proper.

It would only unlock for a Hylar gene-ident. That Tol could have provided, if she removed her suit's gauntlet and pressed her hand against the scan plate. Of course, that could be a death sentence. On the other hand, the interior door was full military grade, and could take hours to carve through, hours they did not have. The Delroc system might have been uninhabited bar this facility, but it was still on the frontline between the ongoing, brutal war between Jol-Nar and the Sardakk N'orr. The last thing any of them wanted was to get caught up between them.

She made a snap decision, applying a double coating of decontam spray and antiviral paste to the scan plate and having Click check it. It came up all-clear. Tol didn't fully trust that, but she wasn't turning back now. There had to be more survivors.

She uncoupled her gauntlet and pressed her soft, wet palm to the now-glistening scan plate. It took a second to come online, before assessing her Hylar genetics and blinking green. Ironic, Tol thought. After her banishment, most other Hylar would hardly have considered her part of their species anymore.

The hatch eased open. Click went first, and Tol followed, pulling on and resealing her gauntlet.

A corridor waited beyond, gloomy in the half-light. There were more bodies, three, two of them sprawled across the deck, one slumped against the wall. Tol hurried to the first.

It was a Jol Hylar. She knew he was dead without recourse to her quintisensor. The water of his containment sphere was utterly befouled, reduced to an opaque muck of infected tissue and decomposed matter. Once, the sight would have made her feel ill. Now she felt only sorrow.

The other two were no better. Infected fluid was still leaking from cracks in their own suits. Unlike the first victim they had encountered out in the access chamber – a station technician – all three of these ones were soldiers, campus-combatant tyros. They had been stationed in the Delroc system expecting to guard the Jol-Nar's flank against the Sardakk N'orr. In the end, a very different and even deadlier enemy had found them.

She moved on, into the first chamber on her right. It was a sensor station, monitoring the system's edges for N'orr incursions. It was abandoned, but for a single Hylar, another technician who appeared to have collapsed at his station, doing his duty to the last.

Tol checked him. A Nar, like her. Scales dry, brittle, but alive. She administered an antiviral injection to his exposed neck. He let out the faintest croak.

"Assistance is at hand," she said, knowing that he was unlikely to be able to hear her or, more accurately, that his dying brain was unable to comprehend her. She spoke anyway.

"You are in safe hands now."

She activated a Hylar-made locator beacon and left it on the blank monitor station in front of the technician.

She moved on, back out into the corridor and then into the neighboring room, exploring the cold, dark, eerie tomb that Arnus Lax battle station had become.

She wondered how the Doolak Plague had first made its way onboard. Contaminated water was a common vector, or an individual carrier. Reinforcements for the station garrison, a new batch of technicians, a visiting officer or official? She set a note on her savant to remind her to search for the station's manifests. Hopefully, if any of the survivors pulled through, they would be able to help.

She made her way through the station, checking the corridors, communications hub, shields and weapons centers, then the barrack domes and food refectory. Some of the hydro chambers had burst, and much of the station was almost knee-deep in murky, infected liquid that flowed out over the lower half of Tol's suit whenever she unsealed another hatch. She was glad her limited Hylar sense of smell was rendered null by her containment sphere.

She found more bodies, everywhere. She kept a rudimentary tally of number, position, and condition via both her savant and Click, and set down locator beacons wherever she found traces of life. There were precious few, but even what she had uncovered so far was better than what she had dared hope for.

It had been like this for years now.

When Tol had first been banished, she had spent decades wandering the galaxy, seeking a purpose. She had worked as a doctor – albeit no longer with her Jol-Nar license – in the Setti system for about ten years, and even spent time as a researcher with a Lazax-run imperial medical college on Worum. In an ironic way, the twin wars that had blazed out across the galaxy had been good for those Hylar not living or working under the umbrella of the universities. Within months of the first fleet action against the N'orr over Terelleum, the Jol-Nar had ordered a total recall of all students and faculty members.

Millions of Hylar throughout the galaxy had packed up and left their technical systems, research stations, medical facilities and advice hubs and departed, almost overnight. The result had been a crippling gulf in knowledge and expertise that the Lazax empire had considered a crisis.

Those few Hylar not under the jurisdiction of the Jol-Nar had found themselves in high demand. Tol had been paid well to work for the empire, but it had done nothing to make her life seem worthwhile.

For a time she had sought out danger and risk, convincing herself that it was on the frontlines of the spreading conflicts that she was most needed. No matter how she raged against her banishment, she could never assist the N'orr in their war against her own people, so she had traveled into Federation space and offered her services. Six years as an auxiliary medic had followed, first in the bloody, brutal trenches on Cyrelum and then as a senior doctoral overseer at the rejuvenation center in the Dantworth system, when the human military had overcome its prejudice against other sentients and realized her worth beyond a frontline combat medic.

All the while, and against her better judgment, she had monitored data packets from Jol-Nar space, hunting for any hint of the fate of KZ80, or the potential spread of Arr's infection. For a while there had been nothing, her hope tempered by her knowledge that the universities would likely suppress any news about an unknown disease.

It turned out the latter suspicion had been correct. The virus had not been exterminated at KZ80. In fact, it hadn't even been stopped from leaving Muaat.

Eventually, the pandemic had become too big to cover up. The disease became known as the Doolak Plague, and its variants proved as devastating as Tol had feared they would. Whole campuses were decimated, with an average mortality rate of twenty-five percent, climbing above forty among Jol-born Hylar. Even worse, the universities refused to acknowledge the true source of the infection – Arr's laboratory – and instead claimed it had developed naturally in water deposits in the Doolak highlands. It was a clever cover, believable from a medical standpoint, but Tol knew better.

She had assessed each update coming from Jol-Nar space with bitterness and sorrow. She had tried to reach out to old university friends to warn them, but she had no access to Jol-Nar FTL facilities or courier ships, and knew that everything she sent as an outsider was monitored and wouldn't be passed on. The truth was being suppressed. She felt as helpless and despairing as she had when she had sat before Enro and tried to convince him of the unfolding disaster. So instead, she threw herself into the midst of the Sol-Letnev war and stayed busy trying to put humans back together again.

She opened another bulkhead. More brackish water poured

out over her slick boots. She took a moment to compose herself, growing weary of the relentless horror of what she was uncovering. So far there had been over two hundred dead Hylar bodies, and she was barely halfway through the station.

Things had changed when she herself had contracted the Doolak Plague. It hadn't been from another Hylar, but from a human, one she had been treating for combat psychosis on Dantworth. She had almost died. Contracting it from a human had seemingly robbed the disease of much of its potency though – it was a latter-stage mutation, and aided by her Nar physiology, as well as her pre-existing knowledge of the disease, she had made it through.

The realization that the virus had mutated into something that could spread to other sentients finally drove her to action. War was a potent breeding ground for disease, and it turned out both the humans and the Letnev had large numbers of troops carrying the infection. So far its manifestation in both species was far less debilitating or deadly, but the fact that it was now moving rapidly through multiple civilizations confirmed Tol's worst fears. There hadn't been a galaxy-wide pandemic for almost half a millennium. She wasn't going to sit by and let the next one spawn right beneath her gills.

Using contacts on Mecatol, she had gone before the imperial council itself and begged for the empire to fight back. To her shock, she had been listened to. One Lazax in particular, named Syd, had championed the creation of a joint imperial research and response unit, pulling together medical experts from across the empire. With Syd's patronage, Tol had been placed in charge, and instructed to wage war on the disease by all means possible, from the lab to the sickbed.

That had been ten years ago, and at first it had all seemed positive. As ever with the Lazax though, help and understanding only extended so far. The new initiative, grandly entitled the Imperial Medical Response Initiative, had been badly underfunded, and its senior doctors, who were supposed to answer to Tol, had fallen to squabbling over strategies and research. Feeling overwhelmed, Tol had taken a cadre of what she considered the best medics and headed to the edge of Jol-Nar space with what treatments she had devised, determined to make a difference. She had tried to reach out to the universities directly, of course, but they had refused all contact, all offers of assistance. So she was reduced to this, making unofficial excursions into campus space, following up reports of contamination and trying to help where she could while avoiding the Jol-Nar hierarchy.

Her comm bead pipped, making her jump and her fins arch reflexively. It was Malik.

"By the Great Learning, what is it?" she demanded, feeling embarrassed.

"We're following up on your locator beacons and collecting the survivors," he said. "But Lakshmi on the *Renewal* is reporting possible trouble. There's a ship headed our way. Hylar."

"Where did it come from?" Tol demanded. "We scanned the system when we broke out of FTL."

"Either it was cloaked, or it was hiding behind one of the outer planets," Malik said. "Either way, it's making a beeline straight for us."

"A what?" Tol asked. Even after all these years, she was still discovering strange new human phrases that Malik casually dropped into his univoca.

"It's coming directly for us. I don't know its class. The *Renewal's* systems are as slow as ever."

"We need a new ship," Tol muttered, turning and wading back the way she had just come. "I'm going to head to the station's scan room. Its arrays will be far more powerful than the *Renewal's*."

"Shouldn't we evacuate?"

"They won't dare board when they discover what's happened to the station, if they don't know already," Tol pointed out. "And it might just be an unmanned scout probe on an automated route, headed here to refuel. I'll let you know as soon as it's scanned."

"Understood," Malik said.

They had first met nearly ten years earlier, when Malik, himself an ex-Sol combat medic, had answered another call from the Imperial Medical Response Initiative. Tol found most humans to be somewhat shortsighted and emotional sentients, but she had grown to appreciate Malik's sense of humor, something other Hylar, especial Jol ones, were clinically lacking.

Both passed beyond the crest of middle-aged, both struggling to make a difference in a galaxy that felt like it was accelerating furiously toward heat death, they had become something more than harried colleagues, a piece of the puzzle neither had quite realized was missing. Without Malik's support, Tol suspected she would have given in to despair long ago.

She returned to the primary scan station and used her gene code again to trigger the systems and lock them on to the oncoming vessel.

As she waited for the feedback, she noticed that the neighboring communications array was blinking. It had to be the approaching vessel, hailing the station. Perhaps they hadn't noticed the presence of the *Renewal* yet. Did they even realize what had happened to the station's garrison?

After vacillating, she decided to accept the transmission. It was a viz beam, so she stood atop the transmission plate and faced the one opposite. As she did so, she saw results ping up on the scanning monitor, the Hylar technology working so much quicker than the mostly human and Lazax-built systems of the *Renewal*.

She froze, disbelief warring with horror as she read the feedback. The good news was that the approaching ship was neither a Jol-Nar war vessel nor an official faculty carrier. It was a small, fast private transport, not formally affiliated with the campuses.

The bad news was that, according to the logs, it belonged to Doctor Atak Arr.

CHAPTER TWENTY-FOUR

QUANN,
CONTESTED WAR-WORLD

Marlo and Zit were given new uniforms for the talks that Holborn had proposed with the Letnev. They donned them for the first time in the dubious privacy of a bombed-out old mechafamiliar shop on what had once been Aruzoe's outskirts.

"I forgot how uncomfortable formals are," Zit grumbled as she battled to button up the starched front of her double-breasted gray Federation Guard uniform. Marlo reached over to help her, feeling the high, stiff collar of his own identical jacket sawing into his throat as he did so.

"How are we supposed to protect the general if we can hardly move our arms or heads?" Zit carried on, craning her own neck back to let her brother do up her collar too.

"I'm not sure we're really supposed to protect the general," he pointed out. "I think we're meant to look pretty. You know, the descendants of Governor Zara Hail, present at the end, the way she herself was at the beginning."

"She was never even governor," Zit said, voice surly. "She was acting governor when she died."

"Confirmed posthumously though," Marlo said. "She was the first martyr. She stayed at her post when everyone else fled."

Of course, they both knew the story well. It was as much family as it was Federation history. The Letnev had started their wicked blockade of the Quann Passage and the planet itself. The colonial governor, Forebeck, had fled, as had most of the administrative staff. Zara Hail had stood her ground, and had been mobilizing to defend Quann despite the odds when Letnev infiltrators had murdered her in the Aruzoe Bombings.

"We're doing her proud by being here," Marlo said, tugging on the bottom of Zit's tunic and taking a step back so he could look her up and down.

"Considering it's you, you look pretty smart," he admitted. Zit made a rude gesture.

"Let's just get out there before they send someone to find us."

It was a short ride along the frontline to the location of the proposed peace talks, via armored carrum. Marlo and Zit shared it with the rest of the honor guard, a surly band of immaculately dressed Fed Guard who seemed to resent their presence. They sat in silence, refusing to engage when Marlo asked them how likely they thought it was that the peace talks would succeed, and whether or not it was true the actual baron of Letnev himself had come to Quann.

They reached their destination and bundled out. From what little prior knowledge Marlo had been able to glean, it seemed the talks were to be held in Quann colony's former administrative center, the so-called Federation Hub. Both sides had avoided destroying it, each wanting the symbolic victory of holding it at the end of the conflict, but despite their best efforts it was still a ruin, its walls now just jagged stumps, its broad stone steps littered with rubble.

To Marlo's surprise, there was a welcome committee already outside. The Letnev had gotten there early, but it wasn't only their own elite shock troopers that were present, but a host of both human and Letnev dignitaries and newscaster reporters. A section of the Federation Guard were detailed to create a proper cordon and keep the civilians back while the rest were ranked up facing the Letnev line already arrayed up the steps, silver armor gleaming in the warm afternoon light.

Marlo had never been so close to a Letnev soldier without them trying to kill him, and he was relieved when both he and Zit were kept aside. General Holborn disembarked from her own armored transport and motioned at them to follow her as she began to climb into the ruins ahead. As they went, Marlo battled his nerves. This was the last place he had imagined himself being just a few cycles ago. He realized he was probably following in the exact footsteps of his grandmother. He shot Zit a sideways glance, and realized she looked as apprehensive as he felt. Their eyes met, and he did his best to appear reassuring.

They were the only ones with Holborn as they entered what was left of the Fed Hub's interior. Shattered stone and twisted, rusting scaffolding was heaped on the floor, but a path had been cleared through it to a flight of stairs that seemed to lead down into what Marlo assumed was a basement or saferoom. Holborn halted and brought them to attention. Her expression was tense, and she spent a few seconds tugging her uniform and brushing at the lapels. It occurred to Marlo that the grizzled officer was nervous as well.

"No matter what happens, you must remain here until I return," she told them.

"Even if–" Zit began to say.

"No matter what," Holborn said firmly. "Is that clear?"

"Yes sir," they both chorused instinctively.

"Very well," Holborn said. Then, after a moment of apparent uncertainty, she began to descend.

As she stepped down, Holborn steeled herself. This was the moment she had been waiting for all her life. The time of reckoning. The little span that would define all that had come before, and all that would happen after. It made her feel sick with nervousness, but she crushed those feelings and masked them with cold indifference, just like her father had taught her.

The Smyths had sacrificed much over the past century. She would not let it have all been in vain.

The meeting place was to be the control center of Quann's old colonial government. It felt eerie, knowing her father had descended into this very room when he had been caught up in the Quann crisis. She hoped desperately that what she was about to do would make him proud, and fulfill the single promise she had made to him before he had died.

The Lazax would pay.

Baron Daz Arrokan the First was waiting for her. He was old now, far older than the stills her father had sometimes shown her when she had been a child, describing how the events of the Quann crisis had unfolded. His flesh was mottled with the age markings that often marred the Letnev, and his long white hair was balding in patches. He still wore the uniform of the barony well though, his breast glittering with medals.

He was not alone. There was one other present, a younger Letnev in a rear admiral's uniform. Holborn recognized him as Vvlos Ssamrac, Arrokan's adopted son. The pair were standing on the other side of an old, cracked viz projector, its surface glassy and blank. As agreed, there were no guards present.

Holborn stopped on the near side of the projector and, as a mark of respect, gave the Letnev salute. They responded in kind with the Federation salutation, a silent relief to Holborn. She had never met either in person, though their reputations preceded them, and they had communicated a number of times covertly. She supposed she would discover soon if their ambitions and interests really did align.

"Well met, warriors of Arc Prime," she said, carrying on with the formalities. Neither replied, letting her continue. "It is a point of great relief among my people that you have agreed to these talks, Honored Baron Arrokan."

Arrokan grunted, seemingly intent on cutting to the chase. His voice came out as a dry rasp. "My people do not feel relief in matters of war until the enemy has been utterly crushed. It seems, however, that will not be happening today."

"No, it will not," Holborn agreed. "Both our peoples have fought long and hard. It became a war without purpose some time ago. It is right that we end it here."

"Oh, it had purpose," Arrokan said with the ghost of a smile. "Purpose especially for a being who is neither Letnev nor human. A mutual acquaintance."

Holborn knew of whom Arrokan spoke. He was part of the reason these talks were happening in the first place.

"Eminent Councilor Zey," she said. "His influence continues, though perhaps not for much longer."

"Your father knew him," Arrokan said. "As do I. He, and the Lazax in general, are the source of all this… discord."

"On that we agree. He has been manipulating events from the beginning. He seeks to weaken both our great civilizations and give the Lazax an excuse to conquer and subjugate us all."

"And we have known that from the start," Arrokan said. "If these talks are to bear fruit, let nothing be obfuscated between us, General Holborn. Your family has done well out of this war. Your father rose to the rank of chancellor, and you yourself now command much of the forces of your Federation. The disgrace your name once held has long been wiped out."

"I could say similar about you," Holborn said, not wanting to overstep, yet also unwilling to let what felt like an accusation pass without riposte. "From grand admiral to baron. There can be no higher rise to power, and all made possible because of the war."

"Baron Werqan was not a wartime leader," Arrokan said. "She was a Lazax lickspittle, not fit to lead our species."

"So you had her assassinated, and used your popularity after the first battle of Quann to assume the mantle."

"Yes," Arrokan said bluntly. "For the good of my kind."

"Zey's efforts to create conflict have suited us both," Holborn said, not hiding from the claim. She knew that now was the time for forthrightness, to go on the offensive, not fight a rearguard action. "But he outgrew his usefulness some time ago. This war has lasted for far too long."

"Perhaps," Arrokan said. "Regardless of Zey's involvement, the barony were not the ones who began it."

"Then you can be the ones to finish it. You know it cannot be won. The more it goes against you, the more tenuous your position becomes."

"That sounds akin to a threat, general," Arrokan rasped dangerously. "You should know better."

"I thought we came here to forge the future, not refight a pointless war," Holborn said, trying not to let Arrokan's prideful recalcitrance get to her. He was coming across as a blunt instrument when she knew he was anything but. "We have always known who the true enemy is."

As she spoke, she noted that Ssamrac hadn't uttered a word, but was watching the conversation play out like a reptilian eyeing his next meal. It was disconcerting, but she kept her attention on Arrokan. He was the key here. She had to keep on top of her own nerves and reservations, and secure what she came for.

"You are aware that the Lazax are voting to mobilize their own war fleet," the baron was saying. "That is why we are both here. Time is running out. They will strike us in a matter of weeks."

"Then let us end this infighting," Holborn urged once more, feeling like she wasn't making headway. "It has cost both our peoples enough already."

"We shall," Arrokan said. "If the terms are correct. You said yourself, my position is based on my victories. I will not surrender it by engineering a dishonorable peace."

"Then what are your terms?"

"There must be reparations, and Quann must be ceded to Arc Prime."

Holborn couldn't help herself.

"You really believe we will surrender Quann?" she snapped, her patience at the end. "The very world this war has been fought over? The world where we are on the cusp of total victory? Where we stand today?"

"You must, or my people will never accept the peace."

"And what makes you think the people of the Federation would accept it if we are seen to give up Quann after seventy-two years?"

"You humans are a malleable species. Honor only matters in the moment. I'm sure there will be some discord, but when the next crisis comes along it will be forgotten. Not so the Letnev. For us, honor is everything."

"Oh, spare me," Holborn all but shouted, her patience worn thin. "I know your currency is acting like the most Letnev of all Letnev, baron, but I am not one of your propaganda drones. Do not pretend that any species can be so easily summarized. Just say what you have already alluded to. You gained power with a coup, and you fear losing it the same way if your position is undermined by peace negotiations."

"How dare you speak to me in this fashion, general," Arrokan snarled, grasping the buckled rail that ran around the viz projector's circumference. "I am Baron Saz Arrokan the First! I–"

There was a hiss, and Arrokan fell, so abrupt it made Holborn jump.

She realized Ssamrac had moved, and that now there was a slender, red knife in his hand. He had just opened Arrokan's throat.

There was no moment of shock on Arrokan's part, no clutching at a wound and choking. He simply dropped in mid-sentence, like a puppet with the strings cut. There was a faint gurgling noise, then stillness.

Holborn stared first at the body, then at Ssamrac. Before she could react – and to her relief – the Letnev wiped the blade on the edge of the viz projector and returned it to its sheath.

"I couldn't endure another of his dull tirades," he said, as though that were sufficient explanation.

"What have you done?" Holborn said, taking a step back. Ssamrac raised a hand, palm open, as though to reassure her.

"Reopened negotiations that were about to close," he said. "Arrokan might have had good ideas once. I would even go so far as to admit he was a good leader. But he has not been for some time. Instead of using this war as a means toward a greater end, he saw the power he could accumulate by prolonging it. It is clear his fear and greed were going to undermine us here today. You know what needs to be done, and so do I. Arrokan did not."

"You... still want to negotiate?" Holborn asked, trying to catch up with the Letnev's thought processes. Of all the moments she had tried to visualize ahead of these negotiations, this wasn't one of them. Her plans felt totally thrown, but she knew she had to regain the initiative, not give in to shock.

"I do wish to negotiate, and so do my people. I am the baron now. We will come to an accord. We must, before the Lazax are ready to strike."

"You don't want Quann?" Holborn asked, trying to feel out the parameters of this new discussion.

"The Federation can have it. The whole damn Passage too. You won it, after all. And there will be no reparations, from either side."

"Forgive me for using a human phrase, but what's the catch?" Holborn said, unable to stop her eyes from darting down again to Ssamrac's knife, sheathed though it now was.

"The 'catch' is that when you go to Mecatol Rex – if your Federation will allow you – it will be without the Grand Fleet."

"That isn't what we discussed with Arrokan. The Phoenix Fleet cannot possibly make war against the Lazax without aid from the Letnev, not after the damage we have suffered over the decades. The imperial fleet would destroy us the minute we translated into the Gul system."

"The Letnev Grand Fleet is in no better state than the Federation's," Ssamrac pointed out. "I will not risk its complete destruction. It would leave Arc Prime defenseless. If what we have previously proposed comes to pass, the uncertainty will be great. Who knows what retaliation Lazax loyalists might take?"

"And how do you expect the Federation to defeat the imperial fleet alone?" Holborn asked, hoping Ssamrac would have an answer. It was clear he had considered all of this prior to striking.

"It may not have to," he said. "There is no indication the emperor has anticipated what we have discussed. Even when news of our peace treaty reaches the capital, they won't expect either of us to be willing to start an even greater conflict in the immediate aftermath of the one we have just ended."

"That is supposition. All you are saying is that you recuse yourself from the dangers involved, and you expect the Federation to take the risk?"

"Yes," Ssamrac said simply.

Despite herself Holborn smiled. She felt sudden relief,

twinned with a wicked excitement. Ssamrac's intervention had simplified things, it seemed. Everything was still on course.

"Don't you think it's ironic?" she asked. "Hundreds of years railing against Lazax control and projecting yourselves as a proud, martial people, and now the Letnev are asking others to fight their battles for them. To do the thing they have always dreamt of doing, but now find themselves too weak and timid to contemplate."

"Oh, there will be battles aplenty, and the barony will play its part," Ssamrac said, refusing to rise to the bait as Arrokan surely would have done. "I am a strategist, General Holborn. I am not simply thinking about war with the Lazax. I am thinking about how things will go when it is over."

"And you want to make sure the Letnev are in the best possible position to capitalize when the galaxy is reborn," Holborn mused. She could see the baron's play now. It was one she could work with. "I cannot begrudge you that. I will be doing the same, for the Federation."

"Do we have an agreement then?" Ssamrac asked.

"I will need to speak with my allies," Holborn said. "But that is a matter for me to deal with. This treaty won't include any of this latter conversation in its public clauses, so let's get it signed."

"Magnificent peace, glorious war," Ssamrac said, and smiled.

CHAPTER TWENTY-FIVE

ARNUS LAX BATTLE STATION, THE FRONTLINE IN THE FIRST JOL-NAR–SARDAKK N'ORR WAR

Tol panicked.

In all the decades since her banishment, she had tried not to think about Doctor Arr. She had tried to seal away memories of what he had showed her, and what he had asked of her. Those hideously carved up and dissected N'orr, his vile quest for a pathogen that would exterminate them, and his cold indifference to it all.

She had no doubt that the Doolak Plague had been born in his laboratories, and that his arrogance, and that of the Hylar hierarchy, had helped ensure it had spread. She had told the Lazax, and anyone else who would listen, of his involvement, but they were powerless to act now against the Jol-Nar for fear that, fully mobilized, they would respond to a developing diplomatic crisis with secession from the empire. At her lowest and darkest ebbs, she found a certain grim pleasure in the knowledge that his efforts to annihilate another species had instead brought his own to the brink. None could say the galaxy didn't have a sense of justice.

While she had been working for the Federation it had become clear that Jol-Nar were supplying the humans with a great deal of destructive, advanced weaponry, which was no small part of their current, hard-won advantage over the Letnev. Arr, she knew, had been a senior Jol-Nar weapons developer before moving into virology, and his hand was clear enough to see. In his own way, he was wreaking devastation across the length and breadth of the empire.

And now, he was here, in the Delroc system. Tol remained frozen as the comms array continued to blink with an incoming transmission. This could be no coincidence. Briefly she knew fear, panic, paralysis.

Then, abruptly, anger burned it all away, like a firestorm on Muaat, surging up the mountainside and engulfing everything in its path.

She hit "accept transmission."

The viz plates underfoot blinked on, her own beaming a transmission of herself to the approaching ship, while the one sent from the ship activated in front of her. A life-sized vision of Arr materialized, the advanced Hylar technology rendering him in full color and enhanced detail. He looked older, more stooped, gills sagging and eyes bulbous. She supposed she didn't look like the fresh-scaled young Nar she had once been either. Still, the mere thought of him made her bristle.

For a second they merely looked at each other, and she found herself wondering if the connection had been disrupted. Then Arr spoke.

"Harial Tol," he said. "I was hoping I would find you on-board. I am assuming given your presence and environmental medical suit, that the station's crew have succumbed?"

"Not all of them," Tol said, her words feeling strangely disjointed as she spoke them. It was surreal, to be speaking to Arr again after all these years, almost dreamlike. The fire hadn't quite worked its way into her speech yet. Instead, she asked the most obvious question.

"Why are you here?"

"Because you are," Arr said.

"How could you have known? We left the medical core on Altalar two weeks ago. It wasn't common knowledge where we were bound."

"But it is common knowledge that you and your task force are in the sub-sector, combatting outbreaks along the frontline," Arr responded. "The faculties of the universities are not as oblivious to your activities as you might believe. I also knew of the plague's presence onboard this battle station. Logically, it was likely that you would arrive here soon. And, despite your indiscretions down the years, you are still logical. You are still Hylar."

"So what?" Tol asked. "You've come here to arrest me? Terminate me for breaking the terms of my banishment?"

"No, former under-doctor," Arr said. "I have come here to ask you to save me."

"There is no cure for the Doolak Plague," Tol said.

"But you have developed means of significantly improving the chances of survival," Arr said. "Certain antiviral cocktails, dehydro therapies, gill-purges."

"So have the universities."

"Not to the same extent. It was decades before what started on Quann spread to the main campuses, decades before the

Circle of Regents took it seriously. Work began too late. But you were countering it from the start. You understand the original virus, before it began to mutate. No one else, Hylar or not, has made as many gains in combatting this plague."

"How do you know?" Tol demanded, repulsed at the realization that, potentially, Arr had still been watching her all these years. "Because of you I was banished from Jol-Nar space. Yet you've still been monitoring me?"

"I have," Arr said. "Once I discovered the extent of the contagion, I expended resources to follow your activities. I hoped that your discoveries could be fed back to the universities and quicken our efforts to combat the outbreak. Following you has not been easy however, especially since Hylar friendly to Jol-Nar were all withdrawn to campus space at the outbreak of the war."

"The war that you've been craving," Tol said. "Isn't it ironic that the plague you tried to breed in order to exterminate the N'orr has instead decimated your own species."

"Your species too," Arr snapped, before falling into a bout of coughing. Tol had already spotted the inflamed nature of his gills, even before he had made his request. He had contracted the Doolak Plague and was in the early stages of viral infection. Tol could not resist a sense of dark delight, and she found herself twisting the knife.

"I couldn't imagine someone more deserving of the Doolak Plague than you, doctor," she went on. "The galaxy has repaid you in kind."

"Nonsense," Arr wheezed as he recovered, his viz projection flickering slightly. "The universe is bound by no such petty laws. The chances of contracting the disease at some point were higher than the balance of probability. And now, you shall cure me of it."

"I told you, there is no universal cure," Tol snapped, willing to make any claim to avoid having to help the despicable Hylar.

"You are being facetious! You have the ability to improve my chances of survival by a significant degree!"

"I could have improved every Hylar's chances of survival if you hadn't banished me," Tol shouted, her fury taking over. "If you didn't continue to refuse me access to university space! I begged all of you. Hundreds of thousands, perhaps millions dead, all on you, Arr! Every last death from this plague, and from this cursed war!"

Arr glared at her for a moment before speaking. "You will assist me, Harial Tol," he said eventually.

"Why? Why would I assist the monster who ruined my life and brought death and devastation to half the galaxy?"

"Because you were, and still consider yourself, a Hylar doctor, and the first act you performed as a doctor was to swear an oath, not only to the universities, but to all species in this galaxy. An oath that binds you to preserve life at all costs. Regardless of who the afflicted is or what they have done, regardless of your personal feelings toward them, if they seek your aid as a doctor, you must assist them."

"You will have sworn that same oath, yet look where we are," Tol said bitterly, knowing that what he said was true. He knew her weakness, and there was nothing she could now do to stop him exploiting it.

"Some can see beyond such foolishness," Arr said. "But I doubt that you can, Tol. Since we encountered one another on Muaat you have consistently proven yourself to be... idealistic.

Fortunately, most Hylar are not like that, but you are one of the exceptions that proves the rule. Now, once again, I am asking for your assistance. Without it I will die."

Tol fought the hardest battle of her life not to deactivate the transmission and storm away. She was shaking, riven with such disgust she thought she might be sick. Even just encountering Arr again was bad enough, but to be manipulated now by him, so brazenly. He clearly had not changed at all. Despite bringing his own species to its knees with his disgusting experiments, he had gained not one iota of self-awareness or remorse. And now, somehow, he had cornered her.

"Are you alone?" she asked, her voice low and firm.

"Yes. My ship is fully automated. I also possess first-rate medical facilities onboard. I will need only the most basic assistance."

As though to make a mockery of his claim, another bout of coughs racked him.

"You are not the only patient here, Arr," she said, speaking over his struggles. "There are survivors onboard this battle station."

"And you have a team at your disposal," Arr wheezed. "I want only you, not them. I imagine the afflicted you have discovered will take time to stabilize and extract. You will have an opportunity to come aboard my vessel and treat me."

"And you simply assume that I will?"

"I consider the likelihood highly probable."

Tol found herself struggling to articulate her thoughts. Instead, she reached out, and deactivated the transmitter.

Arr stared at the space the projection of Tol had occupied a moment before, now empty, the link cut. Then, he screamed, rage and frustration shattering the reserved front he had been putting up.

The shriek became a racking series of coughs, and he collapsed into the high-backed chair behind the projection plate.

He did not have long. He could hardly breathe, and everything ached. This had been his final gamble, a desperate plea he had fought to mask with the confidence that had served him so well down the years. Had his sense of Tol been so wrong? Would she really abandon him and break her oath?

He had feared it would come to this. Concerns about the viral outbreak on Muaat had been lost in the joy and excitement of the war with the N'orr. Even if his attempts at biological warfare had failed, his dream of Jol-Nar dominance was being realized. With Shole's help and direction, he had not only helped provide the campus fleets and armies with the weaponry necessary to decimate the enemy, but had also begun to develop the ultimate tool of destruction.

The first few years of the war had been the high point. Then the Doolak Plague had morphed, spread, and suddenly everything was going wrong. Only Arr's integral involvement in the creation of the super weapon had spared him Shole's wrath, and the interminable university investigations into the causes and origins of the virus.

The outbreak had come at the worst possible time. Torn between total war and a pandemic, Jol-Nar had come dangerously close to collapse. Only now, with victory at Saudor and the worst of the disease having run its course, was the tide beginning to turn.

And all too late for Arr. He had known the disease would find him eventually, though admitting that he had succumbed to it was difficult – it was the most personal example of his failure imaginable, it wounded his pride no end, stoked his rage. He had known too that the Hylar's efforts to treat the disease, hideously under-resourced because of the war, would fail. But he had not forgotten Tol.

He needed to be patient. He allowed his automed to give him another injection and sat, gills wheezing, watching the transmitter, and waiting.

"How can you be serious?" Malik demanded. "He's the cause of all this! Leave him to rot!"

"I would like nothing more," Tol admitted. "But that would go against my oath. It would go against who I am."

Malik just turned away. Tol had found him onboard the battle station and told him in person about the identity of the approaching ship and its owner. She had feared he would react this way. She had almost decided not to tell him, but she had found her courage.

"Would you leave him?" she asked abruptly.

"He isn't the only infected Hylar here, Scales," Malik said, looking back at her. "Our duty is to all of them, not just him."

"I know, but you're avoiding my question."

Malik sighed heavily. "I would probably leave him, yes. Because I'm not as good a person as you are."

The admission surprised Tol.

"I'm not a good person either," she said. "I want to leave him. Let him suffer."

"But you won't, will you?"

She realized he was right. The irony of Arr's infection had, in her mind, become a double-edged sword. It was like the galaxy was testing her, just as it was punishing Arr. Testing her to the limits of her goodness and her honesty.

"I am required to heal the sick, to the best of my abilities," she said. "And that is what I will do. Beyond that, Arr will get nothing."

"You'll allow him onboard?" Malik asked, still with a degree of incredulity.

"No. He has his own facilities on his ship, and I don't want him mixing with the other patients. We don't know which strain he's carrying. Besides, I don't want him anywhere near anything important to me, and that includes my ship and crew. And you."

"Hylar romanticism at its finest." He smirked, clearly trying to pick her up. "I'm not sure you should be with him alone on his ship though."

"Everyone else is needed to finish clearing the station and getting these patients stable and out of the system," Tol said. "I'll be fine. I'll administer the antivirals, monitor him for a few cycles, then call it job done and get out."

"You're implying we should go before you're ready to leave?" Malik asked.

"We knew we couldn't stay here long," Tol pointed out. "Doolak Plague or not, this is still part of the frontline, and I don't want to put you in any greater danger."

"Just inject that slime fish quickly and get back to us," Malik said. "Or do what I'd do, and put him out of his misery."

Tol reestablished contact with Arr via voice transmission. He sounded breathless and only semi-coherent, certainly worse than he had first appeared. Perhaps he was too far gone? She forced herself to set aside such thoughts. If she was going to do this, she was going to do it properly.

Arr's ship had docked against the Arnus Lax, so she boarded it from the battle station. An automed met her in a pristine, white plasticon corridor and led her to a similarly bright and sterile medical chamber.

Arr was waiting for her, slumped in a high-backed chair. She saw immediately that his condition was bad, though not as far advanced as the poor souls onboard the station.

"I knew you would come," the Jol Hylar wheezed, bubbles floating through the increasingly murky water of his containment sphere.

"Be silent," Tol snapped, warding away the automeds drifting around her and pulling her medicum from her back. She had brought what she hoped would be sufficient supplies to treat Arr. If not, too bad – there were enough other patients in need anyway.

She ran a quintisensor inspection, administered the initial injections, and waited. Arr, wisely, avoided addressing her – he seemed to lapse in and out of consciousness, but his vitals remained stable.

Eventually, Malik got in touch, connecting from the station's comms hub via her personal bead.

"That's the last of the living salvaged," he told her. "We've lost one already onboard the *Renewal*, but the rest are receiving treatment. One is even responsive already."

"Good job," Tol told him, stepping back out into the corridor momentarily. Every fiber of her being wanted to leave Arr behind and rejoin Malik, but she knew she couldn't, not if she didn't want to betray everything she believed in. "You should depart now. There's no sense in delaying."

"We can't just leave you," Malik said.

"Every moment you stay places the rest of the crew and the patients in greater danger," Tol replied. "You have to go, for them. I'll be fine."

"So the longer I stay, the more danger I'm in, but the longer you stay, you'll still be fine?" Malik asked. "That's not very Hylar-logic of you."

"Well, I'm bad at being a Hylar. That's why they banished me. Now get going."

"You'll join us at the rendezvous at Capistan?"

"Yes. The station's automated one-shot shuttles are functioning, I checked."

"How long."

"Three day-cycles. Four at most."

"Fine. If you're not there, I'll hunt you to the Jol's deepest depths."

"Don't threaten me with a fun time. I'll see you soon."

CHAPTER TWENTY-SIX

MECATOL REX,
GALACTIC CAPITAL OF THE LAZAX EMPIRE

Atz was still alive when Syd arrived in the capital.

Mecatol had changed. After so long, the decay gnawing away at the Lazax imperium had started to show itself on the surface. With the withdrawal of Hylar loyal to Jol-Nar, the advanced atmospheric scrubbers responsible for keeping the air of the capital clear had started to break down, leading to a perpetual smog that shrouded the city all the way up to the tips of the heavenscrapers. Less money was spent cleaning the outsides of the towering structures as well, leaving their exteriors blackened with pollutants.

Even the imperial gardens, which Syd passed through on his way to the hospice, had started to fall into disarray. Fewer Winnu were employed in maintaining the great spread of horticulture, and plants had started sprawling and growing wild, interspersed with weeds and other invasives. The pathways were overgrown, and even the old moontrees looked sickly and disheveled, hung with dark ivy.

Nobody seemed to care, but then Syd had long reconciled

himself to that. It wasn't so much that they were actively avoiding the steady degeneration, more that they were willfully oblivious. Living amidst it, day by day, year by year, the changes weren't as stark when viewed up close. Viewed with time and distance though, it was all nothing less than tragic.

Even being present on Mecatol made Syd miserable, but he did his best to battle through it. Tutur had been right. He was being a coward, hiding out on Archon Ren, wallowing in self-pity. He still believed there was nothing he could now do to make a difference, but he would at least pay his respects to Atz. He could surely afford that particular debt.

The old Xxcha was in a medical cradle, drip wires coiling from his sagging scales. His breathing was coming in slow, ghastly rattles. Winnu were tending to him, but they stepped respectfully back as Syd entered with Erial in tow. Atz seemed to sense his arrival, and his eyes slowly opened as he looked up with rheumy eyes.

"Syd," he wheezed, attempting to rise with a creak. Syd hurried forward and put a hand on his chest plate, keeping him down.

"You show me greater respect by lying still and conserving your strength, old friend," he told him, mustering a smile. It was hard, seeing someone reduced to this, wasting away in bed.

"I was told not to contact you," Atz croaked softly, with the barest hint of a smile. "They said you would not come, but I knew you would. For the empire."

"For you," Syd corrected, but Atz carried on regardless.

"I am sorry for what I have done to you down the years. How much I have asked. I ruined you. Your career, your life. All in service to the empire."

"I gave that freely," Syd said, as Erial drew up a chair for him to sit in, clasping one of Atz's bony hands in his own. "I was proud to."

Atz said nothing, his eyes becoming unfocused for a moment.

"I know of a Hylar doctor," Syd said. "Exiled by the universities. Her name is Harial Tol. I'm sure she could provide you with the care you need, perhaps even–"

"It is too late for all that, my friend," Atz murmured, becoming lucid again. "I am ready for what awaits me. I wish only to face it knowing I have done everything in my power to preserve our people, our empire. And that, in truth, is why I asked for you to come."

Syd had suspected as much. He did not begrudge it. Time was too short for that.

"Tell me what you wish from me," he urged instead.

"He must be stopped," Atz said. He didn't need to say who "he" was.

"Is he in the capital right now?" Syd asked. He didn't want this. It horrified him, it repulsed him. It was what he had been running and hiding from, for decades now. But he forced himself to stay by Atz's side and hear him out.

"Yes," Atz said. "He and his warmongers are speaking before the emperor tomorrow, in council. They are voting to recall the imperial fleet from its exercises at Myock and prepare it for combat. It will be the final phase before he has the war he's always craved. War, and when it is won, absolute power over all other sentients."

"Only if he wins," Syd pointed out. "There are no guarantees of that."

"So many of the great powers have spent themselves in their infighting," Atz said. "Letnev and human, N'orr and Jol-Nar. Billions dead over the past seventy-two years. Fleets wrecked, planets reduced to ruin. Terrible things have happened while our emperor and most advisors have looked the other way."

Syd knew he was right, and the weight of that acknowledgment was almost more than he could bear.

"We tried," he said, knowing he need not, but unable to stay silent. "Some of us tried."

"I know," Atz said. "And I believe one day others will know that too, and appreciate it. But we cannot stop now. I would do it myself, but…"

"All you need to do is rest," Syd said, voice firm. "I will take care of matters. One last effort, for the empire, for the Lazax… for all the galaxy. It isn't over yet."

He saw light kindle in his old friend's eyes, a light Syd hadn't seen for many years.

"Thank you," he said, settling back and sighing slowly. "Thank you."

Syd told Atz stories about his time back on Archon Ren, describing the Q'waar trees in bloom and the latest debates he had heard in the Ssaalel. He said nothing about the devastation wreaked on Archon Tau – Syd suspected Atz already knew of that anyway.

Atz died that night, with Syd by his side. He stayed sitting for a long time, even after the Winnu had carried the body out, staring at the stripped-down cradle where Atz had lain.

It was all coming to an end. There was nothing to be done now except throw himself into the fire, and see what he could drag out. He had made preparations for a day like this, years before, when there had still been hope.

As the day began to dawn, light fighting its way weakly through the miasma of pollutants, he finally roused himself and called for Erial. The dutiful Winnu had insisted on remaining on call just outside despite Syd's insistence that she go and get some sleep in one of the visitor's suites. She was clearly doing her best to mask her tiredness as she stood straight-backed before Syd.

"I need you to deliver a sealed data packet to eight different addresses today," he said, pausing to calibrate his savant. "Physical copies only, and handed over in person. I will send you the identities of the eight in a moment. It will probably take all day, but it's imperative that it is done with speed and precision."

"My parents were called Speed and Precision, sir," she said. Syd blinked, before realizing she was making a joke. To his own surprise, he laughed.

"I am not sure what I did to deserve you, Erial, but I count myself fortunate to have such a dutiful assistant, especially now," he said, noting how new vigor seemed to enter her tired expression at the rare, unexpected praise.

"Where will you be, sir, if I might ask?" she said.

"I'm afraid you may not," Syd said heavily. "There are some… private matters I must attend. Private, even from a loyal Winnu like you. If you have need of me, ping my savant and I will respond as soon as I am able."

CHAPTER TWENTY-SEVEN

Tol worked to save Arr's life. She knew it wasn't going to be an easy task, even in a practical sense. The doctor had contracted a variant she had labeled as C17, one of the strands most closely related to the original outbreak. It was fast-acting, and produced a number of rare symptoms such as delirium. Beating it required the full gamut of tricks Tol had learned over the decades spent battling the virus.

Arr wisely maintained his silence while she injected him, cleaned his gills, and drained and refreshed his containment sphere. He continued to phase in and out of consciousness. At the end of the first cycle, while he slept, Tol left the automeds monitoring him and went to explore the ship.

It was small and minimalist. She doubted the fact it was rigged out with a full medical operating room was due to the fact that Arr had predicted his own infection, and had wanted the best private facilities available. More likely, he was now conducting his sick experiments from this mobile base, rather than on Muaat. Rumor had it that the Gashlai had rebelled and wiped out the Jol-Nar colonizers while they had been preoccupied by plague and war. Tol hoped it was true. The only pity was that Arr had left before the uprising.

Still, she could find no direct evidence of Arr's grim work, at least not as brazenly displayed as it had been on Muaat. There were no dissected N'orr, for starters. She found her way to the bridge, unchallenged, curiosity mixed with dread over what she might discover. It was nondescript though, the helm overseen by an astral familiar that was currently deactivated as part of its docking protocols.

She checked what she took to be Arr's captain's chair for contaminants and, finding it clear, sat down, swiveling to face the ship's databanks. She had barely done so when the automed back in the operating room pinged her. Arr's vitals were struggling. Sighing – a human habit she had picked up from Malik – she rose once more and hurried back.

Arr slipped deeper into his delirium. He began to speak, just mumbles at first that snapped suddenly into full coherence.

"There's too many," he spat, infected matter from his throat clouding the recently refreshed water of his containment sphere. "I've killed so many and there are still so many!"

"So many of what?" Tol asked, swabbing the clammy gray scales of Arr's exposed upper right arm, stick-thin and frail.

"Insects," Arr hissed. "N'orr. Infestation. They infest everything. Consuming, always consuming. They will eat the whole galaxy if they are not stopped!"

The last thing Tol wanted to hear was Arr's foul ravings, but he was starting to flatline again, and she had to try to bring him back. She didn't, however, have to agree with him.

"They won't eat the galaxy," she scoffed. "Those models have been disproven. The Sardakk N'orr are no more a threat to the other civilizations than any of us."

"Locusts," Arr went on, seemingly oblivious. "Fat-bellied locusts. They will drink our oceans dry, then consume us! But I can stop them. The plague didn't work, so I have used more traditional methods. Beam and bullet. The war sun."

"The what?" Tol asked as she injected a remixoid injection, trying to get him to focus.

"The war sun," Arr repeated breathlessly. "Annihilation for the foe. Not just the N'orr, but all the enemies of Jol-Nar!"

"What is the war sun?" Tol pressed as Arr briefly locked up, his whole body rigid, jaw clenched. He shook before the remixoid kicked in and he was able to answer.

"A ship. It defies classification. The campus war fleet calls it a grade A plus-plus. The perfect death-dealer."

"What's so special about it?" Tol asked as she administered the next injection, anthazine, designed to quell the fever her quintisensor was detecting. She was working automatically, asking questions to keep Arr focused, only half-listening to the responses.

"Vast," Arr spluttered. "Indestructible. Devastating. Quad-shielding, mega-beam lance arrays, FTL-drive missiles. It is beautiful."

It sounded anything but to Tol, but even delirious, she could sense the rapture such weaponry caused in Arr. It would almost have been endearing had the subject matter not been so monstrous.

The last dose of antivirals did the trick. Arr's vitals became regular again. He settled, drifting off to sleep.

Tol realized how exhausted she was. Even accounting for Hylar sleep patterns, which were more forgiving than most, she had been active for almost two full cycles. It was catching up with her.

She found the ship's decontamination suite and hosed her suit, then stripped and, after checking there were no particles in the hydro block, submerged herself. Arr had done a good job at containing his own infection. The sensation of being submerged brought a deep calm she hadn't realized she had been missing until that moment.

She slept, adrift in the silence, dreamless and still. Eventually her savant, still strapped to her wrist, woke her. It was time for Arr's next medications.

Just what the doctor had been talking about during his delirium? His expertise had always been in weapons manufacturing, and doubtless he had played an integral role in arming the Jol-Nar against the N'orr, but what was the war sun?

Arr continued to stabilize, his fever and delirium departing, though he continued to sleep as he entered the recovery phase. It seemed he was going to survive. Tol had never experienced mixed emotions at such a realization.

During the third cycle, she returned to the bridge and accessed the ship's data logs. Morbid curiosity made her do it. She wanted to find out what Arr had been doing in the decades since her banishment. She hoped to find a sliver of good in there somewhere, though she knew in reality it would likely only make her hate the doctor more.

The logs held records of not only Arr's whereabouts, but data he had been receiving and reviewing, catalogued over a number of decades. She started as far back as the systems would allow, and began to work her way toward the present.

Tol was quickly astounded by how integral a role he had played in the initial mobilization and early war years. His presence supplying the Sol Federation against the Letnev was also recorded. Hidden beneath the more mundane reports, however, were hints of what was to come. There were communications with a member of the Circle of Regents, Shole, about a "super weapon" that Tol realized had to be the war sun.

It had taken years of work, based out of New Escha and using the vast resources being pillaged from Muaat. There had been setbacks, delays, and a relentlessly inflating budget. Shole had visited in person to urge the work along as the war had turned drastically against the Jol-Nar. Arr had been repeatedly threatened with removal from the project, but his burning ambitions and his hatred of the N'orr seemed to fuel him through each new difficulty.

Finally, the war sun had been deployed, only a month ago. It had been used in action for the first time at the battle of Saudor, with Arr himself onboard, monitoring it throughout the engagement. Viz streams from other Jol-Nar ships showed the war sun entering combat, and Tol had to spend a moment understanding just what she was looking at.

The war ship was indeed vast, the size of a small moon. Its semi-spherical core was studded, like a Nar spike-blower fish, with shield pylons, defense turrets, beam projection lances, communications arrays and command towers, a leviathan that made even the super-heavy carriers and dreadnoughts that clustered around it seem like mere minnows. As it advanced into the heart of the N'orr swarm-fleet, it seemed to light up like a star, first with the blaze of its potent shields as they deflected planet-killing amounts of energy and ordinance from the N'orr, and then with the brilliance of its own weapon systems as they responded in kind.

The engagement was less a fleet action than a massacre. Tol stared in horrified rapture as the gargantuan warship reduced whole squadrons of enemy cruisers to atoms. A single concentrated salvo of mega-beam fire could sear through a N'orr capital ship's shields and bisect it, leaving it to hemorrhage oxygen before internal detonations wrecked what was left. The N'orr's return fire couldn't even strip away the monstrosity's shields before they had regenerated and were back up again.

The surviving N'orr ships scattered and fled. Tol accessed the after-action reports, including the data breakdown. The estimated N'orr loss of life sickened her. The Hylar casualties were listed only as "minor/negligible."

That explained why Saudor had been such a stunning victory. Arr had turned the tide of the war. What could the N'orr deploy to stop such an engine of annihilation? Once the war sun and its attendant fleet entered orbit above Quinarra, the Sardakk N'orr would find themselves dependent on Hylar mercy. And if it was left to figures like Arr, there would be none.

Tol tore herself away from the logs, shivering. She should not have looked. She should not have further compromised her attempts at caring for her patient. But how could she go on? How could she heal a monster like Atak Arr?

When she next checked on him, he was awake. He looked much improved, sitting up straight now, his eyes focused. He greeted Tol as she entered.

"I take it the prognosis is positive?" he said. Tol composed herself before answering, studying the outputs of her quintisensor reading.

"Vital signs are stable, temperature reading is back within acceptable limits, subject shows full coherency. Inflammation is reduced. Overall improvement stands at twenty-three percent. Likeliness of limited recovery, ninety-one percent, likeliness of full recovery, eighty-one percent."

"I find those odds to be tolerable," Arr said. "You have done well, under-doctor."

For some reason the compliment, coupled with the use of her old title, stung Tol more than Arr's previous arrogance.

"You don't deserve those odds," she snapped. "They're better than the ones you've given thousands of others."

Surprise momentarily broke through Arr's reserved expression.

"You have long known of my work," he said. "Yet now you make aspersions?"

"Just count yourself fortunate that I am not a murderer like you. I have sworn to preserve life, and I will not renege on that."

Arr looked thoughtful for a minute, then offered up a small smile.

"I spoke to you, did I?" he asked. "While I was in a state of delirium? I have a very vague recollection. I can only imagine what I told you."

"Nothing I didn't already know," Tol snarled.

"Then why this renewed aggression? I believed you had come to terms with this... arrangement. Unless you have been looking where you should not?"

"I've seen the war sun," Tol said, giving into the urge to confront Arr.

"It is a weapon, and we are at war," Arr said dismissively. "If I continue to receive support and funding, it is only the beginning."

"You are not content with the deaths you have already caused?" Tol said. "So many millions of your own people, and now millions of another."

"By killing millions, I save billions," Arr snapped. "Or perhaps I should be like you, and stand by as this degenerate empire allows the likes of the N'orr to devour the galaxy. You are too short sighted, your morality too narrow and childlike, to appreciate these things, but history will be kind to me."

"The N'orr's history won't be," Tol said, turning to leave.

Arr continued to improve over the next two cycles. He was even able to rise and move around the medical suite, though Tol kept him contained there, for her own sanity as much as for medical reasons. She returned periodically to Arnus Lax, where she had already prepped a long-reach FTL shuttle for the journey to Capistan. She was intending to leave at the start of the next cycle.

Then, not long after waking from a deep water-sleep, she was alerted by a series of notifications on the scanner system onboard Arr's ship. She checked the display, and froze.

Vessels had translated in-system some time earlier, numerous and large. While the exact classes were unknown, the nature of them was certain – Sardakk N'orr capital ships.

Tol swore vehemently. Malik had been right. They had stayed far too long.

She tried to run the possibilities. Would they simply destroy the station from afar? If they boarded, they would discover the fate of the station's crew and garrison. Maybe she could fire an escape pod, but that felt even more likely to draw the fleet's ire, and consequently their fire. Perhaps she could convince them that she was the only survivor, and that the whole place was quarantined?

She doubted it. Ironically, considering Arr's depraved intentions, the N'orr were one of the species most resistant to the Doolak Plague. If they were intending on advancing through the system en route to Jol-Nar campus-worlds beyond, there was no way they would leave the battle station untouched in their wake.

Would they spare her, given she wasn't Jol-Nar? She had only had a few dealings with N'orr, and she was probably guilty of slipping into an arrogant Hylar worldview that thought of them as mindless insectoid drones. Would they differentiate her from the likes of Arr? And what if they realized just who Arr was? If they knew he was behind the creation of the war sun?

Play dead? Too much of a risk. Too likely the N'orr would open fire, even if the station was unresponsive. She had to reach out.

She recorded a quick audio message, explaining that the station was abandoned and under quarantine and pinging it in the direction of the oncoming fleet. There was no sign of a response. As the other ships moved in typical N'orr swarm patterns to envelope the station, one exotrireme made directly for the strut where Arr's ship was docked.

Tol tried her best not to panic. She would talk with them.

They weren't locusts, like Arr insisted. They were sentients, capable of reasoning. That was what she told herself.

"Were you going to tell me there was a N'orr fleet approaching?" hissed a voice, making Tol jump. It was Arr. She had been so fixated on the scan returns and comms array she hadn't noticed him enter the bridge. He was stooped, one hand supporting himself against the frame of the entrance hatch, his containment sphere water murky with effluvium.

"My savant is linked to the ship's systems," he wheezed. "It alerted me."

"You shouldn't be out of containment," Tol said.

"They will kill me if they discover my identity," Arr said, ignoring her admonishment. "I am known to them. My work is known."

"The war sun?"

A proximity alarm began to ring, warning of the exotrireme, now almost up alongside them.

"Yes," Arr hissed. "Tell them this place carries disease, that they must not step foot onboard."

"I've tried, but I doubt that will make them stop," Tol pointed out. "You were a fool to come here, and I should have left as soon as the station was evacuated."

There was a slamming impact that shook the deck beneath them and made the metal bulkhead groan. Tol steadied herself, while Arr fell, sprawling across the floor plates. After a long hesitation, Tol helped him back to his feet.

"They're boarding," she said, glancing at the ship's external viz displays. A shuttle had been launched from the exotrireme's flank and had latched itself to the exterior of the bridge blister. The realization was accompanied by the thrum of plasma cutters. Tol experienced a moment of paralyzing fear as her thoughts were transported back in time to T19, above Muaat, to the moment the tyros had come for her.

"Tell them I'm with you," Arr wheezed, clutching desperately at her wrist. "Tell them I'm one of the doctors on your staff, and I am sick."

Tol wrenched herself free and glared at him. His words had broken through her panic, revulsion driving out fear. "You want me to pretend you're here to save lives, when you were the one who caused all this? Have you no shame?"

"An invented construct, one of the many that stands in the way of greater progress and, in this case, survival," Arr snapped, still relentlessly clinical.

Tol was spared the need for a reply. There was a clang, and the bridge hatch, its locks broken, swung inward.

The Sardakk N'orr boarded Arr's ship.

They were led by a Tekklar Elite, a subspecies Tol had never before encountered up close, and one she would never forget. The insectoid was huge, barely fitting through the hatchway, his frame armored in scarred plates of green-and-yellow mottled chitin that looked as thick and solid as the prow of a grav tank. His head was similarly protected, with a targeting attachment over one eye and a communications muzzle, complete with ambassador translator, affixed to his mandibles. In one set of double limbs he carried a diffraction shield, the energy sheet activated, while the other set bore a mesh cannon, the flared muzzle swinging round to bring Tol and Arr into its wide arc of fire.

The monstrosity scuttled heavily in, followed by more

regular-sized N'orr swarmers, armed with beam and solid shot rifles modified to fit their insect frames. They spread out across the bridge as the Tekklar loomed over the two Hylar.

"Hands," the N'orr buzzed over his ambassador, the series of ticking noises he had made translated into univoca. Tol immediately raised hers, followed after a brief hesitation by Arr. The doctor was shaking, though she couldn't tell if it was from fear or hatred. Probably both.

"Do you surrender?" the Tekklar demanded.

"Yes," Tol said, as though that wasn't already highly apparent.

"Your battle station reads no life forms," the Tekklar continued. "It is abandoned? Or a Hylar trick?"

"Only the dead are onboard now," Tol said, amazed at how calm her voice sounded. "There has been an outbreak of the Doolak Plague. I was sent by the empire to treat the victims and stop it from spreading further."

The Tekklar looked at her, its one bug-like eye just as inscrutable as the purple glare of the target optic covering the other.

"Would you treat us if we were sick, Hylar?" he asked, the automated tone of the ambassador harsh and uncompromising.

"Yes," Tol said, doing her best not to sound desperate. "I may be Hylar, but I am not Jol-Nar. I heal all."

"We are not sick," the Tekklar said dismissively. "The swarm are not as weak as your water-kind. And you do not look like Jol-Nar, not like most."

That was an unexpected relief, and Tol supposed it made sense. A Tekklar Elite would be used to dealing with Jol-Nar military – killing them, most likely – and most of those were Jol Hylar. Of course, the same could not be said of Arr.

"If you are a healer, what is this one?" the N'orr super soldier said, gesturing with his heavy weapon at Arr. The doctor spoke before Tol could.

"I am her superior on this expedition. I have been sent by the Lazax to oversee her work."

"You are not Jol-Nar?"

"No, I am like her. A servant of the empire. We were both banished for our disputes with the universities. We serve only the Lazax."

The fear Tol felt was eclipsed by her anger at his brazen lying. Of course, she should have expected it. But it was just one more act of deviousness heaped upon all the others. It frustrated her beyond words.

"But you look like Jol-Nar," the Tekklar pressed, looking back at Tol. "Is this true?"

"What he says is true," Tol said. She knew she should stop there, but the words broke free. "About me."

She sensed Arr freeze. She had never felt so liberated, so powerful. She continued before he could speak, or before she herself could pause to consider what she was doing.

"But how he identifies himself is false. He is not my superior, and unlike me he was not exiled by the universities. He is a doctor of Jol-Nar. His name is Atak Arr."

The other Sardakk N'orr surrounding them had been clicking and ticking back and forth between one another throughout the exchange, but at Tol's words there arose a great chirring, an angry susurration that drowned out even the sound of Arr's angry denials.

"Arr," the Tekklar snapped, whole body going rigid, battle-ready. "We know this identity. Arr the warmonger. He who birthed the star of destruction. You help him? You serve him?"

"I told you, I am a healer," Tol replied as firmly as she dared, taking a cautionary step away from Arr, fearing what was about to happen, even as a part of her, buried deep, was exulting. "I am sworn to fight infection and sickness wherever it is found. But Doctor Arr has a sickness I cannot cure. I have done my duty. Now, with your permission, I intend to depart, and return to Mecatol Rex to make my report."

"Then you may include G'Hom T'cha in your report," the Tekklar declared. "And write that he did this!"

He deactivated his detractor shield and slammed the pommel plate into Arr's containment sphere. It cracked, and foggy water came spurting out. As the doctor stumbled, another of the Tekklar's limbs snatched Arr's right arm and, with a crack, wrenched it off with no more difficulty than a child pulling apart an unwanted toy.

Arr's scream was lost in the deafening chitter of the other N'orr as they swarmed in, reaching and snatching at the doctor. Tol stumbled for the hatch leading back into the battle station, terror and revulsion spurring her on. She should have been stronger. She should have matched Arr's malice and manipulation with dignity, to the very end.

But she was weak. Perhaps she could atone for that in time. Arr, however, was making his own bitter atonement right there and then, and it was long overdue.

CHAPTER TWENTY-EIGHT

MECATOL REX,
GALACTIC CAPITAL OF THE LAZAX EMPIRE

After Erial had departed on her latest task, Syd changed into an anonymous set of old clerical clothes, donned a rasping smog nullifier that had the added bonus of concealing most of his face, and took a carrum out of the Core and down into the city's under-levels. He spent a brief period speaking to a similarly shrouded figure outside of a dive bar popular with visiting offworlders of the lower sort, then returned to the high government quarter via an indirect route.

He forced himself to focus on what lay ahead, and not what he had just done. Today would be the final session for the imperial council's debate on the recall and activation of the war fleet at Myock. If Zey and the Accelerationists won the ensuing vote, scheduled to be held some days later, the Lazax would be on a formal war footing. Syd had no doubts about how the other great civilizations would react.

This was the last chance, but in truth Syd held out no hope. He was doing it for Atz, and partly for himself, so he knew that he would at least be able to claim he had tried to the very end.

While he had not visited the capital for a long time, he had retained his primary apartment in the Core, and it was there that he made brief contact with Erial to ensure she was managing her tasks – which, of course, she was – before changing back into his formal robes. At least he would look the part, even if he no longer felt able to play it.

He walked back through the gardens to the imperial palace, passing the monolithic structures of the Tithes and Records Office and the Hall of Cartographers, looming out of the perpetual smog. The palace itself was one of the few places the capital's decay hadn't quite yet touched, its massive permacore walls and golden domes still gleaming despite the foul miasma that swaddled it. Once, the sight of it had filled him with pride in the achievements of his people and hope for the future. Now it seemed like nothing more than an indulgent monument to arrogance and shortsightedness.

A bell began to toll out across the gardens, calling the imperial council to session. A few other Lazax who had been standing outside conversing started making their way into the side annex that contained the council chamber. Syd joined them, unnoticed, and lingered until the rest had entered.

Unlike the vast, circular hall that housed the Galactic Council, the space the imperial council occupied was smaller and more intimate, a rectangular chamber with tiered seating to the left and right of a central aisle that led to a dais that housed another version of the imperial throne. Unlike the supposed equality of the Galactic Council, the tiers were strictly hierarchical, with seating determined by length of service and the number of merits awarded. The most senior members therefore sat on the frontmost tiers and closest to the throne, while the more junior took the rearmost closest to the doors.

The place was almost full when Syd entered, pausing briefly as he was checked by the Winnu guards on the doors. He removed his smog nullifier, and saw a moment's surprise on the Winnu's face before his expression became guarded.

"My apologies, Eminent Councilor Syd," he said. "We have not seen you at the meetings for some time."

"And I suspect you won't again," Syd replied humorlessly, walking past. He would have preferred only to enter once the meeting was actually in session, for maximum impact, but the emperor was always the last to arrive, and after that the doors were sealed.

The chamber was busy with the chatter of the members. Syd slipped up onto a rear bench near the doors, nodding guardedly to the more junior councilors around him. Most of them just stared. Word spread rapidly, and he pretended not to notice the turning heads, the whispers, the subtle gestures. He fixed his gaze instead on the far corner of the chamber.

On Sorian Sai Zey, sitting amongst his cronies, leaning back with casual disregard as he waited for the session to start. Someone tugged the corner of his robes and outright pointed toward where Syd was sitting. Their eyes locked. He was too far away for Syd to be able to tell if there was fear there, but he could make out the other councilor's smile as it slowly spread across his face. Good, Syd thought. Let him be overconfident. Let him feel safe, knowing his enemies only had one card left to play. It would be the final card of this game.

The bell tolled again, announcing the emperor's approach.

The assembly rose with a rustle of robes, a perfect silence falling where moments before there had been expectant discourse. Syd tried to quell the nervousness that had been gradually building, letting his simmering anger toward Zey and his fatalistic disregard for what he knew was coming drown it out. It was much too late for uncertainty.

The emperor's guards entered first, dressed in glittering ceremonial armor. Formerly they were led by a duo of gold-plated Tekklar Elite G'hom, but the N'orr had long withdrawn them from imperial service, throwing every member of the swarm legions into their war with the genocidal Jol-Nar. Now the duty was performed by Winnu guards.

After them came the royal dignitaries who arrayed themselves around the throne – the imperial chancellor, the keeper of the vestries, the imperial cartographer, the galactic consul, and others. Finally, followed only by his pages and the last set of guards, came Emperor Salai Sai Corian himself.

When Syd had been in his prime he had always felt Corian looked so young. He had barely been of age when he inherited the imperial throne, and seemed to have maintained that youthfulness for many years, perhaps by artifice. No artifice could hide the changes of the past few decades though.

His Imperial Majesty had been reduced to powdering his features white and drowning himself in the gold and silver ornamentation of his office in an effort to hide how, just like his empire, he seemed to be withering. Syd caught the sickly sweet smell of the perfumes used to hide the mustiness of his makeup and heavy, fur-trimmed robes as he glided past, standing upon a small, gilded anti-grav unit, staring serenely ahead. In one hand he carried the imperial staff, a grand version of those carried by Lazax dignitaries, while in the other the galactic orb floated just above his upturned palm, its surface studded with jewels representing the homeworlds of the great civilizations. It was a display of pomp and finery that once had thrilled Syd, but now left him feeling cold and bitter.

The procession made its way with painful slowness down the aisle, as behind them the doors were shut and barred with a reverberating thud. Corian's entourage took their places around the throne, the chancellor accepting the staff while the galactic consul took the orb, allowing the emperor to take his seat. There was a pause as the pages settled and arrayed his heavy robes around him, before all was still and silent.

The chancellor struck the base of the staff against the floor, once. The entire assembly cried out.

"Long live the emperor! Long live the imperium of a thousand civilizations! Pax Magnifica!"

"Bellum Gloriosum," a section of the chamber, mostly around Zey, added loudly. The Accelerationist faction had taken to including the second half of the old imperial motto, long discontinued from formal use. Glorious war. Syd felt his anger spike.

The chancellor gave the usual opening benediction, then began to read out the topic of discussion – the final vote on the orders to be sent to the imperial fleet. Wordlessly, Syd stood up and made his way down into the aisle, then started to approach the throne. The chancellor's droning voice faltered, and the rest of the chamber turned their eyes upon him.

Syd knew fear then, but also a vicious, bloody-minded determination. Atz had been right to call on him. Damn all other strategies and ploys, he should have done this long ago.

He advanced on the throne until he saw the Winnu guards begin to nervously reach for their weapons. Then, he halted, and dropped to both knees, like a supplicant.

"My glorious emperor," he said loudly, bowing his head for good measure and spreading all four arms. "I crave your forgiveness, and that of my fellow councilors, for this unscheduled interruption. With your imperial permission, I request that I be allowed to make a short address prior to the commencement of today's debate."

Stunned silence greeted his words. He kept his arms wide and eyes down. He had been tempted to forge straight into what he had planned to say, but better to at least try to show a degree of respect, even if he no longer felt it.

It was the imperial chancellor who recovered first.

"This is an outrageous break in protocols," he began to angrily declaim, but the voice of the emperor silenced him.

"It is... unexpected. But you have served me well for many years, Eminent Councilor Ibna Vel Syd. I did not know you had returned from Archon Ren. I trust you would not make this interruption without cause. You may gaze upon me, and speak."

Syd did so, rising with some difficulty. He took only a second to collect himself before he began to address Salai Sai Corian.

"In truth, Your Imperial Majesty, I am not here to debate the rights and the wrongs of the fleet's presence in Myock, or even to decry the decay and stagnation that has befallen our once-proud empire. I come only to impart facts. The fact that there are some within this chamber who have neither your benevolent rule, nor the preservation of the Lazax imperium in their best interests. The fact that those self-same so-called councilors have brought war upon this imperium, and intend to bring it upon our species and perhaps this very world."

"Ridiculous," called a voice. Syd recognized it immediately as Zey, but refused to deign to turn his head toward where he sat on the benches, instead keeping his eyes fixed firmly on the emperor as Zey continued.

"Is this really what you have dragged yourself off Archon Ren for, Eminent Councilor? To waste the time of this chamber and His Imperial Majesty with your tired old conspiracy theories?"

"Tired and old I may be, Your Majesty, but the only conspirator here is Eminent Councilor Sorian Sai Zey," Syd exclaimed, quick as a flash. "He and the Accelerationists have been undermining the Pax Lazax for almost a century. He has fomented unrest among the civilizations great and small, among species that look to us in this chamber to ensure peace and stability. We have turned a blind eye while the traitors in our midst breed internecine conflicts, wars that now engulf more than half the galaxy."

"The eminent councilor has taken leave of his senses," Zey barked. Syd half-sensed that he had risen from his bench.

"I wish that were the case, Your Majesty," he responded, still looking to the emperor. "I wish, in my old age, that I were reduced to witlessness, and that my knowledge in these matters was misplaced. But it is not. Zey is a traitor. He has conspired with fellow Accelerationists in the Letnev and the Sol Federation, and quite possibly with the Universities of Jol-Nar, to cause chaos. He hopes to use this chaos to agitate for greater control from Mecatol Rex. He wants to create an empire based not on peace, harmony, and common progress, but one founded in the tenets of military rule and iron Lazax domination. That is not this empire, Your Majesty. Not your empire. Not the empire we founded, by mutual consent with our fellow sentients, after our brave, wise ancestors overthrew the tyranny of the Mahact. Zey's empire would just be another form of that tyranny."

"Your Imperial Majesty, I demand that Syd be removed from this chamber," Zey said, voice hoarse with fury.

"I am not the only one who believes all this to be the case," Syd went on forcefully, resolving despite his anger to plow on and ignore what was happening around him. "Others are aware of Zey's destructive goals. In fact, it was no less than Eminent Councilor Atz, late of this chamber and respected by all, who first showed me the reality of what was unfolding, right beneath our eyes."

"Not only do you disgrace yourself, but now you seek to disgrace the late Eminent Councilor Atz too?" Zey shouted. "A noble Xxcha beloved by so many in this chamber, and so recently deceased! Do your depravities know no limit?"

"You disgrace him with your lies," Syd snapped, finally turning to confront Zey.

"He knew almost everything, from your liaising with the Letnev Resurgentists to your lobbying of those Federation politicians who wanted a military intervention at Quann. He sent me to monitor you, to find out the truth. My only regret is that I failed him, like I failed so many others. Well that ends now. I have come back from Archon Ren to destroy you, Sorian Sai Zey, and destroy the plot you have so long woven about us all. I will do that for our emperor, for our imperium, for the entire galaxy, and for all the billions who have lost their lives these past seventy-two years in wars that monsters like you have spawned."

The two Lazax glared at each other in the stunned silence that followed. It was all Syd could do not to stride to Zey's bench and strike him. Eventually, it was Zey who spoke, and now his voice was low and deadly as an envenomed dagger.

"Proof. If you are making these disgusting accusations, you must at least have proof."

Syd felt like the silence that hung on the end of Zey's words was so heavy it would crush him. He forced himself to answer.

"I do not have hard proof," he said. "Because you have always made sure there isn't any. But you know that I speak the truth, and I suspect others in this chamber do too. Your schemes lie exposed, Zey. The light shines upon you. You shall be allowed to skulk in the darkness with your sycophants and co-conspirators no longer."

"There you have it," Zey snapped, now addressing the rest of the chamber. "By his own admission. There is no proof, because everything Ibna Vel Syd has just said is a work of fantasy. A derangement born out of his own repeated failures. It is foolishness like this that has seen the irreversible decline of his career. None of us can blame him for his failure at Quann. But the truth is, he himself had a hand in creating the devastation we now must endure. Were it not for his incompetence, perhaps the crisis at the Passage might have been averted. It is understandable that it has weighed so heavily on his mind, understandable that it should erode him, year after year, as the empire plunges ever deeper into this crisis that we must now extract ourselves from. But to project his own failings into these fevered accusations – as inventive as they are…"

He trailed off rhetorically. Syd took a step toward him, done with debate, but the voice of the emperor stilled him.

"I have heard enough," he said, his voice frigid. "Eminent Councilor Zey is indeed correct in at least one matter. These accusations are outrageous. This chamber has never known anything like it. I will not deign to indulge it a moment longer."

In his own anger, Syd dared to try to interrupt the emperor, but Corian kept going.

"It is only because of your long legacy of service that I am not ordering you to be arrested immediately. As it stands, Syd, I command you to remove yourself from this chamber. Once today's matters have been dealt with, this council session will be extended and we shall vote on whether you should be stripped of your titles and membership. I expect you to await our verdict without making any further accusations."

Syd knew he had failed. It came as no surprise. Perhaps, in a time long past, he would have bowed toward the imperial throne, turned, and departed, as ordered. That was what his instincts wanted him to do, even now. But he did not.

"I intend no disrespect to you, benevolent emperor, nor your office, nor your retinue, nor my fellow councilors. But I will not adhere to those instructions, believing as I do that they come from your current misguidedness. Instead, I beseech my fellow councilors – consider what I have said. Consider how low we have all fallen, how far we are now from those bright ideals we once grasped firmly, with four hands. None of you will speak out in my defense, I am sure, but I hold out hope that many of you suspect, in your hearts, that there is truth in what I have said."

"Seize him," shouted Corian. The armored Winnu rushed

forward. Syd did nothing to oppose them, but continued to speak as they snatched him and began to drag him toward the door, his tone rising until it was ringing from the walls.

"You have to stop him! Don't recall the fleet! Don't feed the monster he has created, or it will consume us all!"

The doors were unbarred, and he was hauled out before they slammed in his face. The guards carried on, ejecting him beyond the palace steps and into the gardens. Without a word, they turned and marched back into the vast structure. Syd watched them, then took a few steps toward the nearest garden bench. He was able to make it before he collapsed.

It was over. Emotions surged, and he bowed his head as tears filled his eyes. Regret, rage, sorrow, shame, and with it all, an ugly relief that he tried, but failed to deny. He had done all he could. Or almost all. There were two parts left to play, two further actions that, in truth, he had long considered, but always rejected. He had already laid the groundwork for both. All that remained now was to follow through, and forever sully the name of Ibna Vel Syd.

"I saw what you did," Erial said later, when she rejoined Syd back in his apartment. "Other Winnu are talking about it. You've been removed from the council. There are reports all over the newscasters."

"Then that's something," Syd said stoically, not really wanting to discuss what had happened.

"Did you think it would make a difference?" Erial asked with a forwardness that surprised him. "Did you think the emperor would listen?"

"No," Syd answered bluntly. "But I had to try. For Atz,

and for myself. Or, for my past self. Right now, I don't care whether or not the emperor listens to my warnings. It's too late anyway."

"Maybe not," Erial said. "The final vote isn't for another three days. It might yet go against Zey and the Accelerationists."

Syd knew it was best to say nothing. He didn't want to implicate Erial in any of what was about to happen, at least until he could guarantee her safety.

"Your deliveries today were all a success?" he asked instead.

"All but one. The Hylar doctor, Tol. She's offworld. Her office said she is absent on business, but she was scheduled to be back yesterday."

"Doctor Tol's work often takes her to the edge of the Jol-Nar N'orr frontline," Syd said. "It is not unusual for her to be absent for extended periods. I am helping to fund her efforts combatting the Doolak Plague. Everyone else took receipt of the messages I gave you?"

"Yes, sir. It's quite the spread of contacts you still have here on Mecatol. Two freight hauler captains, a retired politician, junior administrators, and envoys."

"And you want to know what they've all got in common, and why I'm contacting them now, after I've been removed from the council," Syd surmised. "But you're too good a Winnu to actually ask."

"And you're too clever a Lazax for me."

"Clever enough to disregard flattery, anyway. You'll find out just what is happening soon enough. Until then, I have more contacts for you to reach out to."

He sent a series of identities and locations to her savant. She glanced down at them, then froze.

"The first one on this list," she said slowly. "Is Eminent Councilor Zey."

"It is," Syd acknowledged, "and you are to deliver that message to him directly. Be careful though. I have no doubt you will be followed."

"Understood," Erial nodded and, to Syd's surprise, grinned. "No offense, sir, but this is much more interesting than watching games of escar in a Q'waar tree."

"Interesting is one way to describe it," Syd allowed. "I fear it's going to become something a lot more than that very soon."

CHAPTER TWENTY-NINE

MECATOL REX,
GALACTIC CAPITAL OF THE LAZAX EMPIRE

Zey's response was slow, but when it came, it was just what Syd had hoped for. Zey agreed to speak with him in the imperial gardens, just across from the moontree where the two of them, with Atz and Marchu, had first discussed the matter of Quann.

Syd didn't tell Erial the meeting was going ahead. He told no one, bar the contact he had met in the dive bar down below the Core, just after Atz's death.

He considered dressing in his old, white ambassadorial robes, but rejected the idea. That was what he would have chosen to wear once, but that Syd was about to die. It would be wrong to try to emulate him.

Instead, he wore the brown clerical robes again, though he disdained the smog nullifier. He wanted Zey to look him in the face.

The meeting was set for dawn. Syd ensured he arrived early, standing in the half-dark beneath a row of sickly looking hifa trees, facing toward where the moontree still stood. Slowly, daylight began to struggle through the pollution, picking out the features of the surrounding garden, thick and overgrown.

It was cold. He drew his robes tighter, not wanting to be seen to shiver. He forced himself not to look too hard at the moontree across the path from where he was standing. In fact, he turned so that his back was to it, and Zey would have to face it when he arrived. There was no point in worrying now, he told himself.

Zey came alone, materializing slowly from the smog. He was wearing the golden formals of an imperial councilor, and a data circlet. His expression was neutral, but his eyes smoldered with angry triumph. Syd suspected he had only agreed to meet so that he could gloat over his victory face-to-face. That was fine. Syd didn't have anything to say to him anyway.

Zey stopped before him. Before he uttered a word, the councilor pressed his savant. There was a crack followed by a low thrum.

"A disruptor?" Syd wondered, realizing Zey had just triggered a program that would scramble any audio recordings taking place, as well as the signals of most communications and tracking devices.

"You expected anything else?" Zey asked. "I am not a fool, Syd. I thought, after all these years, you might have finally started to appreciate that."

Syd was glad the signal he was intending to send was going to be a physical one, and not something like a savant ping. He thought about giving it right away.

"Well?" Zey demanded imperiously. "Did you come here to surrender? Or did you just want to shout some more?"

"I just want to know why?" Syd found himself asking instead.

He didn't really want to know, or at least he hadn't until that moment, but the question still found its way to the fore. Zey let out a short laugh.

"Well, that's rather broad, isn't it?"

"You consider yourself an intellectual. Summarize."

Zey sighed, looking suddenly weary, frustrated almost. He spread his arms to gesture at the overgrown garden.

"Look at this. All this. It's all going to ruin. We both want to stop that happening. We just believe in opposite processes. This empire was built by us, and it can only be maintained by us. You think this imperium will heal itself through benevolence, but we're too far gone for that. It was too late, even before Quann."

"How much of Quann was your doing?" Syd pressed.

"Enough," Zey said. "But probably less than you think. I know you believe I'm some force of evil, pulling the strings of destruction, like some painted Mahact villain in one of the Liberation Day street plays. But I'm just one piece in the machinery of change. Exposing me wouldn't stop what's going to happen. In fact it would only make it worse. I wish Atz could have understood that before the end."

"Were you onboard the *Magnificatum*?" Syd asked.

"Yes. I'm sorry about what happened to your Winnu."

"And what happened to yours? Nauru?"

"She's dead. Obviously."

"I shouldn't have asked her to spy on you."

"No, you shouldn't have."

He had anticipated that Zey would gloat, in fact he had hoped he would. Instead, he was being candid, almost conciliatory. Syd supposed that was natural enough at the end, when it was so obvious that Zey had won. He had been correct at the start of the conversation. These were the mere formalities of surrender, not to Zey, but to events now unfolding.

"So what happens next?" Syd asked. "You win the vote, the imperial fleet is recalled from Myock and makes ready. The Letnev and the humans make peace, if they haven't already, and we see a civil war that eclipses everything that has happened over the past seventy-two years."

"Nothing quite so grandiose," Zey said. "The Federation and the Letnev have crippled each other, as I knew they would. The N'orr and Hylar too, for that matter. We will never have a better opportunity to assert our control. And once we do, we will never allow the other civilizations to become so powerful that they can threaten us again."

It was Syd's turn to sigh. For all the logic of his words, Zey's inner being was as twisted and dark as any Mahact caricature. He was everything Syd stood against, everything he had struggled to defeat for most of his life.

He reached out, placing two hands on Zey's shoulders, and looked him in the eye.

"I want you to know this," he told him. "I believe, with utter certainty, that you have destroyed not only our empire, but our very species. It may not happen now, or even soon, but the path you have helped to set us on has guaranteed that one day the Lazax will be held as detestable and vile as the Mahact once were. Every civilization, great and small, will despise us, and they may be right to do so."

The anger rekindled in Zey's eyes, and he opened his mouth to speak. Syd let go of his shoulders and moved a fraction to the left. A heartbeat later, as the first word left Zey's lips, there was an ugly, wet cracking sound.

Syd took a full step back, looking at the long, slender shaft of wood that seemed to have suddenly sprouted, quivering, from Zey's left eye. He stood perfectly still, words unspoken, his other eye wide with shock. A single line of crimson ran slowly down his pale left cheek.

There was a humming discharge as his shimmer shield ignited, far too slow to deal with the low-velocity projectile. It shone around him before blinking out again.

Zey collapsed, falling straight back, dead before he hit the ground.

Syd looked down silently at the body, not turning even as he heard footsteps approaching him from behind.

Wordlessly, the Shikrai – Syd didn't know her name – stalked past and bent over Zey. She grasped the shaft of her arrow and, with a soft crunch, tugged it free. Then, glancing only briefly at Syd, the avian slung her needle bow, ruffled her black feathers and walked away into the smog.

It had been fitting, Syd thought, that Zey's killer had perched in the boughs of a moontree to take the shot.

He felt a sudden surge of sorrow, twinned with panic. It gave way to revulsion, and then a cold and empty void. He continued to look at the body for some time, wondering if he would ever truly feel anything ever again, then turned and forced himself to start walking.

He had done the unthinkable. Once it would have filled him with disgust, but he knew there was nothing left there to feel anymore.

In truth, that morning the assassin had killed both Sorian Sai Zey and Ibna Vel Syd.

•••

Things moved quickly. A Winnu security detail raided Syd's apartments, but he was no longer there. He had reached out to Marchu, who had given him sanctuary in one of her Hightown properties, overlooking the ship yards north of the Core. Syd was thankful more than ever that, seemingly against all odds, he still had good friends on Mecatol Rex.

News of the killing made headlines for days, and there was a media furor, but no officials directly blamed Syd – he suspected the imperial council didn't want to name one of its own members in the murder case of another, not publicly anyway. He wasn't sure how Erial would handle the realization that he had become a murderer. He knew that she was within her rights to leave, or even report him, and he refused to have her confined. In the end he needn't have worried. She clearly noted the news about Zey's death, as well as the fact that their location and activities had gone covert, but she never asked him anything specific.

Thanks to her, communications were kept up between Syd and his other contacts. Erial reported that the Hylar, Tol, had just made it back to Mecatol, seemingly after a close encounter on the frontlines of the Sardakk N'orr–Jol-Nar war. That was good news. Most of the other pieces were moving into place. He hoped that, with Zey's death, he had bought time. The Accelerationist faction had been thrown into disarray, and that would surely hamper the efforts to push the empire into war with its own subjects. At the very least, it stopped the mobilization of the fleet – the vote went against recalling it from Myock to Mecatol.

A week after Syd went into hiding, Marchu brought him the star charts he had requested.

"They're direct copies made at the Hall of Cartographers," she told him. "So they should be completely accurate and up to date. The only problem is these scans were logged, as you predicted, so they'll have a record of what I was looking at. Chief Cartographer Garr was also aware."

"It's a risk we have to take," Syd replied, beaming a miniature hologram of Marchu's findings from his savant. "Thank you for doing this. Now we'll be able to plot a course with confidence."

"If we have to," Marchu clarified. "Hopefully, it still won't come to that."

Syd said nothing. He was beyond hope.

CHAPTER THIRTY

New Port,
Sol Federation War Dock

The priority message for Holborn arrived late in the cycle, just as she was preparing for bed. She took one look at it and changed back into her uniform, then ordered a shuttle from the docking strut to take her out to the *Pride of Jord*, Admiral Trelo's flagship.

"Is it true?" she asked as she arrived on the bridge. At dock, and with the night cycle now underway, the nexus of the Phoenix Fleet's flagship would ordinarily have been a quiet, contemplative place, but right now it was bustling with crew members, the air filled with nervous, excited energy.

"It's true," Trelo replied, clearly doing her best to appear calm and collected before her flustered subordinates. She was a kindred spirit, another senior Federation officer who saw the decay and hypocrisy of the Lazax, and how they were dragging the galaxy down. Holborn had been working with her toward this end for years now, and trusted her completely.

"It's been confirmed by Selwin, the Federation delegate on

Mecatol," the admiral went on. "The imperial council has voted not to recall the Lazax fleet from Myock. They won't mobilize."

Holborn took a moment to digest the news, forcing herself not to get carried away. This was so much more than she could ever have hoped for.

"Why?" she found herself asking. "Does Selwin know what happened?"

"The councilor, Sorian Sai Zey, was assassinated," Trelo said. "Another councilor called Syd accused him of treason during a session just beforehand. He's now wanted for Zey's murder, but has disappeared. The Accelerationist faction lost all confidence, and the anti-recall side scraped the vote. Apparently, the capital is in uproar."

Despite herself, Holborn began to laugh. Trelo looked on, nonplussed, until she had recovered.

"That scheming rat finally got found," Holborn said eventually, still smiling. "Zey's been trying to play everyone on a galactic scale for decades now. My father talked about him. He was agitating even during the Quann incident. It seems someone on Mecatol finally had enough. Wasn't that other councilor, Syd, at Quann when the war began too?"

"I don't know," Trelo shrugged. "History was never my strong hand. All I know is that the Lazax have just voted by committee to leave the capital of their damned empire defenseless."

"Has Jord been informed?" Holborn asked, urgency starting to take hold. "What about the king?"

"The king will do whatever the Federation government tells him to do at this point," Trelo said dismissively. "I'm told they've been made aware. I'm expecting a sealed data packet containing orders within the next day. In the meantime, I'm putting the Phoenix Fleet on high alert. We can be underway before the week is out. In less than a month, we can be in high orbit above Mecatol Rex."

"The pro-Lazax faction on Jord may try to stall," Holborn pointed out, trying to cover all eventualities in her mind. She was suddenly desperate for this to succeed, to go ahead. She couldn't stop herself from running it through and seeing success at the end of it, but she knew that was still not necessarily the most likely outcome. "Some of those sniveling traitors may even try to warn the emperor."

"We'll go ahead regardless, as soon as we're ready," Trelo said, the certainty in her voice redoubling Holborn's own determination. "We'll never get another chance like this. Never. We strike now, for freedom's sake."

CHAPTER THIRTY-ONE

MECATOL REX,
GALACTIC CAPITAL OF THE LAZAX EMPIRE

Marchu brought Syd news he had not been expecting.

As the weeks had passed he had started to feel increasingly isolated, reliant on Erial to maintain any semblance of contact with the world beyond. A part of him wished he was still on Archon Ren, playing escar amidst softly sighing Q'waar boughs while enduring Tutur's morality lessons. That was foolishness though. That Syd, just like all the others before him, was gone. In his new reality, he disavowed such weakness. He did what had to be done.

His newfound certainties fell away when Marchu visited him in the lower rooms of his apartment one morning, just as he was finishing breakfast.

"There are strong rumors that the Phoenix Fleet has left its dock at New Port," she told him. "Some accounts are claiming they're already underway with a course set toward the galactic core. To Mecatol."

Syd finished the ri fruit he was eating and sat back in his chair, pondering the news.

"Was it not commonly believed the Phoenix Fleet would be docked for months, if not years?" he asked. "The damage sustained during the war with the Letnev was astronomical. It will be a long time yet before Sol's naval assets are restored."

"Fully restored, yes, but the last report from Ambassador Kero on Jord claimed they still had over a dozen serviceable dreadnoughts and two spaceworthy carriers at New Port," Marchu said. "Those are the elements that appear to have departed."

Syd's sense of unease began to grow. He had long worried that the humans couldn't be trusted, but he had not anticipated any rebellion coming so soon.

"What of the Letnev? Were they not still keeping Federation fleet assets occupied above Quann?"

"The Letnev seem to have withdrawn all their vessels to their territories. The elements in this system are also thought to be about to depart, destination unknown."

"Why is the Federation fleet coming here?" Syd wondered aloud. "Have there been recent courier deliveries from Jord?"

"None that I've heard of."

"And what's the council saying about this? Have the Federation delegates been questioned?"

"As far as I'm aware, the emperor is still digesting the news. The delegates can't be found."

This was a problem. More than that. The war fleet of any great civilization approaching the imperial capital unannounced was cause for concern. Ordinarily, the Letnev were the most powerful naval force in the galaxy, and their presence helped keep the others in check, while the threat of an alliance between those same powers in turn stopped Letnev aggression. But the recent wars had upended things. Syd had assumed the pieces were still settling, and that both Jord and Arc Prime would take time to recover. He had certainly not anticipated a unilateral move by the Federation in the direction of Mecatol Rex so soon.

"We need to find out their intentions," he said, still turning over possibilities in his head.

"They cannot pass into the Gul system without imperial authorization," Marchu said.

"I'm not sure imperial authorization carries the weight it once did," Syd pointed out. "Especially with the fleet still on maneuvers at Myock."

That was the real crux of the matter, the one that he suspected Marchu had been deliberately avoiding mention of. Because Syd had assassinated Zey, the move toward having the Lazax fleet brought back to Mecatol in preparation for war had collapsed. In that sense, Syd had just ensured that the capital world was defenseless. But surely there was a reasonable explanation for the battered remnants of the Phoenix Fleet making a move toward the galactic core?

"We have to accelerate our plans," he told Marchu.

Syd's old friend did indeed keep him updated, and none of the news was good. The Phoenix Fleet's course was undoubtedly set for Mecatol Rex. All attempts by Lazax authorities, both private and formal, to reach out to either Jord or the fleet itself met only cold silence.

Even worse, there were other movements underway, ones that, when added together, spelled out the possibility that there was a disaster unfolding.

Letnev ships in the Gul system had departed, without

explanation. The absence of the Hacan Freeguilds on Mecatol had also been noted. There had been many departures throughout the decades of warfare, as species sought to protect the interests of their own kind back on their homeworlds. The N'orr were now wholly absent from Mecatol, bar the presence of a few at the Galactic Council, though that itself was rapidly emptying. The lack of N'orr, along with that of the Hacan, meant the only armed forces on the surface of Mecatol were the Lazax Capital Guard, Winnu, and police forces, and there was even less in the way of manned orbital defenses.

A growing sense of unease was spreading through the capital. Syd felt it himself, a sickly sense deep in his gut, a crawling unrest in his mind that made him perpetually nervous and on edge. He tried to master it, but it was a struggle.

"The humans mean war," Syd finally told Marchu over dinner one evening. "Or worse. I think they mean to exterminate us. To destroy the empire."

Marchu said nothing for a while, seemingly considering Syd's opinion.

"Why would they seek to destroy us?" she asked eventually.

"Power," Syd said. He felt as though that word alone explained everything, but after a pause he continued. "Whether we like to admit it or not, there is a notable vacuum of it right now. The Federation have bested the Letnev, and if the peace between them both is anything to go by, the Letnev have remembered that they hate us more than the humans. There is no authority emanating from the imperial throne right now. No decisiveness."

"Recalling the fleet from Myock would have been decisive," Marchu noted.

Syd didn't begrudge her that. She was right, and deep down the knowledge terrified him.

"But that would have meant war," he pointed out.

"A war the empire would likely have been able to win swiftly. The Phoenix Fleet is in no position to resist the imperial armada. But that armada sits at Myock, while we are here, defenseless."

"Unforeseen circumstance," Syd murmured, unable to stop himself from raising some defense. He felt a growing sense of horror at what was happening, and how he had become involved in it all, but all that was left was to push forward and trust that he had done what he could. Still, the urge to deny involvement was strong. "I doubt things would have played out as simply as you claim. The last time the empire made war on its own subjects was when the last Letnev rebellion was put down, and even then it was only a response to outrageous provocation."

"Well... I fear you're right about the Federation's intentions," Marchu said. "And I suspect they're about to give us a provocation even more outrageous than the Letnev's."

"We need to accelerate our plans. Drastically. I will contact the last ones on the list, make sure they're ready to move. Everyone else who wishes to join us, this is the time."

"I'll help get the word out," Marchu said, rising. "Try to focus the minds of those who are wavering."

"As long as our efforts go undetected," Syd added, finding some solace in focusing on the details.

"They will, I promise."

As Marchu made for the stairs up into the apartment proper, Syd called out to her. He spoke impulsively, for the first time giving a voice to the fear and shame he was working so hard to hide.

"I'm sorry. For all this."

Marchu paused, glancing back. "It's as you said, my friend," she replied, offering a shrug. "Unforeseen circumstances. We must all do what we can."

Syd did not feel ready when he gave the order.

A final, frantic flurry of calls and message pings went out to the group Syd had been trying to assemble almost since his return to Mecatol Rex. He had thought he would have many months, even years, to see this done. Instead it had been weeks. So much was still unfinished. So many would be left behind. But it was now or never.

He did his best not to consider his own complicity in it all, the fact that the Phoenix Fleet were only able to bear down on Mecatol Rex unopposed because he had fatally undermined efforts to defend the capital. If he stopped to think about any of that, he knew he would not be able to carry on with the task before him. He could not stop. It was about more than just him. It always had been.

"You're sure you wish to come?" he asked Erial as they waited for a shuttle sent by Marchu. She shook her head.

"What choice is there?"

"You could risk staying," Syd pointed out. "We can't be certain of the Federation's intentions. And even if they mean harm toward the empire, as long as you're not at the Core I'm sure you would be fine."

"I don't have anything here," Erial said after a moment's thought. "No family, few prospects. I'm considered something of a liability as an aide, apparently."

"You've been an excellent assistant," Syd told her, speaking the truth. "And I'm proud to be taking you with me. I'm not sure I could have done this without you."

The shuttle carried them to Marchu's private cruiser, currently hanging in low orbit above the Core. She greeted them onboard the bridge.

"I've renamed this ship the *Syd*," Marchu said, apparently serious. "It seemed only right given it's going to be the flagship of your new fleet."

Syd laughed, though the humor was bitter.

"Are the others ready then?" he asked.

"Yes. *Manda* and *Hurwana* are on-station just above us. They've taken on the last of their supply shuttles. The refugees are all here and assembled."

"I want to speak to them before we depart."

"Do you think there's time?"

"I'll be brief."

The hold of Marchu's cruiser had been transformed into a meeting place for a nervous, restless gathering. Most of those present were Lazax, but there was a section of Winnu, mostly aides and their families, and a small coterie of Hylar and others. Syd passed among the crowd, offering greetings and reassurances that they would be underway soon. He spoke briefly to the most prominent Lazax present, including Councilor Yarrai – the only other member of the imperial council to agree to this – and Zunz, an imperial representative on the Galactic Council. He paused too among the Hylar, identifying Doctor Tol. She looked tired, reserved, speaking only to a human beside her, her partner on her medical staff.

"I'm glad you could make it in time," Syd told her. "I'm sorry

I've been so… unresponsive in recent years. I hear there was trouble on the front?"

"A ghost from my past caught up with me," Tol said, abandoning the Hylar love of logic and precision for a moment of hyperbole. "But I banished him. In fact, it helped make up by mind about joining you here. I received your message when I got back to Capistan."

"Then I'm glad," Syd declared. "Many in here will count on your talents before the end."

He mounted the stairs to the hold's gantry, which he used as a makeshift platform to address the crowd. An expectant hush fell.

"Friends," he began, making a Lazax gesture of greeting. "Family. Thank you, all, for being here. I know it is no easy thing. Many of you have had to leave those close to you behind. All of you are making sacrifices none of us would have dared dream of just a short while ago. We are united by that, just as we are united by our commitment to the future.

"You all know me. It is the privilege of my life that you have chosen to follow me in this endeavor. I am unworthy of that backing. My own failures are too numerous to list, certainly if we want to set off in a timely fashion! I played my part in the disasters that led us to this place. I won't deny that anymore. My only redeeming quality is that I have decided not to give up. By being here, all of you have decided that too.

"Some of you are likely still hoping that the worst does not come to pass, and that this voyage proves unnecessary. I am with you on that. But we can no longer live our lives based on assumptions, assumptions that the empire is still strong and stable, that 'glorious peace' still holds a meaning for our fellow sentients. If we are guilty of one thing collectively, it is standing by, doing nothing, and hoping for the best. That can no longer continue.

"In truth, I had lost all hope before today. I did not know if this plan would succeed, if any of you would come. But seeing you all here has changed that. You represent the future. You represent the survival of our people and, more importantly, the survival of our empire and the ideals that once underpinned it – honor, justice, and peace. And while those still exist, the whole galaxy can have hope. So, thank you."

There was no applause, no acclamation. Syd stepped down and headed for the bridge.

"Is the incendiary round locked on?" he asked Marchu when he arrived. The Lazax merely nodded. Though it was a private luxury cruiser, Marchu's vessel did possess a prow cannon, ostensibly for self-defense.

"And did you send the message I prerecorded?" Syd pressed, ignoring the unwillingness he sensed from Marchu.

"Yes. The Hall of Cartographers thinks a bomb has been planted somewhere within the archive stacks. They're currently evacuating."

Syd fought one of the hardest internal battles of his life, trying to convince himself they could wait a little longer. Every minute gave those in the Hall of Cartographers more time to evacuate. But every minute also raised the danger that they would be locked on to by orbital defense systems. He couldn't risk that, not after all that had been done.

"Fire the shell," he told Marchu. He could see how she was struggling too. He placed one hand on her shoulder.

"You know we cannot risk being followed. When this is

over, they will come for us. All of them. If we do not destroy the records that show where we are going, we may as well ground this ship right now and accept our fate along with the rest of the empire."

Marchu nodded. Unable to speak, she gestured toward the fire control officer.

The newly renamed *Syd* fired its prow solid-round cannon. In terms of ship-bound weaponry, the range to the Hall of Cartographers was point blank. The Core was well protected by defensive shields, but none of them had been raised. The shell cracked through the Hall's grand facade and detonated somewhere within. Syd watched on the bridge's displays, seeing the first flicker of flames within, presaging an inferno that would sear away all record of where they were bound. He wondered about the outrage this act of barbarism would cause. He hoped that history would forget this particular moment, but knew it would not.

"It is murder," Marchu said quietly.

"It is necessary," Syd responded, conciliation giving way to coldness as the need for action gripped him. They had to keep going. To stop now would mean disaster.

"Signal the *Manda* and *Hurwana*," he said. "And engage on the course we agreed. Let us be gone, while we still can, or this will all have been in vain."

CHAPTER THIRTY-TWO

Six Months Later – Mecatol Rex, Galactic Capital of the Lazax Empire

Like a small flock of oceanic predators disturbing a great shoal of prey-fish, the Phoenix Fleet arrived in high orbit above Mecatol Rex, scattering trader and civilian craft in all directions.

Holborn stood on the bridge of the *Pride of Jord*, hands behind her back, unmoving in the midst of frantic activity. Before her, Mecatol Rex filled the primary viewing port, a great arc of blues, grays and greens, swirled with white cloud cover.

It was the first time she had ever gazed on the imperial capital, and it was breathtaking. To be here, at the heart of the empire, at the heart of the galaxy, and with her finger on the trigger. She had never known exhilaration like it, and knew she never would again. It was all she could do to remain still and seemingly emotionless.

She assessed the readouts on the screens on either side of the view port, hardly daring to believe that the imperial capital had yet to ignite its shields. During the voyage she had constantly expected to receive a communique that the imperial fleet was rushing back from Myock to defend the capital, but there had been nothing. Once they broke into the Gul system, she had anticipated being challenged or, at the very least, that they would arrive to find Mecatol Rex's prodigious defenses prepared and its orbital weapons platforms run out and primed. None of that seemed to be the case though. She had held her breath as they had slid in under the outer guns, anticipating an annihilation that never came.

It was as though the Lazax had given up, as though they were welcoming their own destruction. She could only imagine the fear and chaos that had paralyzed the workings of the imperial government.

Since setting out from New Port, the fleet had been receiving a bombardment of a different kind, from councilors, politicians, and eventually even the emperor himself. They had demanded to know where the war fleet of the Sol Federation was bound, what they were doing in the Gul system, why they had come to Mecatol Rex. They ordered them to change course, to submit to Lazax authority and obey imperial edicts.

Neither Holborn nor Trelo had answered even a single missive. Communications channels had been left open, but were unmanned. The time for talking was long past. All that remained, before the end, was a token gesture.

"Transmit the declaration," she told Trelo. "And anchor us directly above the imperial palace."

After a few moments, Trelo confirmed the missive had been sent. It was a brief message stating that the Sol Federation henceforth declared itself independent from the empire, and demanded that the empire recognize it as such. It also gave the Lazax thirty minutes to do so.

Holborn raised her wrist to consult her savant, realizing as she did so that she was shaking. She forced stillness upon herself, before triggering the encrypted, sealed data-message she had received from Jord just prior to departure from New Port. It had been weighing on her since setting out, the monstrous unknown at the heart of a labyrinth of uncertainty. It contained the Federation's formal instructions to her concerning the actions to be taken upon arriving at the imperial capital.

The majority of the message consisted of the digital signatures of the king and every senior Federation politician. The actual text itself was just a single sentence.

If the emperor will not recognize the independence of the Sol Federation, you are to destroy Mecatol Rex.

She couldn't resist letting out a heavy breath of relief. It was finished.

"Turn off the comms array," she said to Trelo. The admiral showed only the briefest moment's hesitation, knowing what that meant. Holborn was about to snap at her, but she obeyed.

"Ignite shields, run out all guns," Holborn went on. "Target-lock the imperial palace, the Chamber of the Galactic Council, and the government Core."

"Should we not wait for the thirty minutes to elapse, at least for show?" Trelo asked. It seemed, here on the edge of destiny, that she was getting cold feet. Holborn had no time for such weakness. Her life, and those of her forebears, had all led to this one moment, this point of decision that would change the fate of the galaxy forever.

"Destiny waits for no one," she said, loud enough for the whole bridge to hear. "Tell me when the target locks are complete."

She steeled herself, thought of her father, of the uncle she had never met. Thought of the power and the glory that awaited both her, and her species.

"Target locks complete," Trelo said breathlessly, the weight of the moment too much for her.

"Then in the name of Jord, the Sol Federation, and a free galaxy," said Holborn. "Open fire."

The first blow was by the *Pride of Jord* against the imperial palace. The Phoenix Fleet were on the cusp of low orbit, and the energy beam fired from the *Pride*'s prow lance struck the imperial council chamber. Permacore seared apart and then exploded around the line of crimson, eye-aching brilliance before it blinked out, flaming debris clattering off the palace's central dome and arcing out over the gardens.

Destruction followed, terrifying in its scale and raw intensity. Hundreds of thousands of tons of munitions were unleashed by the human warships on the Core, solid shot and energy, plasma and quake-bombs. Government buildings that had stood for over a thousand years were ripped apart or demolished. The vast dome of the Chamber of the Galactic Council – long abandoned by its delegates – was staved in and wrecked. The burned husk of the Hall of Cartographers was wiped from existence by a shell from the dreadnought *Executioner*. A firestorm swept through the imperial gardens, the overgrown groves becoming a furnace, the clids and moontrees blackening, cracking, and falling like lit torches.

The imperial palace suffered the worst. In a matter of minutes it was demolished, its ancient permacore pulverized by explosives or melted by blasts of energy.

Before the deadline for their acquiescence had even passed, the Sol Federation had ripped the heart out of the Lazax empire, forever.

Syd received visual confirmation of the fate of Mecatol Rex a little over six months after fleeing the planet. A looping news reel seemingly of Hacan origin was picked up by the sensors of the *Manda*, with footage purported to have been recorded from one of Mecatol's orbital weapons platforms.

Syd watched it all on his cruiser's primary bridge display.

He had steeled himself for this moment. A part of him had expected to feel nothing, much as the time after he had killed Zey. That hollowness was still there, but it shared his thoughts with an icy pain greater than all before it. It was one thing imagining this, planning for it, even accepting that it would happen. But to actually witness it – there could be no preparation. Syd knew it would remain with him forever, the haunting sight of the Phoenix Fleet silhouetted by a silent firestorm, blossoming across his people's homeworld, the capital of an empire that had started to fall long ago, and had now finally struck the ground.

A few of the other refugees watched it, but most could not bear the sight. Marchu stood beside Syd, silent for a long time as they saw the destruction spread, and tried not imagine the horror of the millions that had already played out. Syd found himself closing his eyes, struggling against tears, feeling sick. He only opened them again when Marchu finally spoke, voice a dry, dead whisper that brought with it the crushing weight of reality.

"This is the end."

"No," Syd found himself responding as he finally discovered the strength to turn his back on the destruction of all that his people had spent a millennium building. "This is only the beginning."

ACKNOWLEDGMENTS

My thanks go out to everyone involved in bringing this novel to life, particularly my ever-brilliant and patient editor Lottie, and the always-approachable FFG team – alongside Katrina Ostrander – who make this all possible.

ABOUT THE AUTHOR

ROBBIE MacNIVEN hails from the highlands of Scotland. A lifelong fan of sci-fi and fantasy, he has had over a dozen novels published in settings ranging from Marvel's X-Men, to *Descent: Legends of the Dark*, to *Warhammer 40,000*. Having completed a doctorate in Military History from the University of Edinburgh in 2020, he also possesses a keen interest in the past. His hobbies include historical re-enacting and making eight-hour round trips every second weekend to watch Rangers FC.

robbiemacniven.wordpress.com
twitter.com/RobbieMacNiven

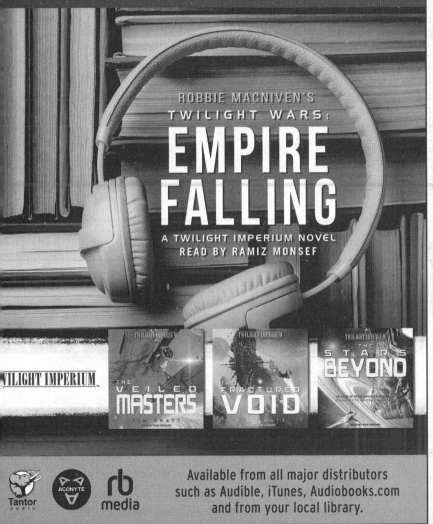